The Blossom
or the Bole

By Pheme Glass

About the author

Pheme Glass is a native of Cookstown, County Tyrone but moved to Omagh after her marriage to Peter (deceased 2010). She has three daughters and two grandchildren.

She writes poetry and has successfully published a collection of her work 'Seeds of Memory' in 2013.

'The Blossom or the Bole' is her first novel. The setting for the book draws strongly from school holidays spent on her Grandmothers farm in the foothills of the Sperrin Mountains.

The book is purely a work of fiction but with reference to actual people in the public eye of the day. All other characters are fictional and bear no resemblance to anyone living or dead. The headlines from the two local newspapers are as published over a century ago.

Published in 2017 by Shanway Press, 15 Crumlin Road, Belfast BT14 6AA

Cover design: DavidLee Badger

ISBN: 978-1-910044-15-5

This book is dedicated to
Timothy Stewart Glass
1967-1969

Acknowledgements

My thanks go my family and all my many friends who have encouraged me in my efforts to write this book.

In particular, Nicole Watt for her invaluable help as the story emerged, Kathy O'Donnell for her constant support, and Lorna Martin who taught me all about commas and apostrophes.

Denis Whelan, my son-in-law who read my early musings and kept pushing me to finish.

Marella Fyffe, who made it possible for me to visit Belgium and World War 1 sites in 2008, where the first seeds of the story began, and for giving me a place of solitude in The Bamboo Loft & Mindfulness Retreat, to complete the story.

John Harding a great master of creative writing, who has been my mentor and guide over the past twenty years.

Omagh Library for its amazing archive of newspapers and reference material.

The Tyrone Constitution and The Ulster Herald, for their newspaper headlines of a century ago.

The Open Door Poetry Group.

Omagh Library Creative Writers Group.

Abercorn Estates, Baronscourt, Newtownstewart.

Among School Children
by W.B.Yeats
published in 1926

8th Stanza

Labour is blossoming or dancing where
The body is not bruised to pleasure soul,
Nor beauty born out of its own despair,
Nor blear-eyed wisdom out of midnight oil
O chestnut-tree, great-rooted blossomer,
Are you the leaf, the blossom, or the bole?
O body swayed to music, o brightening glance,
How can we know the dancer from the dance?

Book One

Prologue

A full moon cast four shadowy figures into bright relief as they climbed up the side of the mountain carrying a long box between them. The night was still, apart from their short white puffs of breath, which filtered into the cold air.

Halfway up they stopped at a low wall surrounding a cairn and left down their burden.

An owl hooted three times. One of the four put his hands to his mouth and hooted three times in reply. They waited, neither moving nor speaking.

A blanket of fog rose from the valley further down, creeping closer to where they stood swirling around them like a veil.

Out of the fog four more figures appeared. The box was passed across the wall to waiting arms.

No words were spoken. The first four turned and disappeared into the fog. The new bearers moved slowly up the mountain and were soon lost in the shadow of the thick gorse that surrounded them.

The first light of dawn broke on the muddy street of the small thatched house. A dog growled but was silenced by a low whistle from a man as he crossed the street to the front door. He lifted the latch gingerly to avoid its noisy clatter.

Stepping into the kitchen, he stooped to warm himself over the dying embers of the fire. The night had been successful.

The guns had come at last and were now in safe hands.

Chapter 1

The sky held all the promise of another fine spring day. A will-o-the-wisp fog was slowly melting away revealing the yellow flower of the broom on either side of the lane leading up to the school.

The building was typical of small rural schools consisting of two classrooms divided by a black stove. A curtain hung in the middle which, when closed, divided the pupils according to their age. Girls sat on the left and boys on the right. A door at the end led to a small store room which was also used by teachers as an office.

It was Ash Wednesday and the Roman Catholic children from the school were coming up the lane after attending nine o'clock mass at the chapel in the village. Master O'Brien followed them as they walked in twos, their heads down, their hands in supplication of prayer, though some of them were having difficulty in keeping their heads bowed as they entered the school yard. They looked forward to displaying the black ash clearly visible on their foreheads.

Groups of Protestant children were gathered in the yard. They stopped to stare at the procession. The younger children were whispering, curious about the black marks.

Elizabeth Granger who at five was the youngest child in the school spoke up.

"Josie, your ma didn't wash your face this morning, it's all black." Laughter broke out in the playground and calls of "black face, black face" from some of the older boys echoed around the yard.

"Shush now, Elizabeth," the teacher, Miss Finley, said gently taking the child's hand. "This is Ash Wednesday and Josie has just been to mass."

"Can I have a mark on my face, miss?"

"No, Elizabeth, you don't go to Chapel. You go to the Presbyterian Church. Now come along, children. We need to get inside and finish the morning lessons. Line up now."

There was some jostling and pushing among the older boys as they prepared to enter the classroom. Master O'Brien called one of the boys out of the line.

"William Johnston, is it your turn to fetch the turf in from the stack and stoke the fires in the classroom?"

"Yes Sir," William replied. "It's me and Paul this week. I was waiting for Paul to come from the Chapel."

Paul came and stood beside William. "Aye, we were just goin, Sir."

"You boys will soon be leaving us. Is it your plan to behave like infants all your lives?" The boys' faces reddened. Looking sideways at each other.

"Well, has the cat got your tongues? I could hear yours earlier, William, as we came back from mass. Now you appear to have lost your voice."

"We were only actin' the eejit* sir. Didn't mean no harm."

"No sir. The Protestants always give us a poke about the black faces. It's just a bit of fun."

"You will soon be out in the real world, boys. Comments made without thought have a bad habit of coming back to haunt you. We live hand to mouth in this small community, respecting our differences. You will both soon be away from the school yard, but until you are, I expect you to behave and to set a good example to the younger children you leave behind. Now get on with your chores."

William always enjoyed this annual ritual on Ash Wednesday, chiding Paul about his black brow and pretending not to recognise him. Such jokes were well worn among the boys and girls in the senior class, but not always treated as a joke with some of the Catholic boys. The O'Neil brothers, in particular, were scathing in their comments about Protestants and these disputes often erupted into fights. Such battles left many a black eye but over the years had no effect on William and Paul's friendship. The boys escaped to the turf stack and began to fill the baskets.

"Jaysus, William, your big mouth will get you into trouble yit."

"Ach sure it wouldn't be the same if you papists didn't get a touch when you appear at school with black faces," William laughed.

Paul lifted his basket and, as he passed William's, he kicked it over, spilling the turf in all directions.

"See if that'll keep you busy, big mouth. I'm away in.."

"Ach, Paul, you wee shite! That's not fair."

"All's fair in love an' war, Willie boy. Who's laughin' now?"

William caught hold of the basket Paul was carrying and tugged it hard. Both boys fell in a heap in the middle of the turf, laughing and throwing handfuls of turf dust at each other. They were so caught up in the carry-on they didn't hear the master approach.

"What is going on here? Is it too much to ask you pair of hallions* to do a simple task? Get on your feet and fill those baskets immediately. I will deal with you both after lessons." Mr O'Brien turned and left them red-faced again, brushing the thick dust off their clothes.

"Ach God, William, another slappin'. Our hands will have permanent calluses when we get away from school in June."

"Did you not put some meths on your hands like I told ye? It hardens them up for the cane or maybe you're takin' a wee swig instead." William staggered, rolling his eyes.

"Your hands must be like leather now. The master will have to buy a new cane for the bad weans* in September."

The baskets filled, they entered the classroom. The other children looked up from their books, some with open hostility. Josie O'Neil caught William's eye then bowed her head over her slate, a ghost of a smile still on her face. They stoked the fire and stacked the turf before taking their seats to begin lessons. William and Paul sat together at the back of the class as did all the children of a similar age. They were fourteen now and in their final weeks of school.

Over the years their free time had been dominated by avoiding any unnecessary work at home and fishing together on the Glenelly River. Those carefree days were now short lived and like so many boys in the small rural community they were destined to become farmers and work the land.

The young voices of the children echoed from the yard. It was lunch break. Master O'Brien carried the school books into the store and stood waiting as Miss Finlay stacked her papers on the shelf.

"I had to speak to Johnston and McGovern this morning again. I have kept them behind after lessons. I know those two are great friends but I have concerns about the fights between the older boys which are becoming more frequent these days with regard to religious differences."

"I agree with you Master, it is a worry."

"There is trouble brewing in the country, Miss Finlay. The paper says there is a train going to Belfast on Easter Tuesday to rally Protestants against the Home Rule Bill. They say Edward Carson has the government running scared and is planning large scale disruptions."

"You can hardly blame people when they see their entire way of life threatened by this bill."

Miss Finlay blushed, turning her back to the master. She realised she had spoken out of turn. Their respective politics had never been spoken of before in the schoolroom much less discussed. "Excuse me, Mr O'Brien. I apologise for my outburst. It won't happen again." She slipped past him and went out to the yard leaving Mr O'Brien to weigh up what he had discovered about his normally quiet and agreeable colleague.

Easter was only a week away and, with the prospect of a break from school, the boys were planning a fishing competition. The rules were simple, only they could enter the competition, the biggest catch of the day was the winner and if caught by the bailiff you were on your own.

Paul and William had been busy over the winter tying flies and repairing their very meagre fishing tackle in readiness for the holiday. They were in the hut they had fixed up with bits of corrugated iron and fallen trees. It was more of a shelter than a hut but it was somewhere out of the rain to meet and talk, away from the prying ears in the cramped kitchens at home. The table was an upturned animal feeding trough, rendered useless by the large hole at one side.

The boys were perched on two roughly chopped branches, engrossed in the task of binding their fishing poles with new gut.

"I hope there comes a big flood before the holidays. It'll clean out the rubbish lyin' on the bank. Did you see the dead sheep, William, up beyond the turn?" Paul bit into the piece of gut with his teeth.

"Aye, I've seen it. That's the fourth dead sheep this month. Pity the man who owns them when he goes luckin' for them. I think they were in lamb, too."

"That was some fight at the mart last Thursday. Seems Hughie Kerr and Column Girvan kicked the shit out of each other."

William spat out onto the grass. "Aye, though it's not the first row there's been this past while."

"Are you going to Belfast on Tuesday, William, to hear Carson?"

"I don't think so. The rest of them are goin' with a crowd from the Orange Lodge. Ma didn't want to take them for fear of trouble, but Da told them they were goin' on an excursion and now she can't back down."

William cast a sideways glance at Paul, "Is your Da goin'?" Then he took off at a run stopping at the edge of the field. Paul didn't follow, but stood watching him as he turned and walked back. For a minute or two neither of them spoke.

"I'm sorry, Paul. I didn't mean to hurt your feelings. Sure you know me, always stirrin' it."

Paul farted loudly then took to his heels laughing. "Try stirrin' that, smart ass," he shouted back.

William followed, a huge grin on his face,

"You're a wee shit, McGovern. You'd better check your breeches."

BALMORAL DEMONSTRATION
Thousands of Ulster Protestants expected to
converge in Belfast on Easter Tuesday.
The parade will march to Balmoral to hear
Sir Edward Carson and Mr Bonar Law begin the
campaign against the Home Rule Bill

Tyrone Constitution, September 1912

Chapter 2

The house was in turmoil from five o'clock on. Ann was in the middle of buttering bread, wrapping it in clean muslin squares when John and William came into the kitchen from the milking.

"John, you'd better get a move on. It's almost six and the cart will be here by half past."

"Aye, all I need to do will only take a minute of two. I could be doin' with a cup of tae?"

"Get dressed first, John. If we miss the train we will be having the picnic at the station."

"Are you sure you can manage the jobs today, William?" Ann asked as she filled the basket.

"Aye sure there not a lot needs doin' till milkin' tonight. You get off and enjoy the day, the weather is fine so far."

"Will you go out and keep the wee John from getting dirt on his good clothes. He's like a butterfly with excitement. Elsie is away to get dressed."

"Aye, I'll keep him occupied till you're all ready."

The father and son met in the narrow doorway as William went out.

"Well, that's me ready. Any chance of that tae ye promised? It's a shame that lad's not coming with us. It's about time he started to pay attention to what's goin' on around him instead of loiterin' about at the river with young McGovern."

"Please don't start that now, John. He made his choice and aren't we glad he'll be here to keep an eye on things."

The journey on the train was like a Sunday school outing. It stopped at all the stations along the route to pick up passengers. As the train passed through the countryside people along the way stopped and waved. The Union Jack flags streamed out of many of the carriages. Hymns and the national anthem were sung with great gusto. As the train pulled into Great Victoria street station the whistle sent out three sharp blasts and smoke belched from the funnel filling the platform with clouds of soot as the crowds spilled out of the carriages. The Johnstons were swept up in the vast crowds on the streets of Belfast, all making their way to the city centre where the parade to Balmoral was due to begin.

Men in uniform were lining up four abreast to march past the saluting base where Sir Edward Carson and Andrew Bonar Law stood. Brass bands played hymns as the solemn parade made its way to Balmoral Showgrounds, the crowd of spectators pressing forward, eager to be part of it.

John was finding it difficult to keep up. His leg was stiff after the long journey and he refused to use the aid of a stick. Ann tried to keep them together. Mesmerised by the mass of people on the streets, wee John dropped his flag and cried so much that Ann had pushed her way back to try and find it. She had to give up in the end and eventually caught up with the family and her sobbing seven year old. Elsie was carrying the basket of food and was trying to comfort him.

"We'll get another one, wee John and then we'll have some ice cream."

Balmoral was a heaving mass of people all trying to get near to the platform, some more successful than others. The band played hymns in the distance and a sombre atmosphere descended on the crowd.

"John, let's go to the edge of the crowd and find a place where we can sit down and eat."

"I want to hear the speeches, Ann, why don't you go on with the weans and I'll catch you up later."

Ann frowned and spoke into his ear, "No drinking, John, please."

"Where would I get a drink here Ann? It's a strict no alcohol day. Go on and get your tae." he kissed her on the cheek and melted into the crowd.

The crowd near the platform were mostly all men and John found himself standing next to a man drinking from a small silver flask which he had produced from the inside pocket of his coat.

"Are you a local man?" John asked, the familiar thirst twisting in his gut. "I am indeed, Belfast born and bred. Have you travelled far yourself?"

"Aye, I'm from Tyrone, a long journey on the train but worth every mile. I try to go to as many meetin's as I can get to but it's not easy. "

"Indeed. We need every man to answer the call. These are testing times." He took another long slug from the flask.

"Are all the public houses closed?" John asked getting a strong whiff of good whiskey.

"Yes, I'm afraid they are closed for the afternoon on orders from on high to avoid any unnecessary boisterousness in the crowd. Good thing if you ask me," and with this last remark, he quickly replaced the flask in his pocket and walked away. John cursed under his breath, his need for a drink getting stronger by the minute. He moved back towards the edge and came across a group of men he recognised from the mart in Strabane.

"Well, boys, you're a welcome sight. Have ye seen any sign of a shebeen* around here?"

"It's as dry as a bale of straw. Ye can buy tae like the dregs of a shugh*
over at the back, but nothing stronger."

John thanked them and resigned himself to tae. In his wanderings he found
himself once again near the front of the platform. Suddenly, a group of
policemen appeared and, following them, the platform party of robed clergy
and the tall figure of Edward Carson. The man next to him nudged his arm.

"Here he is, boy! The man sent by God to save Ulster."

A roar went up in the crowd and a chant began "Carson! Carson! Carson!.
No surrender! God and Ulster!" Edward Carson raised his hand and the
thousands of Ulster Protestants lapsed into a reverent silence.

His speech lasted for over an hour and he ended by saying: "I know the
responsibility you are putting on me today. In your presence, I cheerfully
accept it, grave as it is. And now I enter a pact with you and everyone of you,
and, with the help of God, you and I joined together – I giving you the best I
can, and you giving me all your strength behind me – we will defeat the most
nefarious conspiracy that has ever been hatched against a free people."

A pandemonium of cheers erupted from the tumult of men, women and
children gathered in the area around the platform. It took several attempts for
the marshal on the platform to bring order to the gathering. Men wearing
uniforms saluted as the din subsided and the band played "Oh God our Help
in Ages Past," the crowed singing loudly with one voice.

The Conservative leader, Andrew Bonar Law, whose father had been a
Presbyterian Minister in Coleraine, County Londonderry, was introduced.
Another roar of approval rose from the gathering as Bonar Law stood and
spoke at length, ending with: "Once more you hold the pass, the pass for the
Empire. You are a besieged city. The timid have left you; your Lundies have
betrayed you; but you have closed your gates. The Government has erected,
by their Parliament Act, a boom against you to shut you off from the help of
the British people. You will burst the boom."

The speech ended with uproarious cheering and applause. The band
played the National Anthem and the fifty thousand voices again echoed the
resolve and tenacity of their leaders.

John went in search of Ann, his heart filled with all that he had heard.
William should have been here standing next to him showing his solidarity.
He knew it was time to talk to William if he was ever to become a son he
would be proud of.

Ann had heard little of the speech. The walk had taken three hours. Wee
John had slept on the grass after the picnic. It would take the same time again

15

to get back to the train. She hung around the gate for a good hour after the Anthem and then decided to go back to the station. They were all tired and trying to locate one man in a crowd of this size would be impossible.

"What about Da? How will he know where we are?" Elsie asked

"Your Da said last night if we got separated to go back to the station." The lie was easier than the truth of telling Elsie that if her Da found a public house they would not find him till home time.

"He will miss the train, Ma. We can't leave without him."

"Don't worry. The train is not leaving for a while. Did you enjoy the day? I saw you chattin' with a crowd earlier. Some fine lookin' cubs, did you know them?"

"Naw, I didn't. We were just talkin'."

"So you did enjoy the day then?" Ann was smiling down at her beautiful daughter who was blushing bright red.

"Aw, Ma, stop teasin' me. We were just talkin'."

Her surprise was genuine when she heard John calling out her name as they reached the station. He was hanging out of the door of a carriage, waving frantically.

"Come on! I have got a good seat. Where did you get to? Wasn't it a great day? That'll give London our answer to Home Rule. Did ye hear him? Carson has the power and we will stand with him."

"I never heard a word, John. We were too far back. You missed the food. I kept you your share and there's milk if it hasn't gone sour. How is your leg?"

"Ach, it's not good, but I would suffer any pain just to say I heard the great man's words." He stood up and people turned to listen to him."We're on the brink of civil war. Ulster will not bow to Home Rule. Carson will stand by us. We will stand by him. God save Ulster."

The passengers in the carriage cheered loudly as the whistle blew and the train shunted out of the station.

The Blossom or the Bole

The Blossom or the Bole

17
17

Orangemen as Home Rulers
Anti-union Resolutions Passed in 1800
"Ireland as a Nation"

How many Orangemen of today know that the most
bitter opponents of the Act of Union of 1800 were to be
found in the ranks of the Orange Order?

Ulster Herald 1912

Chapter 3

Mary filled the pails at the well. It was early. The sun might come out from behind the thick cloud later in the day and hopefully she would get the washing outside to dry. Drying it in the barn left it damp and smelly and took days. She went back to the washing and began to rinse it out before she put it through the mangle. She loved this time of day when she had time to herself. Padraig was off up the mountain to dip sheep so, when she heard footsteps in the lane, she stood upright and waited to see who was calling at this early hour. Paul came onto the street with a big smile on his face. He turned to reveal a large salmon hanging from a stick.

"You must have been up early?"

"Early bird catches the worm but in my case a salmon. We'll be atin' well the nite. It's my best catch yit"

"Where did you get it or maybe I should ask how did you catch it? Were you poachin', Paul?"

"Ach don't be so goody, goody. Who's to know if we don't tell them"

"If the bailiff catches you, you will end up in court. Did you clean it out at the river?"

"Now, Ma, I'm wise to that one. I left no evidence on the bank and the cat'll soon get rid of the guts."

"You may get it done then and I'll salt it later."

"Can we have some for the dinner? It's all I thought about since I caught it."

"Aye, but I'll keep some salted for the hardship days." "Don't worry. There's plenty more where that came from."

"Luck, Paul, you know poachin' is against the law and if Simpson catches you, you'll be up in front of the magistrate. We have little enough without havin' to pay a hefty fine."

Just with that Padraig came back from the mountain, carrying a lamb under his arm.

"Has it been injured, Padraig?"

"Naw, just a bit thin, we could use it for the pot."

"Now, Da, aren't we the great hunters home with food for all?" Paul held up the salmon waiting for his Da's approval.

"How did you catch it?" Padraig asked.

"Ach, just the way you taught me. I lay on my belly and watched the bank under that oul stump at Bradley's corner. He was lyin' in tight to the bank and, cool as ye like, I slide my hand in under his tail and catch it tight the way you showed me and lifted him clean out of the water and hit him hard with a stick. He's a big one, Da, bigger than thon one you brought home."

"Padraig, have you had a hand in teachin' our cub to poach?"

"Aye, and he is better at it than me I can tell you. Well done, cub."

"I'm away to the back of the house to gut him. Ma wants to salt him, but will ye remind her to leave a steak or two for the dinner today. Could you keep a wee one for William, Ma. I can't wait to tell him. He'll be as mad as hell." he went off whistling to himself.

"That's a fine catch Mary, and sure where's the harm? I fancy a bit of salmon for me dinner. I need some milk for this wee waif and a warm spot by the fireside. It needs feedin' up. Oliver can have it for a pet, Where is he?"

"He's in the house atin' his breakfast. Call to him. He shud be outside this nice day. There's a box in the barn by the door and some empty sacks for the lamb. I left fresh bread on the table for you. The kettle just needs brought back to the boil. I'll be in shortly. I want to finish the washin'."

"You're a wonder to behold, Mary, The more work we heap on ye, the more lovely you look" He set the lamb down and caught her around the waist, lifting her high in the air, the water running from her hands.

"Get away, Padraig McGovern. When the compliments fly, I get worried for what's to follow. Put me down at once! I'm soaked to the skin!"

He let her down and lifted the shivering lamb and went towards the barn, he turned speaking in a half whisper,

"No need to keep fish for young Johnston. He's fit and able to catch his own."

Before she could answer him, the barn door closed. She could never make out what went on in his head. He was a good man but something always changed in him when Paul showed his friendship for William. Later in the morning, she gave Paul a muslin parcel with a cut of fish inside.

"Don't let on to your Da, son, you know what he can be like. Some things are best kept between you and me."

"Thanks, I know what you mean. I'll give it to William later."

"Mind where you put it, that cat has been on the prowl since you came back with the fish. Did you give her the guts?".

"I did surely and if you can find a single fish bone I'll be surprised. She tore into it as if she had niver seen a bite before. I'm away now to clean out the hens and then meet William. I'll be back early."

"School tomorrow, so be back before dark."

"Aye, Ma, school. Whoever thought up that idea should be in the river with the fish, I'll be glad when I'm done with all that."

"Don't say things like that, Paul. You need to learn your lessons if you are to get on in life."

"That's what bothers me, get on with what, cleanin' out dung all day?"

"Life might seem like that now but when you're older you will need your letters to make a life for yourself". She smiled at his furrowed brow, "Get on now to those hens and be sure to check for eggs."

He finished cleaning out the hens and slipped two big brown eggs into his pocket. That was breakfast sorted as well as dinner. He headed off over the field towards the river. He saw Simpson the water bailiff, along with another man crossing the ditch. His heart skipped a beat, thankful that he had no evidence to get him into trouble until he remembered the parcel for William. He couldn't turn now for they had seen him.

"Good day, young McGovern. Are you makin' for the river?"

"Aye, I surly am, Mr Simpson. Are you comin' away from it?" Paul knew he could get into trouble for cheeking back but he smiled brightly in an attempt to divert their attention.

"Now then, my lad, let me take the wind out of your sails or, in your case the fish out of the net. I want to introduce you to Mr Colgan. He's the new bailiff for this part of the river and he has a sharp eye in his head. You spend a lot of your time at the river, cub*, so if you see anyone poachin' or nettin' you can let Mr Colgan know. Isn't that right, Mr Colgan?"

"Aye, I'm a great believer in spreadin' the work load so if you see anything out of the way you would let me know, wouldn't ye, cub?" Colgan smiled and stepped closer to Paul "Your Ma got fish for your tae tonight? Ye smell a bit fishy to me."

Paul pulled back.

"Hope you're not guilty of taken fish from the river? He stepped closer.

Paul was about to take to his heels when Simpson laughed.

"Too young Mr Colgan, poachin's a skill that's learned but yer best to keep an eye on this wan. He's growin' up fast. Good-day till ye, Master McGovern."

Paul didn't answer back but walked on towards the river, their laughter following him till he was out of earshot. He was glad he had held his ground not wanting to think what might have happened if he had run off. The sweat was running off him when he reached the hut. William wasn't there and he sat down on the log. He took the parcel from his pocket, the smell of it turning his stomach. It was a close shave. "Did you meet oul Simpson?" Paul jumped up.

"Holy shit, William, where did you come from? I didn't hear you."

"What's up? You're as white as a sheet."

"Aye, I met him alright and the new bailiff, Colgan's his name. I had a parcel of salmon for you in my pocket and I'm sure he smelt it. Jaysus, I was sure I was done for."

"When did you catch the salmon?"

"I caught it this mornin' about seven o'clock. He was the best wan I have iver caught. Nose ta tail a good three fut."

Paul extended both his arms, smiling proudly at William "I wish you could have seen him, William. Even me Da has niver got wan this big."

"Jaysus, it's a good job it wusn't later or ye wouldn't be here to brag. I seen them comin' I had the rod out when I heard them talkin in the next field. I dropped the rod in the ditch and climbed the Chestnut tree. They niver seen me. I stayed up there till you came. That's why you didn't see me."

"We'll have to be more careful, William. This new boy's smart and he's young and fit, not like oul Simpson, who couldn't outrun a snail."

"Aye, anyway, where's my share of the catch?" William took the parcel and undid it.

"I hope I don't meet them boyos on the way home. This must have been a big wan alright, Paul, luck at the size of that Fin."

"Did ye not believe me? I told ye he was a big wan."

"Aye but I always leave room for exaggeration and your bad sums, Paul. Are ye sure it wasn't layin on the bank or maybe it just jumped out into your arms because you're such a good catch"

"You're just jealous, William. Be sure ye don't choke on a bone when you're atin' it"

William lunged at him and they tumbled to the ground, "Get off me, you savage."

"Is that what the poor fish said this morning?"

Their laughter was caught on the wind. A flock of starlings perched above them flew off, screeching across the river. Later that night Paul found the sticky remains of the eggs in his pocket.

NO HOME RULE
Are Ulster Men drilling?
Columns of men have been seen drilling in formation
in many villages in Tyrone.
Broom handles used to replicate guns.
Tyrone Constitution 1912

Chapter 4

William and Elsie trudged home from school through a heavy drizzle of rain. William welcomed the rain and fresh floods in the river. School was coming to an end soon and they would have more time for fishing.

There was a cart and a small black trap on the street, the horse and the pony attached to the shafts, grazing at the ditch.

"Uncle Jack and Aunt Allison must be here. Wonder who the other fancy trap belongs to?" Elsie remarked as they approached the front door.

"Aye and I suppose they have scoffed the bread for our supper. I'm starving."

"Aw, stop mitherin*, William. You know mammy always keeps back our share."

They came into the kitchen and were immediately struck by the silence that fell as soon as they came through the door. They greeted their Uncle and Aunt who nodded, avoiding eye contact.

There was a young man sitting at the far end of the table. He was thin faced with dark hair and a sour expression. He nursed his hat gingerly on his knee, his eyes alert to the people around him.

"Come up to the fire weans and take off those wet clothes. There's bread on the table." Their Ma fussed over them while they cast sidelong glances at the stranger.

Aunt Allison was sniffing back tears. William lifted a slab of soda bread and ate hungrily, fresh crumbs falling from his chin. "Is there something wrong, Ma?"

His Da spoke sharply to him, his face bloated and red.

"Don't speak with your mouth full, cub. Get on your oul duds there's jobs to be done in the byre."

William could smell the drink on him and knew it was better to get out of the way. Whatever was wrong, he would hear it soon enough. He lifted another slab of bread and went off down to the bedroom. Elsie followed him.

As soon as they had left the room, the silence was broken by the babble of angry voices. Then the front door closed. William and Elsie pulled aside the curtain and watched as the stranger climbed up on the trap and guided it out of the gate.

"God, William, who was he and what's this all about? Have you been in trouble again?"

Elsie was almost two years older than him. At fourteen she had an irritating habit of following him around. He had banned her from the hut at the river after he had found her poking around in their things. He hated girls, especially sisters.

"Why is it? That as soon as something goes wrong around here, everyone looks at me? No, I have not been in trouble. Not enough to have some stuck up wee shit callin' at the house. Get out of my room. I need to change before the oul boy starts in on me."

Elsie left William and slipped back to the kitchen. No one seemed to notice her. She filled the basin from the kettle on the stove and began to gather the cups that were on the table. She had a nose for gossip and had found early in life that the less you interfered in the adults conversations the more you heard. Today was no exception.

"What can we do, John?" Allison was asking looking at her brother, her tears never far from the surface.

"Get him away for the time being. Send him up to Jean's in Cookstown till the dust settles. Is your man away out there to be trusted?" John nodded to the door.

"Aye, he's Mabel's young man, Albert. He's not too happy getting involved, but she made him come with us to the minister. He's good enough, but a bit above himself if you ask me. He's getting his education in Belfast." Jack McCrea wrung his cap around in his hands. "They arrested two others as well and took the guns. We're not sure how many there were on the cart. Tommy McFarland's goin' mad. He said that's the third lot we have lost in the past month."

"McFarland's useless. He has no head on him for this sort af thing. I know a man who might be able to help but I make no promises." John finished the last of the porter in his glass and rose to get his coat. "I might not get anywhere with this tonight, but I'll try my best."

"Are you leavin now, John? I'll be makin the tae soon. Will it not wait till then?"

"Naw, Ann, strike while the irons hot. Don't worry, Jack. We'll get this sorted out in no time at all."

Jack got up. "I'll come with you. We can take my cart."

"I could be a while. Hiv you got time?"

"Aye, I need to do something. All this sittin' around is no good." As they went out to the street, Ann followed them.

"John," she spoke sharply under her breath, "Don't let this lead to a drinkin' spree in the village. Do what you need to do and come back early. There's milkin' to be done."

"William can do that. We won't be late."

The men climbed up unto the cart and left Ann feeling helpless. She knew what would happen and as usual she would be left to pick up the pieces.

She came inside and sat down beside Allison. "What did the Minister say?"

"He said he will speak for him at the barracks. Sure our Walter is only a wean" Allison buried her face in Ann's shoulder. Ann looked up and caught Elsie standing listening.

"Elsie, you should be out helpin' William. How many times have I told you not to eavesdrop on grown up conversations?"

"Is Walter in trouble, Ma?"

"Your cousin is reaping the rewards of listening at doors. Go on now. Do as you're told and no repeating what you heard here."

Elsie left the kitchen and raced out to the byre. "Was that them away?" William asked.

"Just da and Uncle Jack. They're away towards Newton' "

"What! For feck's sake! That means I'm stuck with the milkin' again." Elsie was smiling.

"What's so funny?"

"I know something you don't know, William."

William ignored her, caught up in the way he was always left to carry the load. His da and his drinkin' spoiled everything.

"Go an' get the milk pails ready and stop prancing about."

"Wait till ye hear, William! Walter has been arrested." William stopped and stared at her.

"Stop talkin' shite, Elsie. What would they arrest Walter McCrea fer?"

"It's true, William, honest to God, something about guns. Da and Uncle Jack are away to see somebody."

William pulled at the cow's teats harder than usual. He had not seen much of Walter since he had been hired out to a farmer in Antrim last year. He had come home two months early with a black eye and a broken rib. Ma told them he had a falling out with the farmer and that Uncle Jack had to repay part of the hiring money. He liked Walter. He felt sorry for him being in trouble again.

"Go back to the house Elsie. See if you can hear anything else."

"Aye, I thought that bit of news would get you goin. I have my uses, William Johnston. You owe me a favour."

He aimed the teat at her, the milk missing her back as she ran laughing from the byre.

"Where are we goin', John?" Jack asked as they made their way up the steep brae.

"We're goin to see a very oul friend of mine who, if my information is right, we'll find in a field beyond the Orange hall."

"I heard the UVF were drilling there and down at the big house. There could be trouble if they're caught."

"It's not agin* the law, Jack, if ye hiv a licence signed be a JP and where there's a will there's a way."

"Do you go to these drills, John?"

"Naw, me marchin' days are long gone but I try to do my best to keep up with what's goin' on."

"Alison has bad nerves. She couldn't deal with it if I got involved in that sort of business. Ye seen yerself what she was like the day, I thought she would have a heart attack when the constable came to the dur. Does your Ann know you're involved?"

"My Ann wouldn't stop me even if she cud. I'm me own man, Jack. I might be a cripple but I'm not useless. Stop here, Jack, it's a tight wee step to the field. We'll need to walk from here."

They had been walking for five minutes when they heard the sharp voice coming from behind the wide ditch.

"That sounds like me man, Jack. Let me do the talkin'" Jack was breathing heavy, beads of sweat breaking on his brow. They rounded the ditch and came face to face with a crowd of men formed in ranks along the field.

Alan Campbell recognised the towering figure of John Johnston. He had put on weight, but at six foot four, he carried it better than most men of his age. They had served together at the Orange River in 1899, but John had been injured and shipped back barely six months after they had arrived. Alan acknowledged him and motioned him to wait.

He completed his assessment of the men before standing them down then headed across to meet Johnston.

"Johnny boy, how the hell are you? You're still standin' tall." They shook hands and back-clapped their greetings.

"I heard ye were back in these parts. It's great to see you again." John said still holding on to Alan's hand. "Weren't you livin across the water? Was the pull of a good fight too great for you?"

"Aye, it was something like that. I'm back to do some training for the lodge. Seems Tyrone set an example when they paraded at Craigavon and the demonstration in Omagh has made men stand up and stop this Home Rule bill. We need to turn banners into guns. The lodges in Tyrone have set the standard. So we need to live up to our reputation. How's the leg?"

"A feckin' curse if I'm honest. But I'm not dead yet. Could be of some use if you need a hand. I can still shoot a gun."

"Ye always had an eye for the bull's eye, Johnny, it's a pity you're out of action. You're lucky to be still here to talk about it. There are many we knew lyin' out under the desert sands. What are you doin' with yourself these days?"

"Farmin' and rearin' weans."

"Jez, bad leg wasn't a drawback in that department. How many have you?"

"We had six but lost three to the typhoid in '08.

"God, Almighty. I didn't know, I'm sorry for your loss Johnny. It hit the country badly. I lost three cousins around the same time. You haven't had your troubles to seek. Was it Ann Crawford as was that ye married?"

"Aye, the very same one. What about you? Are ye married?"

"I married the army. She's the only woman that would put up with me, but I'm not goin' short if ye get my meanin'. The loss of the weans must have been hard on yis.*"

"Aye, very few families escaped. It was hard on the Missus but ye have to get on with it."

"What brings you out here, Johnny?"

"I was wonderin' if you could help an oul pal, Alan. It's a bit of family trouble. Ann's sisters young cub got himself into a bit oh trouble with the law over one too many guns in his cart. He's only sixteen. Headstrong and easy led. You know yourself how these young wans are. I have the father with me. This is Jack McCrea. Jack this is Alan Campbell, the man I was tellin' ye about."

The men acknowledged each other with a nod.

"It's a bloody disgrace. We need every man we can get before this is all over. Give me his name Johnny. It might take a day or two but keep it to yerself and I'll do my best. Now, I need to get on. I'll let you know. Good luck."

"I owe ye one, Alan. Don't forget my other offer. Any time, any place. I'm yer man." John stood watching his old friend as he lined the men up for the drill. He missed those days. He wanted to become involved in this latest struggle, a fight for King and country, but here at home where it mattered most. He limped back to the cart, his thirst for a drink growing stronger.

"Now Jack, that's all taken care of. Keep it under your hat for a day or so and the boul boy will be back home safe and sound. I think it's the pub now for a porter or two to celebrate."

"I'm grateful, John, but I had better get back to Allison and tell her the news. I'll drop you off in the Plumb. I have no help at home with him in the barracks and the milkin' needs to be done."

"We'll be signin' the covenant soon and there will be less of this arrestin' young cubs who are only doin' what is right. These Liberals need to sit up and take notice. Ulster will not be subject to Home Rule. You must be proud of young Walter?"

"Aye, but his ma is not happy. The women don't see this like we do, John. She says he learned all this UVF stuff when he was hired out up in Antrim. He came home with all these plans to join up, but he's too young to join anything yet. This gun runnin' is getting very serious, I'd be happy to see him home and so will his Ma."

They had reached the village again and Jack stopped the trap. As John stepped down, Jack slipped a coin into his hand.

"Sure there's no need to do that, man. We need to look after out own, but my thanks to you. Good luck and don't be hard on the cub. I wish I was that age again."

The horse and trap rolled away and John opened his hand and smiled. A shillin', bright and new, lay on his palm. The thirst for a porter was about to be quenched.

ULSTER DAY

Sir Edward Carson spoke to the nation on
the eve of Ulster Day. Calling on all responsible
men from every district in Ulster – "That it is their
duty when they enter this solemn obligation, that it
is the most serious matter that has ever confronted
them in the course of their lives."

Tyrone Constitution, 4th October 1912

Chapter 5

It was Ulster Day, 28th September 1912. John and Ann climbed up on the cart beside their neighbours. The Orange Lodge had arranged transport and a succession of carts had been driving back and forth on the road all morning. Every cart was decorated with banners and bunting and, as carts passed back and forth on the road, there were loud cheers and calls of 'No Home Rule! Home Rule is Pope Rule!'

"You didn't bring wee John, Ann?" Lizzy Crawford asked as they made their way to the village.

"No Lizzy, William is in charge while we're away and wee John is happy to play out in the fields on such a good day besides it's nice to get an hour to ourselves."

"What a day it is! A day our children will remember for the rest of their lives. It will go down in the history books as the day Ulster men and women put an end to any talk of home rule. God and Carson have called on us and we must answer." Ann made no reply, recognising the criticism that lay in the remark.

John squared his shoulders and began singing the national anthem, his fellow passengers joining in.

The roads around the church were packed with carts. A long line had formed leading up the drive. The mood became solemn with conversations carried out in loud whispers. Children were playing in the hay field next to the church under the watchful eye of Miss Finlay the schoolteacher.

John stepped into the porch followed by Ann and each were directed to their specific document. Men signed the main Covenant and women signed a separate women's Covenant, pledging their support.

After signing they both moved outside to the sunshine passing the time of day with people in the line moving forward to the church porch.

"Lizzy was right. We should have brought wee John. He would have enjoyed playing with the other weans," Ann said. She hated being away from him even for a short time.

"William should be here even he can't sign."

"Aye, maybe so, but he's old enough now to make up his own mind and the likes of Lizzy Crawford should keep her nosy opinion to herself. It's none of her business."

"Ach, don't mind her, Ann, just enjoy yourself for a while," John said, putting his arm around her. "We could go for a stroll down by the river if you fancy a wee kiss and a cuddle." He tightened his hold on her waist and smiled. "John Johnston, keep your voice down and behave yourself. We will do no such thing!"

"Well you can't blame a man for tryin' when he has the best lookin' woman in the county by his side."

Ann was trying hard not to smile. "Be serious, John. Today we are meant to be serious about this and you want to fool around."

"I am serious about this. Now will you walk with me or not?"

"We can walk home together if you like and not take the lift."

"Ahh, that's a bit of a problem. I'm not going straight home. I have to go to the hall in half an hour to meet a couple of lodge boys. We have some business to talk about."

Ann tried hard to stay calm. They were in the middle of a crowd and these people had enough to talk about. She stepped away from his embrace and whispered into his ear, her hand over her mouth.

"Don't come home the worse for drink, John. The boys don't like it and neither do I." He caught her hand and she was aware people were looking at them.

"Don't make a scene here, please John."

"I'm going to the hall. Honestly, and I'll be back at tea time."

"I'll believe that when I see it. I'm away on home. You suit yourself." John watched as Ann climbed up on the cart parked across the road, smiling her thanks to the driver. She didn't look back.

He was unaware of a group of men in conversation with the minister when he crossed the road to the pub, emerging half an hour later to make the short walk to the lodge.

The hall was small with wooden benches around three sides and a storage area for three furled banners.

A cluster of men sat in the benches at one corner. Their conversation stopped and they rose to their feet as John approached.

"Ach, sure there was no need to stand for me, boys. Have you started without me?"

Some of the men turned and left, muttering apologies, avoiding eye contact with John.

"Is everything alright here? Have I missed something?" He began to sweat, sensing the tense atmosphere. Derek Boyd and Malcom McConnell remained, both men now struggling with an explanation. Derek Boyd spoke.

"We have a problem here, John and I'm sorry to have to be the one ta tell ye. There's word around the country that you can't be relied upon, given the dangerous times we're living in."

"What word? What are ye talkin about, Derek I'm a loyal protestant, I served Queen and country and carry the scars to this day. Who says I'm not reliable? Let them say it to my face and I'll show them both my fists."

"It's not your loyalty that's in question here, John. To be blunt, it's your drinking habits we object to. Even on this auspicious day in our history you have chosen to imbibe in strong drink. As Master of this Lodge, I have been asked to speak to you and to tell you that your drunkenness can no longer be tolerated. It contravenes the laws of Temperance and Sobriety within the Orange Institution and therefore we must caution you that unless you control your drinking, we will be forced to suspend your membership of this lodge, which means we cannot permit you to sit on committee. We're sorry it has come to this. You have the right to have this decision reviewed in July 1913, when we renew membership applications. We hope you can understand our decision. Rev Bowman has asked me to tell you he will be happy to talk to you at any time. Good day to you."

The men left, the door slamming shut behind them. John sank down on a bench, his head in his hands.

Home Rule Campaign.
Record Fund Wanted.
Appeal to Irish People.

A manifesto to the Irish people, signed by the Most
Rev. Dr O'Donnell, Bishop of Raphoe; Mr J. E. Redmond,
MP and Mr J. Fitzgibbon MP, National Trustee, has been
issued: "Once again," it says, "the duty devolves upon us
of making an annual appeal to you for subscriptions in
aid of the Home Rule Fund....."

Ulster Herald 1912

Chapter 6

It was a month since Ulster Day and not a day had passed that John had not considered the consequences of the warning from the master of the Lodge. He had been filled with rage and disgust. How could he be treated like a criminal by his own people. He was not the only member of the Lodge to take a drink or two but no one was standing in judgment on them.

He had not told Ann. He was ashamed and as the days past his need for the drink became worse. He knew he was spending money they didn't have and yet Ann never complained. He had thought about going to the minister but his pride and stubbornness stopped him.

He needed to relieve himself. He slipped out of the bed and pulled on his trousers leaving the bedroom quietly so as not to disturb the rest of the house. The cold morning air cut him as he went up the yard. Another day dawning. He cupped water from the barrel into his dry mouth, had a pish then went to the barn. The half naggin* bottle was warm when he pulled it out from its hiding place in the bale of hay. He drank quickly, finishing the last drop with guilty relish. He would have to get a fill later when he was coming back from Newton.

"You were up early." Ann was in the kitchen stirring the pot of oats.

"Aye, I thought I had better get an early start so I have time to take Elsie over to the big house. Is she all packed?"

"Aye, for all she has to pack." Ann burst into tears again. She had hardly slept a wink knowing that it was the last night she would hear Elsie's sweet breath as she lay in the bed next to her.

"I just hope she is happy. I'm going to miss her." Her sobbing began again. "I just want her to stay with me. I need her."

"Ma, please don't cry." Elsie had come into the kitchen unnoticed to them. She hugged her Ma, her own tears not far away.

"Now girls, don't be standin' there cryin into the porridge. I like to add my own salt." John laughed at his own joke. Mother and daughter broke away from their embrace, wiping away the hot tears.

"Mrs Harbinson, the housekeeper, told me not to pack any clothes. I will get a bath in a proper bath house after I arrive and my hair washed. I'm getting all new shifts and everything," she blushed. "Mrs Harbinson said I can bring my Bible and a prayer book and one special personal ornament from home, but no clips or hairbrushes."

What's all this bathin' about? Do they think you have fleas?"

"No. All the new staff comin' in do the same and anyway I don't want to be any different from the rest. What will I bring for my room, Ma? I wish I had a picture."

Ann smiled and reached down behind the table and handed Elsie a small parcel wrapped in brown paper.

"This is for you, Elsie, to remind you of home and how much we all love you."

"Oh, Ma, what is it? Can I open it now?"

"Aye, open it for Gods sake. I just hope you're not getting away with the gold we had saved for our oul age."

"Och, John be serious! Go on, Elsie, open it. I hope you will be pleased."

The paper fell away from the parcel to reveal a small pincushion of red velvet with the name Elsie stitched into the centre of a heart.

"Oh, Ma, it's beautiful. It's the most beautiful thing I have ever seen. Thank you. I will keep it safe forever." The tears fell again and she clung to her mother sobbing.

"I'm sure you will put it to good use and your work will make us all very proud. I got you a pad of writing paper and envelopes as well so you must write as often as you can and tell us how you are. Now, I have made a pot of soup and fresh bread for us before you leave. Can't have you going away hungry. Go and put those things in your bag so you won't forget them."

"I hope the cook's as good a baker as you are," she said as she went off humming to herself.

The cart set off at midday. Elsie watched her Ma's waving figure until she disappeared from view. She had said goodbye to William and wee John before they went to school. There had been some tears but William had teased Elsie about her nosey ways, warning her not to be caught listening at doors in the big house. The two boys made up a rhyme and left her on the step laughing as they chanted, 'nosey girls with big big ears will get pushed in the midden* in floods of tears'. She was going to miss William and wee John and all their daily banter.

The journey was a bumpy ride until they got to the gate lodge of the estate and the gatekeeper directed them to the servant's entrance. A curving drive flanked by neat lawns led them down into the estate and several hunting dogs greeted them at the rear doors. "Here we are then, Elsie my girl, all present and correct. Here let me help you down." Elsie hesitated.

"Will the dogs be cross?"

"Not at all, lass, they're the welcome party. Come on. Get down and make friends with them. I see someone comin' from the house." John removed his cap. "Good day, Missus. I'm John Johnston, I'm just leavin' off my girl Elsie. I was told I had to sign a paper."

"Good Day, Mr Johnston. I am Mrs Harbinson, the housekeeper. Elsie, you can go into the house once you have said your goodbyes to your father. Mr Johnston, will you call with Mr Billings at the estate office, which you will find behind that green door to the right. He will see to the paperwork. Good day to you."

"Good day, Missus. Now, Elsie, it's time to say goodbye. You will be on top of the world here lassie! It's a fine house with lovely gardens. I best get to see this man Billings. Give me a hug now and get away into your new quarters."

"What have you to sign, Da?"

"Your indenture papers to say we accept the estate as your guardian for the next three years. Sure I thought you knew about it?"

"Aye, but I didn't know you had to sign anything." Elsie shuffled her feet as she stared at her Da, "Does that mean if I don't like it I can't go home again?"

"Now, Elsie, this is not the time to be havin' second thoughts. These people will be good to you and you will learn a lot from them. As for goin' home you will be able to visit us on your days off. This was all arranged. Things cannot be changed now. Write to us and let us know all the news. Now I must get on and you had better see to your duties. Give me a big hug and try not to worry."

They parted and John watched her disappear through the door.

It was a good thing that Ann could not come with them today for he was sure she would have lifted Elsie back onto the cart and taken her home with them again.

He went off to find Billings and receive his first payment for his daughter's hiring.

Constable Campbell was doing his rounds of the public houses. There had been a lot of after hours drinking lately and he was determined to stamp it out. He had just crossed the road when he was nearly knocked off his feet. The constable straightened himself, a scowl on his face. John Johnston was swaying on his feet and knew a lecture was on the cards. It would not be his first lecture from the constable and one time he nearly spent the night as a guest of his Majesty in the station's only cell.

"Now, now, Mr Johnston here we are again. Are you on your way home?"

"Sorry, Constable, I niver seen ye. My eyesight is not what it was."

"You have a bit to go to get home. Will you be able see your way up the road if your eyes are that bad?"

"Ach sure I could get home blindfolded, I'm so used to the road."

"That's no surprise to me, Mr Johnston, your eyes have been giving you trouble for some time now. Ye would need to get rid of that blindfold, you should try some syrup of figs mixed with water twice a day and total abstention from porter. You'll feel like a new man in no time. Goodnight, Mr Johnston."

"Goodnight, Constable, and I thank you for your kind advice." Under his breath John cursed his bad luck at meeting the constable. He was the greatest gossip in the village and kept the minister up to date with any late night drinking. He had stopped going to church every Sunday and only went when Ann got upset and begged him to think of the cubs.

His drinking was well out of his control. The past weeks and months had slid by in a haze of alcohol. He had tried, but the need for the drink gnawed at him and it eased the pain in his leg.

Christmas had been hard on Ann. She missed Elsie. On the one day that she might have got home to visit over the holidays, it had snowed hard and the roads were impassable in places. That and the fact that John had lain in his bed drunk over most of Christmas put the dampers on any festivities. He hadn't gone to church either. When they took their seats, she sensed the disapproving stares of those around her. After the Christmas service Reverend Bowman had shaken her hand with his usual question about John's health and his continued absence from church. The congregation queued up behind her as she tried to cover her embarrassment. To her relief, there had been a commotion along the drive when one of the horses, frightened by a stray dog, reared up overturning the trap and they were able to slip away unnoticed.

Wee John was oblivious to everything. He had got a book about Cowboys and Indians in his Christmas stocking. He and William had spent two days out in the barn making tents out of meal bags, bows and arrows with bailing twine and sticks cut from the hedge. They ran in and out of the barn whooping and howling, and when the snow appeared they made a sleigh of the turf creel and slid up and down the steep bank behind the house. William was back in his boyhood again and Ann wished she could stop the clock and hold unto these moments with the sound of their fun and laughter filling the darkness of her days.

Alison and Jack had called on Boxing Day. Alison was quiet. Ann tried her best to cajole her into singing them a song like she used to when they were young, but they had to listen instead to John in one of his few lucid moments trying to sing and dance a jig almost falling in the fire. Wee John had clapped and tried to copy his da and the adults laughed, trying to hide the undercurrent of their disapproval of John's behaviour.

"How's Walter these days, Jack, is he keepin' out of trouble?" John winked, knowing he was not supposed to mention Walter's run in with the police.

Jack stood up and pulled on his cap.

"It's time we were away home and in answer to your question, Walter is doin' what every Orangeman shuld do in these times. He's joined the Ulster Volunteer Force. Tyrone is the first County lodge to organise and other lodges will follow our lead. Then Carson will have his army. Barnonscourt is preparing to show the British Government that we will not stand for Home Rule. We are as Irish as them down in Dublin. We belong in the British Empire and we will fight to the last man for it. Come on, Alison. It's a pity ye'er not allowed to, John, after your wee problem."

"What problem is that, Jack?" Ann asked.

"Did he not tell ye, Ann? He was suspended from the lodge on Ulster Day for his drinkin' and about time too. The whole country is talkin' about him. Can't understand how ye put up with it."

Ann stood up, her hands closed in fists, her face white with rage. William came and stood beside her.

"I think ye have said enough, Jack. Ye have no right to come here to our home and speak about things that don't concern ye and yes, John did tell me, but ye have no right to speak ill of John in front of his weans, especially after all he did for Walter when he got in trouble."

"Good for ye, Ann. I have served my country and I would do more if I was fit. So don't get on yer high horse with me."

"You could do more, John, if ye kept away from the drink. You're a ruined man. Ye ought to be ashamed af yerself, leavin' Ann to face the music on a Sunday morning while yer lyin' drunk in yer bed. Take my advice for what it's worth and sober up for the family's sake. I'm sorry Ann."

As Jack moved to the door, John caught his coat and punched him to the

41

ground. The two women screamed and William jumped forward trying to pull his Da away from his uncle who was now lying on the floor, blood running from his nose.

"Leave go, cub, I'm not finished yit."

"John!" Ann was on her knees beside Jack, covering his bloody nose with the end of her apron.

"Go away to yer bed, I'll have no more of this in my house in front of the weans. Go now." He staggered out of the kitchen and they heard the front door latch clatter as he went out into the street.

"Go after him, William. See he's alright, I'll see to Uncle Jack." She pulled a cloth from the line and wiped away the blood. He got up on his feet and clutched the cloth to his nose, mumbling incoherently.

"Come on now, Jack, I know ye mean well but this is something I have to deal with and I take comfort in the teachin' of our Our Lord who said 'Let him that is without sin cast the first stone.' A lesson a lot of people round here seem to have missed." Allison gave him a drink of water and reached for Ann's hand.

"If I can help, you will let me know."

"Aye, Alison, I will. The bleedin' seems to have stopped. Are ye all right to get home, Jack?"

"Aye," was all he said as he left holding a fresh cloth to his nose. Wee John climbed onto her knee.

"Why did Da hit Uncle Jack, Ma?"

"Ach, ye don't need to worry, wee John, he will be sorry when he's feelin' better."

"Is he sick?"

"Aye, he is son, and we will have to help him get better. Now ye need to get to bed. I'll come down and say your prayers with ye."

She heard raised voices outside. William came into the kitchen followed by John who grunted an oath and went down to his bed.

"Did you know Da had been thrown out of the lodge?"

"No, he niver told me."

"Aye, there's a lot he's not tellin'."

"What do ye mean, William?"

"Ach, ye have enough to worry ye. I shouldn't make it any worse."

"Tell me, William."

"The barn an stable are full of empty bottles up behind the stacks and in the loft. Wee John found them when we were playin' out there. Where is he getting the money fer it all. I asked him there now but all I got was a swearin' match?"

The restraint she had been holding back came in long silent sobs. She buried her face in her hands and took comfort in her son's strong arms as he held her, rocking her to and fro as she had done for him so many times in his childhood. After a while she pulled away and kissed him on the cheek.

"Thank ye, son. I needed that."

"Ach, I wish I could do more."

"Aye, I know, but better times will come. God will be our strength but now I think we need a bite of supper and wee John is waitin' for me to say his prayers with him. Ye could fill the water bucket and the kettle and the turf box is empty." She smiled at him. "Ye did ask if ye could do more."

He went off to do as she bid him. She knew about the bottles hidden around the place. She had found a half full one under the mattress one day when she was changing the bed. It was poteen, clear as spring water, but as potent as the poison it was. She had tried to talk to him about it but all her efforts ended up with his denial and promises to stop.

The snow stopped early in the New Year. John had stopped drinking long enough to clear the snow away from the lane, but in truth he had run out of his supply in the barn and was soon off to the village to replenish his stock.

William and Paul met in the Plumb and had moved under the bridge for shelter, their breaths turning into white puffs from the cold.

"How was Christmas for ye, William?"

"Miserable most of the time, Ma misses Elsie and Da niver sobered. If it hadn't been for wee John I would've gone mad. What about you?"

"Ach, the usual, quiet, Da got a goose given to him and by New Year I thought I was beginning to grow feathers and talk with a gobble. Ma says I was talkin' in me sleep."

"What were ye sayin?"

"She couldn't make out what I was sayin' but I told her I was likely dreamin' I was a goose."

"Do you have funny dreams?"

"What? Dreams about Geese!"

"Naw, dreams about lassies. About kissin' them an all?"

"Jez William, I have not. Have you?" Paul laughed.

"Who were you kissin? Miss Finlay by any chance."

Then they both roared with laughter that echoed down along the river.

"Are ye havin' me on, William?"

"Ach, I just thought I'd ask ye'. Who else could I ask?"

"Sure we all have dreams. What's different about yours?"

William jumped up from the stack, realising Paul's dreams and his were not the same.

"Forget it. I'm only foolin' ye. Come on! We need to get down to the hut and get a bit of work done. I found a great oul beam in the orchard we could use for the roof."

Paul followed William down the riverbank, all talk of dreams and kissing soon forgotten.

The O'Neil brothers were standing on what was left of the hut. Although the storms of the winter had caused some damage, the roof had been intact last time they had been here. Now it lay flattened and the collection of odd seats and meal bags had disappeared.

William let out a roar of anger and charged Fergal, knocking him to the ground. Cahill O'Neil lifted a stick and attacked Paul, landing heavy blows to his back and legs. Paul managed to grab the stick and pulled Cahill to the ground. They rolled around the bank of the river each trying to gain the upper hand. It was then that Cahill fell into the fast flowing river. The water was high and the three boys watched, helpless as he was pulled under the water by the current.

"You bastard, McGovern!" Fergal shouted as he dived into the water cutting across the raging current to reach his brother who had surfaced and was clinging to an overhanging branch on the far bank.

William and Paul cheered and taunted the pair as they pulled themselves out of the river. Cahill was limping badly and there was blood running from a cut on his forehead.

"This is not over, ye feckers! "You'll pay for this," Fergal shouted.

"Stay away from our land or he will be held under the water next time!" William shouted back, slapping Paul on the back and they shook their fists in the air at the two figures disappearing out of sight.

"That'll teach them to mess with us, William. Come on! Lets get this mess sorted out."

Over the river, Fergal heard them laughing and cheering and vowed their victory would be short lived.

DEATH OF THE 2ND DUKE OF ABERCORN
James Hamilton, 2nd Duke of Abercorn, died aged 73 in
London on Monday 13th January. Burial will take place
in the family plot at Baronscourt Parish Church.

Tyrone Constitution, January 1913

Chapter 7

A letter arrived from Elsie a week after the death of the 2nd Duke of Abercorn.
The papers had been full of the news. It had been reported that members of
the Royal family were in attendance at the funeral. Ann had worried about
how Elsie would cope with being so close to a house in mourning, recalling
the horror they had all gone through just a short five years ago when they had
buried the little ones. She need not have worried.

Dear Ma and Da and brothers,
　I know you would have heard about the death of the Duke. We were
all shocked when it happened even though he had been sick for a long
time and he was very old. We were kept busy with all the very special
visitors who came for the funeral. I cannot say who they were except that
we had to bow a lot.
　Mrs Harbinson was never off her feet as the Duchess took to her bed
for three days after all the fuss was over and needed tending to a lot.
Mrs Harbinson said I was a great help to her and she is going to let me
go home for four days next month. She has arranged a cart for me on
12th of Feb at 8 in the morning so I'll be home early that day and leave
on the fifteenth. She asked if Da could bring me back.
　There is a lot of coming and going now since the funeral as the
workmen are changing the stables into a canteen.
　This is going to be a training camp for the officers in of the UVF
and we are getting our own post office so my letters will get to you
faster.
　We are getting a new woman into the household, she is going to train
women and girls in first aid and Mrs Harbinson says all the maids
will have to attend the training. Just imagine Ma me a nurse.
　I hope this finds you all well as it leaves me. God Bless.
　Your loving daughter, Elsie

Ann folded the letter and put it behind the clock to be read aloud later.
Elsie sounded happy and seemed to be doing well but the talk of her training
to be a nurse made Ann afraid of what would come out of it. Elsie was still
young and easily influenced. Maybe it was time to meet this Mrs Harbinson.
She would try and go with them to the big house when John left Elsie back

after her holiday. In the meantime she had to make everything nice for Elsie coming home.

Elsie was in a flurry of excitement. She was going to learn all about being a nurse. Well in truth she wouldn't be a nurse exactly but they were going to be taught how to bandage wounds and care for injured soldiers.

It was all part of the new camp being set up on the estate. All the women and girls had to be involved and were expected to attend training sessions two evenings a week. A fully trained nurse had joined the household called Miss Georgina Althrope. She was very nervous on her first day and Elsie had tried her best to make her feel at home, remembering her own first day in the big house. Georgina, as she asked to be called when she was not on duty, had a room away from the servant's quarters near the nursery. As their friendship grew, and when her duties allowed it, she spent more and more time in Georgina's company.

For months the buildings around the estate had been filled with carpenters and builders. Now that the renovation to the stables were almost complete, Elsie and the other maids had been set to cleaning the rooms in readiness for the first intake of soldiers.

Newly installed electric lights had become the talk of the kitchen and viewed with mixed feelings.

"It's not right," the undercook had declared. "Now we have light all the time there'll be no time to rest."

"I hope we get electric light here in the house," the housekeeper remarked. "Just think how easy it would make our lives, not having to light the lamps every evening. I'm told the electric also heats the water. The telephone and post office will also be great conveniences. Imagine being able to speak to someone in London."

"It'll only be convenient if the body ye want to speak to owns a telephone. How many of you know someone who has one?" Mr Billings remarked.

And so the debate went on.

There was no shortage of admirers on the estate. Men, young and not so young flirted with the maids every time they appeared until, Mrs Harbinson complained to Mr Billings. Then the workmen were banned from whistling and passing remarks. Elsie kept well away from any trouble.

Mrs Harbinson was good to her and if she was to do well for herself she needed to keep in her good books. The idea of being a nurse appealed to her. In her short time on the Estate she had begun to realise how sheltered her life had been at home. The opportunities that were open to her seemed endless.

She felt guilty and knew how much it would hurt her Ma if she knew how she felt. Best to keep things to herself for now and have patience.

UNITED IRISH LEAGUE
KNITTING THE RANKS

Greencastle Branch Re-organised

An Enthusiastic meeting was held in
Greencastle to bring together nationalists
within the district to enrol in the Irish Volunteers
in defence of Home Rule and to veto Partition.

Ulster Herald, Saturday, February 22, 1914

Chapter 8

Padraig crossed the road to the hall in Carrickmore. He cursed inwardly at the way things were going between the Brotherhood and the Hibernians.

This past year it seemed that Nationalists had been forced to pussy foot around the protestant band-wagon. Left standing on the sidelines while unionists paraded the country, flaunting their illegal guns in full view of the law.

It was time to put an end to the small talk and cosying up to the Protestants. The Irish Volunteers were now an army; but who would they be fighting for? The meeting started with a heated discussion revolving around the call from John Redmond for Irishmen to join the Irish Volunteers. In the opinion of many Nationalists, Tyrone was caught up in a war of words with the Hibernians and the Brotherhood would not be in a position to move forward unless they got over their differences and joined forces. The division of opinions at the meeting threatened to become a rabble. Patrick Mulryan stood up and in the silence that ensued he spoke.

"Be warned that the time for action is coming close when all Irish men should search their souls for the strength to commit to the battle we all face for Ireland to be free from oppression. The UVF are at our doors, armed and ready to fight. Are we going to argue among ourselves while our protestant neighbours march armed to the teeth, in full view down our streets while the British argue and slice Ireland up like a cake to deliver it to Carson on a plate? We need to be ready to stand back to back in defending our Irish heritage. We need Irishmen to put aside their differences to stand together to fight together and to rid us of this boil on our country's back. Let us show the UVF our strength, let us show them we will not be bartered over in the halls of Westminster. Are ye with me?"

The crowd erupted.

Mulryan raised his hands and silence restored.

"Drilling will begin immediately, every man should report to his circle. Marches have been arranged in all districts. You will not show open aggression at this time. We will behave in an orderly manner but the message must be clear. The guns are on their way. Our day will come."

After the meeting, Padraig waited for the crowd to leave. Five men remained behind representing the circle's council for action. Patrick Mulryan, Packie Monaghan, Tip Sweeney, Sean Quinn and Padraig. Mulryan spoke again.

"Well, boys, I thank you for your support this evenin'. What I am about to say is to be treated with strict confidence. Plans for a rebellion to end all rebellions have been set in motion. We have been defeated, in the past, by poor planning not enough men and not enough guns. That will not happen again. We are bound by the oath of the Brotherhood and we must be actively involved in recruitment and training in the coming year. Redmond has an army of Irish Volunteers but they fall very short in numbers to match Carson's Ulster Volunteers. We need young men to answer the call so when the time comes we will have a force to match any army not to fight in a foreign war but in a war for this island of Ireland.

"These plans for the rising throughout Ireland are well underway but we lack the commitment here in the north and that must change in the near future. Dublin is to be the target and central to the strategy for an act of rebellion in every county of Ireland. Agents are active in Germany buyin' a shipment of guns. Planning and patience are to be the motto for us all.

"Tyrone will play a pivotal role in the insurrection through a communication network, already in place. Important to this is secrecy. Tell no one, not even your wives of what we, as a nation, are about to do."

On the way home Padraig was fired up with a new resolve, that he and his family would not be found wanting when the call came to defend Ireland.

If only Mary would forget the past and give him her support. He had met a lot of women at meetings who stood side by side with their men and their bravery and courage impressed him.

Mary had turned her back on all politics after the death of her father when she was fifteen. She had been devoted to him and had attended meetings and rallies with him as a child. He had been heavily involved with the Irish Political Party leader, John Dillon, when a split had occured with Tim Healy.

Healy had accused Dillon of selling nationalists to the Liberals and questioning their loyalty to the cause.

Her father had taken the scandal which followed as a personal slur on his name and had fallen into long periods of depression from which he had never recovered.

He passed away just two years later and Mary had sworn that she would never become involved in politics again.

Padraig felt frustrated that all his efforts to do what was right were being hindered by Paul's friendship and loyalty to William Johnston, who had a strong influence on him. It was time to remind his son of where his loyalty lay.

ARMY RECRUITMENT ADVERTISEMENT
The Royal Inniskillen Fusiliers
Recruits are now wanted for the above
regiment, also for all branches
of His Majesty's Army.
Young men of good character between
the age of 18 and 25 years are invited
to join and have good prospects.

Tyrone Constitution, March 6, 1914

Chapter 9

"Hope ye have all your work done before ye go out?"

William kept his head down concentrating on trying to tie the broken laces on his boots. His Da leaned forward on his chair. "Did you hear me, cub? I won't ask again."

"Aye, I'm all done. And I did my own work. Ma has enough to do." He stood up, his tall frame filling the space beneath the low ceiling. "I'm going to the Plumb."

"Did you feed the horse? We need to keep him in good trim. Talk is that the army are coming round the fairs looking for horses for the war effort. They say we could get up to two hundred pounds. But they only pay the top money for strong cart horses."

"Aye, I fed the horse, as I always do. Have you thought about how we are going to cope without a horse if you do sell to the army?"

"You mind your business, cub, and let me mind the rest!"

Ann Johnston came into the kitchen carrying a basket of turf, her thin frame stooped under the weight of the burden. She set it down on the hearth and looked at father and son, sensing the now familiar hostility between them.

"What are you two chitterin'* about now? Are you going out, William?" she asked, ignoring the snort from her husband. "Take the lamp with you. There's a mist coming up from the river."

John Johnston rose and knocked his pipe out on the hearth, scattering burning ash onto the stone floor. "I'll walk down with you. I'm going to Bradleys." William ignored the last remark, lifted the lamp and walked out of the kitchen door slamming it behind him. John snorted again and lifted his coat from the back of the door. "You can't say I don't try. The sooner he gets himself some decent work the better. There's a hiring fair coming up soon. It's time he earned his keep."

"Don't you dare speak of hiring him out to strangers? There's plenty of work to be done here at home."

"Aye, but there's no money coming in. He's not a wean anymore, Ann. He'll be seventeen on his next birthday. I was hired out and had three years under my belt at his age. I had to earn my keep. And times are no better now than they were then."

"If you spent less in Bradleys on drink we might have a bit more to come and go with. I've already had to part with Elsie. And how would we manage here if it wasn't for him?"

"Aye, rub it in you're married to a cripple."

"I didn't mean that and you know it, John. I miss Elsie. And you would soon know how that feels if William wasn't here to help out."

"Stop your yappin*', woman! You talk as if our Elsie was dead; she's only gone into service at the big house."

She was silent, knowing she would lose any argument on this subject. "Are you going to fix the thatch tomorrow? That leak is getting worse."

"It'll be done when it's done. I still have the ploughin' to do on the bottom field."

He pulled on his cap and limped out of the kitchen, the door slamming for a second time. She could hear him now out on the street, shouting William's name.

Ann knelt down at the fire, stacking the turf into the dwindling glow of orange ash. She missed Elsie. John couldn't understand her grief and he was drinking more than ever now. The loss she had felt when Elsie had left that first day on the cart, her small bundle clutched on her knee, and her face red from crying had broken her heart. It wasn't like her first day at school – she had to be gone for weeks now. Her time off from her duties didn't allow her to travel home and back. She had a half day off every six weeks and had managed to get a trap ride home for the afternoon a couple of times.

She began to gather up the ingredients for the morning scone of bread and the pot of porridge, her final jobs of the day. She had been on her feet now since seven this morning and she was tired. Wee John was fast asleep and the house was quiet, apart from the chirping of the crickets behind the chimney. She started on the bread, her mind wandering to what the future months would bring. All this talk in the papers about guns and war filled her with dread.

Jack's boy, Walter, was in England at a training camp. He had joined the Belfast Battallion. Allison couldn't be consoled. Walter was always going to be in this war. He had always talked about fighting, guns and war and never grew out of it. Now it was gun running, when other lads his age were fishing and climbing trees.

She thanked God that William had shown no interest in the UVF. She had lost too many of her children already. The epidemic in '08, seven years ago, had robbed her of her three beautiful weans.

Annie would be thirteen now, Martha eleven and Thomas nine, all gone from her in those three terrible weeks. Part of her had never accepted their loss. She had not left the other children out of her sight for a long time and they had carried her through despite her grief. John had the drink but it had taken its toll on him as well. They were not alone in the parish. The sickness had filled many graves that year, when death had walked among them without a backward glance.

The talk of civil disobedience against Home Rule was on everyone's lips. The men coming and going over the summer at hay time had talked of nothing else. She had seen it for herself in Newtown, men parading up and down the street, most of them no more than children. At the beginning of the year they had no uniforms and they had used broom handles for guns. Now, they had the full regalia, and the broom handles had been replaced by real guns. It wasn't a toy army anymore and even the look on their young faces had changed. The embarrassed flush had gone, replaced by a new confidence that shone like the buttons on their new uniforms.

The Con was full of it; pages and pages of news from the front and talk about Home Rule. Carson was calling for men to join up. The UVF were mobilised. She was thankful for John's bad leg. At least he was unfit for the army but she could see it was affecting William. He was changing. He kept secrets now. He was growing up. At sixteen he had the look of his father, tall and well built, with too much of his father's temperament. He had an eye for the girls now and they had an eye for him, especially the wee girl in the shop. He never had to be asked twice to go to the village. She was one of the O'Neils and Ann hoped he would stay well away from that sort of trouble. She shivered and prayed a silent prayer. Maybe John was right about the hiring out, it would keep him near and at least she would know he was safe and out of harm's way. She put the scone into the pot oven and swung the crane over the fire, piling the hot turf on top of the lid, another task done. She eased herself into the chair. It was just past nine; John would not be home for a while yet. She took down the Bible and flicked through its familiar pages, stopping at Ecclesiastes: 3: *To every thing there is a season and a time to every purpose under the heaven.*

TYRONE STANDS FOR IRELAND
Enrolment of volunteers.
Greencastle, Carrickmore, Sixmilecross
and Omagh fall into line. Eminent speakers propound
their views; Nationalists fall into line

Ulster Herald 1914

Chapter 10

William had stood outside the door for a minute and listened to the voices of his parents. Then, leaving the lamp at the gate, he skirted down the field, heading for the river. The oul boy had threatened to hire him out before. Mammy had always been able to stop it happening, but William knew he was on borrowed time. He had plans of his own, and they didn't include being a dog's body for some oul' bugger up the country.

He could hear his Da calling his name as he jumped the low ditch, scattering a flock of sheep as he went until the sound of his Da's calls had got fainter and was soon lost to the welcome sound of the water flowing over the stones. He was meeting Josie. They met whenever they could but they could not be seen together. Lately things had begun to get serious between them but she was a Roman Catholic. They were not supposed to get friendly with Catholic girls. One time, Paul had been caught by the priest passing one of William's notes to Josie at chapel and had kicked up an awful row, threatening to tell Josie's Da. She worked at her uncle's shop and she said she would meet him under the bridge on her way home.

He waited for over an hour but she didn't turn up. He was raging with frustration, his body urgently needed to lie with her and feel her softness under him. Now he faced another restless night until they met again. On his way home, he heard his Da whistling as he came down the road. He didn't want to talk to him. There had been enough talking for one day.

In the kitchen the smell of soda bread filled his nostrils.

"You're home early, son. The bread's not ready yet."

"Da's on the road. He must have got threw out of Bradley's. I'm away to my bed. Goodnight, Ma.

He was meeting Paul the next morning but as usual his Da had a list of jobs to be done before he could get away. He followed the river upstream to the foot stick and crossed to the other bank. Paul McGovern was already there fishing, his dark head just visible above a deep ditch under the bridge. William called out to him and he turned to greet him.

"You're late." Paul cast his line again and snagged it on the Rowan bush. "Now look what you made me do! Damn to hell, that was my best fly! I'll have to go after it! What kept you anyway?"

William was struggling to keep himself from laughing. It was always the same. Paul was hopeless at fly-fishing, but he persisted, even though the rod was one made from an old hazel cut from the hedge wrapped with gut. Paul turned to face William and had caught William's silent amusement.

"What the hell are you laughing at?"

"I'm not laughing at you. I'm laughing at the poor fish that can't understand what it's supposed to do, sink or swim!" Paul leapt at him and they both fell into the long grass of the bank, each straining to get the upper hand. "I give up! I give up! Stop! I'm lying in cow shite, let go!" William pushed Paul's heavy frame off him and they both lay panting on the grass. "Well, what did keep you?" Paul asked again.

"Just the usual, do this, do that.' He always seems to have another job that needs doing, just when I'm about to leave the house. I'm fed up with it all. I'm fed up with him. Now he's talking about selling the horse to the army."

"Is he serious do you think? Jeez William. Your oul' boy never misses a trick."

"Oh, he's serious alright. No discussion about it either or how we're going to manage."

Paul had heard it all before. William and his Da never saw eye to eye. He was lucky; his Da gave him plenty of slack, just as long as the work was done on time. But times were hard and he didn't know how they managed.

"Aye, I know what you mean."

"No, you don't know what I mean, Paul, You get on with your oul boy. At least he listens to you. Mine just wants to grind me into the ground. I heard him tell me Ma he's going to put me to the next hiring fair."

"God, William, he wouldn't do that. Sure hired help has no life at all – it's pure slavery!"

"Well, it won't happen and it's not going to happen." William stood up, scooping a handful of stones, and began chucking them into the river.

"What are you going to do?"

"I'm going into the army. They're recruiting up at Omagh barracks. You've seen the posters."

Paul joined him at the riverside and bent to gather a handful of stones chucking them with some force at the water.

"Does this mean you're joining the UVF?"

"I don't think it makes any difference what they call it. UVF, IVF – they're all going to be in the same army. Did you not see the picture in the Con? They marched to the station and saluted each other. I wish I had been there to see it. William bent and scooped up more stones, skimming them up the deep pool beside the far bank, a game he and Paul had played endlessly since they were children.

The silence between then was marked only by the plop of the stones in the water. Finally, William spoke.

"Will you come with me? Will you join up as well? Pals can be together. It says so on all the posters. We could go up to Omagh next Saturday. What do you think?"

Paul threw his last stone across the water then turned to face William. "I can't, William. My Da would feed me to the pigs if I even mentioned it. He says that this war is just another excuse for the British to push through the Home Rule Bill. Redmond was in Carrickmore talkin' to the Irish Volunteers. I didn't go but Da was mad as hell when he came home. He says it's Carson's Army no matter what Redmond says about it."

"Luk, Paul, Nationalists are joining in their droves in Dublin an' all round the country. Redmond has backed the war himself. What's so different about here? We'll all be on the same side, wearing the same uniform."

"That's alright for you to say, William, but I'm not as sure as you." Silence fell again between them like a dark shadow.

William lifted another handful of stones, tossing them from hand to hand, his frustration and anger not far from the surface.

Finally Paul spoke.

"You have to understand the way things are with my Da, William. He's a Republican through an through. He sees no good comin' out af this war."

"It's what you think that matters here, Paul. What else has he said?"
"There are things I shouldn't be talkin' about to you, William. Things I don't want to get mixed up in."

"Do ye not trust me, Paul? Is that what yer sayin' ?"

"Jesus, William, that's not fair. It's not that I don't trust ye. My joining the Brits in this war would kill him and that would be after he killed me! He has a lot of connections around the country with the Brotherhood and he wants me to join them now I'm sixteen. How the hell could I do it to him?"

William spat at the ground.

"Don't tell him. We won't let on till we're soldiers and there's nothing they can do about it." He was flushed now, his fear of Paul's rejection pushing him. "The money's good. We can look out for each other. We're too young to be buried in the bog. We need to see the other side of things."

"I don't know, William. Even talkin' about this scares me. We're goin' to a meetin' tonight. He's put my name down for the Brotherhood. He wants me to be like him but I've no time for it. I just wish I could do what I want for a change."

"Then come with me, Paul. Do it for us. Our oul boys have had their day. All mine can do is drink an' talk. He's not able to join anything with his bad leg. But if talk could win a war it would be over by now. Will you at least think about it? I'm going anyway, with or without you. I can't stand it at home anymore. There's no future in that farm. I'm not going to slog my guts out for nothing and get hired out to some oul shit, who will just work me like a horse. Will you think about it?"

"What about the age limit? We're too young."

"That's easy! I'm going to lie about my age! I won't be the first to do it." "What if they know we're too young?"

"How the hell would they know and if they don't take me in Omagh then I'll go to Strabane or Cookstown."

"What about Josie? Have you told her about your plans?" William kicked the bank, his anger flaring up.

"Josie will have to get used to it, she's not my keeper." He threw the last stone into the water.

"I'm going, Paul, no matter what. You're either with me or you're not. It's getting dark. I'm away home. Let me know by tomorrow, one way or the other. Goodnight."

Paul watched his friend walk back over the bridge and disappear from his sight. He couldn't imagine not having him around. He had been jealous when William had started to spend time with Josie O'Neil. She had been in the class below them and he knew she had always had a soft spot for William and if he was honest he had a bit of a notion of her but until recently he had not thought much about it. William had laughed when he had objected to Josie coming to the river with them but he didn't want her mooning over William. Him and William had shared practically the whole of their lives in one way or another. Now a girl and religion threatened to come between them.

He had heard enough fireside talk at home to know that there was trouble brewing, and it was closer to home than people realised. He had his own views. He saw no need to always be at odds with the people around you. But his Da was a strong Republican and he expected Paul to follow him into the Brotherhood. His instinct was to go with William and be a part of a great adventure. To see the world before marriage and weans tied him down. But he had a loyalty to his own family, and he couldn't allow himself to forget this.

He slowly wound up the loose line on the spool and headed back for home the long way, hoping the extra time would help him to think what he was going to do. Despite the fading light, he walked along the bottom field with a familiar step. He knew every hump and hallow on this well-worn path like the back of his hand. He and William had spent their childhood building small dams along the banks, and floating boats made from bark and lichen. They'd caught sticklebacks in the narrow channels of shallow water. As they got older they'd made rods from strong hazel cut from the hedge and hooks from chicken wire, digging the empty potato drills and soft earth along the river for fat juicy worms that wriggled in mass indignation as they were lowered into the deepest pools.

He was passing the chestnut tree and remembered how they had both climbed up through the canopy, impatient to harvest the best chestnuts that grew high up on the top branches. They were never ripe enough when they got them, their inner core soft, pale and disappointing. The first to find the hard brown nut was a challenge they looked forward to as each Autumn approached. Now there was a different challenge.

TYRONE FALLING INTO LINE
Onward march of the Movement.
Corps springing up throughout the County.
The Volunteer Movement is rapidly spreading
throughout the O'Neill County, and today
almost every parish has its own corps of
Irish Volunteers drilling each evening.

Ulster Herald 1914

Chapter 11

Paul's name was on the list going forward to the circle meeting for approval to join the Brotherhood. He didn't want to join but his Da was set on the idea. He was to be interviewed tonight by the selection panel. He hadn't mentioned it to William and now he felt guilty about keeping it from him.

They had gone one night last month to a public meeting just to see what was happening. He knew some of the crowd. The McHugh brothers from Gortin were there and Josie's brother Fergal O'Neil. Fergal was a bully and was never done baiting for a fight. There was no love lost between them.

There had been a crowd standing round the door. He kept trying to get away from the clamour. He spied Fergal in the crowd watching him and before he realised it he was standing beside him.

"Ach, here's wee Paul, the Protestant's front man. No sign of King William tonight, Paul? Did he not come with you to hold your hand? Maybe he wants to join the brotherhood?"

"Mind your mouth, Fergal. One of these days it'll get you into trouble." He had tried to move away and Fergal had stuck his foot out, tripping him. He staggered but, before he could react, his Da had Fergal by the scruff of the neck.

"You got a problem with your feet, O'Neil. Maybe you have too many toes. I could sort that out for you if you like. Now get out of my sight!" He dropped him back on his feet. Fergal's face was red with rage as he made for the door. He had turned back and hissed at Paul.

"I'll get you for this. There are circles within circles. You're a marked man."

There was no doubt what was meant by the remark.

Paul knew his chances for admission to the Brotherhood were poor. They had certain rules. If there were any objections it ended any chance of ever becoming a member.

He was too friendly with William and it didn't bode well with some Catholics. It didn't bother him, but his Da would be angry and hurt by any decision to bar him.

He was waiting to be called into the room at the back. He had watched other boys coming out after their interview, their faces lit up as if they had been given first prize at the feis*.

"You'll be ok son, just concentrate on what we talked about. Keep your answers clear. Be in no doubt that you believe that any action the republican movement take in the face of the British back peddlin' on the home rule debate is the right one." His da rambled on and on but he just wanted to go home and forget the whole thing before he got in too deep.

He was called next and his stomach lurched as he entered the room. There were five men sitting behind a table. The man at the end pointed at the empty chair. He knew Packie Monaghan and Tip Sweeney from the farmer's mart in Gortin but the other three were strangers. The man in the middle spoke and all eyes were focused on him. The sweat broke out on him. He had to clench his knees together to stop them from shaking.

"Well, Paul, no introductions needed here tonight except to say we're all Irishmen and we're all prepared to fight to the last man for the freedom of our country. What would you do for the cause?" The silence that followed the question was magnified by the loud rain beating on the window of the small room.

Paul coughed to clear the sudden ball of phlegm that was gathering in his throat. A second man spoke his voice quiet and soothing.

"Now, lad, I know this can be a bit daunting for a young wan like you, but all you need to do is to prove to us that you're true and trustworthy and that you will abide by the decisions of this circle in all that you may be asked to do in the future for the cause of freedom from oppression."

The man at the end of the table looked up from the paper he had in on the table in front of him.

"You're on friendly terms with a Protestant named William Johnston?"

Paul reacted immediately. "What has that got to do with anything? My friends are my business."

"Not anymore. We expect you to put aside all other allegiances towards the fulfillment of the aims of this circle. This means you will continue your friendship with William Johnston and any members of the Johnston family you come into contact with. You will report all conversations you may be a party to with regard to information on the Ulster Volunteers and their movements...."

Paul jumped up, overturning the chair.

"No! I will not be a snitch for you or anyone else. What do you take me for? I have been friends with William Johnston for all my life and you expect me to betray him and his family. Who are you anyway?"

Tip Sweeney rose and walked around the table, lifting a chair, and setting it behind Paul.

"Sit down. It's in your own interest to be calm and listen to what we have to say."

Paul sat down on the edge of the chair, his mind whirling, trying to understand what these men were suggesting. He was scared. He felt the world around him shifting. He didn't want to be here but he knew he had to put a good face on and pretend to agree, at least until he could think straight.

The man at the end turned the papers around to face him. It was a list of names. His heart hammered in his chest.

"Take a long look at this list. These are our enemies not our friends. These are the people who will take up arms against you and your family. This is not a betrayal. This is about looking after your own kind. Do you recognise any of them apart from the Johnstons?"

The phlegm rose up again and the cough he had held back before made him choke.

"Do you want a drink?" Packie Monaghan spoke for the first time. Paul nodded, unable to respond, his hand covering his mouth.

"Maybe we need to convene another meeting. You seem to be under the weather." Paul swallowed hard, the sweat bubbling up under his collar as another fit of coughing made him rise and stoop over as he tried to control it. "Aye, I think you're right, Packie." Tip Sweeney lifted the papers on the table. "Can you come back in a fortnight? That should give you time to get rid of that cough and have a think about what we have discussed. I would warn you to avoid repeating this conversation to anyone outside the brotherhood. Do you understand? "Yes."

"Have you any questions?"

"No."

"See you in a fortnight, Paul. Don't let the side down."

He walked past his Da, ignoring him and all the eejits* hanging around the front door. He headed up the hill to the cart.

He wretched and threw up into the sheugh*. As he wiped his mouth, Packie Monaghan's voice carried up to him in the cold night air. He jumped the low hedge and ducked down.

"It's time you had a sharp word with him. He has a fortnight to pull himself together then he will have to be dealt with. I bid you goodnight."

"Good night, Packie, I owe you one."

The footsteps receded down the road, the horse snorting as his Da climbed up into the cart.

He came back onto the road again and climbed up on the cart.

"What the hell happened in there, son? What did you say? You came out of that room like the divil was at your heels."

"I didn't say much. They did all the talking. I don't want to talk about it now. I want to go home."

The cart jolted over the rough road. Their only light was from the tilly lamp swinging from its hook, casting long shadows on the ditch. The cloud broke for a moment, filtering moonlight on the silhouette of the mountains. The heavy breathing of the horse and the rattle of the harness was the only sound in the still night.

"Are you alright, son?"

"Aye, why wouldn't I be?"

"Luk, son, I know this is hard for you, but you can talk to me. Tell me what they said."

"Stop the cart."

"I will not stop the bloody cart, not till you explain what happened in that room. Is this anything to do with that O'Neil cub, the one who annoyed you at the last meeting?"

"Fergal O'Neil has made it his mission in life to annoy me as often as he can. I could have dealt with him myself. There was no need for you to get involved then and there is no need for you to get involved now."

"I saw him trip you up. It was deliberate."

"I know, but it's not the first time and I'm sure it won't be the last. He's a bully. Look, Da, forget him. He's not worth troubling about."

"Don't let the likes of him put you off. He's an arrogant wee git."

"Isn't that what I just said? He's not worth the trouble."

"Ok, son, we'll leave it at that for now. Packie had a quick word with me after you left. He said they want to see you again in a couple of weeks. He said you had a coughing fit and they had to postpone the interview. You seem to be alright now?"

"Aye, something caught me in the throat." He coughed again but it was a poor effort compared to earlier.

The cart stopped abruptly.

"What's goin' on here? Are you keepin something from me? Having doubts about joining the Brotherhood?"

He could feel his stomach turning again. The thought of lying to his Da was against all he had been taught.

"I'm not sure. I don't understand it sometimes. I can't just hate somebody because they think different to me."

"You're talking about Willie Johnston, I suppose."

"William is my best friend. I couldn't go against him in this or anything else. He's like a brother to me."

"The time has come to put your schooldays away now, Paul, and grow up into a man's world. You're the next generation. It's your job to take up the struggle in the cause of Irish freedom. Willie Johnston will look at things differently when he sees the way things are going in this country. He won't ask you for permission to follow his own side when the time comes."

"His name is William, Da, not Willie and he never pushes his side at me, not ever. We don't do sides."

"We are fighting a war here, Paul, in our own back yard. A Brother was killed in Dublin and hundreds wounded on Bloody Sunday last year. This is where you should be and where your allegiance should lie, not with the likes of the Willie Johnstons. His family all signed the Ulster Covenant in 1912. His Da signed in his own blood if he is to be believed, thinned down by spirits no doubt." Padraig laughed at his own joke.

"That's not fair, Da. Mr Johnston has had a bad leg for years since the accident. He's in pain a lot of the time and William says that's why he drinks."

"It was no accident."

"What do you mean, 'no accident'? What happened to him?"

"Sorry, I spoke out of turn. It's none of our business, son. Just you remember where your loyalties lie. I'm depending on you for that. Now, we had best get home. Your Ma will be worried. Don't repeat any of our conversation to your Ma. This is between ourselves, Paul."

"More secrets."

"What's that supposed to mean? I have no secrets from your Ma."

"If I'm old enough to join the IRB, then I'm old enough for you to trust me a bit better than you do."

"It's not that I don't trust you, you're my son, but there are some things that we should never share, especially where women are concerned."

"Like what?

John laughed. "You'll find out some day."

BARONSCOURT VOLUNTEERS CAMP
English Press Opinion.

Reports in Unionist and radical newspapers say the camp
is purely for instruction purposes. All who attend are
fully aware of that fact. It was from start to finish run on
military lines. There were no free spells from work,
except between tea hour and lectures each evening.

Tyrone Constitution 1914

Chapter 12

William leaned on the gatepost outside the house, the lamp in the kitchen spilling soft light out onto the street. The anger he had felt earlier was gone and he was now filled with regret. Paul was his best friend since they had met at school that first day and they had been inseparable ever since. This was the first time he could ever remember that they had fallen out. He knew he had become pigheaded this last while, snapping at his Da more than usual, and needing to be on his own without any of the other distractions that went on around him. His thoughts kept going back to the fair day in August.

They had been sitting on the bridge in the Plumb, watching the parade of girls who were there for hiring. There were men and boys up for hire as well. But William and Paul ignored them, trying not to think of what their own future might hold if things didn't get better for the farmers around the country. The place was jumping with noise from the cattle and sheep, the auctioneer's chanting rhythm calling out bids ten to the dozen in the ring. Hawkers and tinkers roared and shouted and, now and again, if you were lucky, a fight would break out among the tinkers and then the whole place erupted into an uproar.

A poster on the wall opposite had appeared all over the place last week saying: "Your Country Needs You." They had both studied the poster making little or no comment. But for William something about the man in the uniform looking directly at him had made him feel important. It implied that he, William, would have a part in bringing about the defeat of these foreigners who wanted to ride roughshod over other countries. This was something he could do and earn good money at the same time. He tried to imagine being free from the boredom of the farm, the day after day sameness of cows and shit.

A fight had broken out among the tinkers over near Patterson's shop and the poster was forgotten in their eagerness to get a good view of the two burly men rolling on the ground, blood pouring from a deep cut in one man's head. The police arrived and the fight soon broke up. They wandered on, weaving their way among the familiar faces gathered around the pens, chatting and fooling with other lads they had known from school.

Over the bridge they came across the Army recruiting tent. The tall man in uniform called to them to come forward and talk to him about the benefits of joining in the war effort. Paul held back, but William was intrigued and crossed the road looking back encouraging Paul to follow, but he waved him away and moved on back over the bridge without looking back. His anger at Paul had flared in that moment but the soldier at the recruitment tent drew him in and he had forgotten about it until now. He had told Paul later about his conversation with the Sergeant, about the pay and all the perks of being a soldier, but he began to realise that Paul was not as fired up about it as he had been. The thought brought a lump to his throat. It wouldn't be the same without Paul.

The next night he waited until the house was quiet then crept out. He had been able to get a message to her and they were meeting at the usual place under the bridge. She sat with her back to him looking down the riverbank. He crept up behind her and clapped his hands hard inches from her ear. She jumped with a squeal that echoed over the water.

"Aw God, William, you scared the living daylights out of me! Look I'm shakin' like a leaf. Don't do that again." But she was smiling and he slipped his arms around her and she melted into them.

They stood there for a time just listening to the water trickling over the stones. He kissed her on the top of her head his hand caressing her breast. She turned and he pulled her close to him. He knew she could feel how much he wanted her. She began to respond. Her hips moving in an expectant rhythm against him. He lifted her skirt, his hand moving in between the soft warmth of her thighs.

She moaned softly, pulling him down until they were lying on the soft mossy ground.

"Do you want me Josie?" he asked. She kissed him full on the mouth. "Stop talkin' William."

Later, as they lay in each other's arms he stroked her arm and kissed her again.

"I'll have to go now, William. I wish we could stay like this forever." "Aye, but we can't. I'm joinin' the Army, Josie."

She pulled away from him and stood up. He stood up and caught her arm.

She was trembling, the fear in her voice filling the space between them. "You can't do that, William. Not now, not ever. There's a war on. Men are dying out there. You can't go, William. Do you not read the paper? They print out casualty lists every week. Andy Morton from Corrick was killed. I know his Auntie, she comes into the shop, she says her sister can't stop crying."

"I have to do this, Josie. My cousin has joined up and here's me sittin' at home. I'm goin', no matter what. The money is very good and I'll be able to save a bit for when I'm home again. The papers say it'll be over by Christmas."

"That's just not true, William. Anybody with any sense could tell you they're just more lies from the government. My Da says this is another way to kill Irishmen."

"Your Da would say that. Sure we know where his loyalties lie."

"What do you know about my Da, William Johnston? At least he's not sittin' in a bar getting drunk every night...."

William pulled away from her. They had never discussed the politics that separated them, nor the problems they may have at home.

"Leave my Da out of this. It's not about him. This is about me, about us and our future. If we are to get out of this village and lead our own lives then we need to look to the future."

"I'm sorry, William. Sorry for talking about your Da like that, but I'm scared of losing you. I love you."

Before he could stop her, she turned and ran. He watched her disappear up the road into the village. He couldn't follow her in case they were seen together.

The next night, Paul was waiting down on the riverbank. No fishing rod. He was sitting with his head in his hands and didn't look up as William sat down beside him. Neither of them spoke for what seemed an eternity to William. What if he said no? It wouldn't be the same without him.

His heart was pounding. He rose to his feet. "Well, have you decided yet?"

Paul stood up his eyes downcast. William turned away disappointment rising up in him. Then Paul punched him on the shoulder.

"I'm your man, William Johnston. Me and you is going to war and when them Germans hear about it, they'll shite themselves!" And with that he broke into a run, singing.

"We're in the army now, we're not behind a plough, last one in the river is a dead Hun!"

They sat on the bank and began to make excited plans for their future as soldiers. They talked until well after dusk had fallen and hunger made them think about home.

"What made you decide to go, Paul?"

"Things I don't want to talk about now. When are you going to tell Josie?"

"I have already told her. She was raging and ran off home crying."

"You mean you told her about our plans?"

"What else could I do?"

"You could have waited. Jez, William, what if she spills the beans? What if my Da hears it before I can tell him?"

"She won't do that, but I need to get a message to her. Will you give her a message at chapel on Sunday?"

"I'm not carrying any more messages between yous two. I got into enough trouble with the priest the last time and I don't want to run into her mad brothers either."

"Sorry, Paul, I shouldn't have asked. I'm going into the village in the morning. I'll try and see her if she's on her own in the shop."

"You might be more than sorry if this gets out. You shouldn't have told her. I'm prepared to take a big risk for you, not telling them at home. What happens if they find out? You'd better get it sorted out." He walked away, his hands dug deep in his pockets.

William was shocked. In less than a week they had disagreed twice. He went after him.

"I'm sorry, Paul, I niver thought. It'll be alright, honest to God. I'll talk to her in the morning, first thing."

"Aye, well, you had better or we're both in for it. I'm away home."

"What about Omagh next Saturday? Are we still on for it?"

"Aye, I'm still game as long as she hasn't squealed on us."

Paul had hardly slept since the meeting. He was more afraid now of the brotherhood and their requests to be an informer on William and his family than going off to fight a war. He wished he could talk to him, warn him, but he knew that he could never do that. He had made up his mind to join up. At least he and William would be together and away from here and the threats to them both.

William was in the Plumb early and waited at the corner in the hope of seeing Josie before she started work. Two of her brothers appeared crossing, the bridge making straight for him.

"Are you waiting for somebody, Willie boy?" Fergal shouted. "What business is it of yours?" William asked.

"If you're waitin' on our Josie you'll be waitin' a long time. Keep away from her, you proddy* bastard, or you'll feel my fist in your face."

"You're all mouth, the pair of yous. We're not in school now. Ye can't hide behind the master."

They were face to face now and people were turning to see what all the noise was about. The parish priest came out of the post office. He stopped and called to them.

"Good morning, boys. Are you looking for me by any chance Fergal? I'm on my way over to the parochial house now. You can talk to me as we go. Good morning, young Johnston. How is your mother?"

William felt his face flush down to his neck. "She's in good health, sir. Thank you for askin'."

"Good. Pass on my best wishes. Good day to you." He turned and walked on. The O'Neil boys followed, casting sideways looks at William.

The shop had opened and William crossed the road and went in. Josie's Uncle Sean was behind the counter and filled out his order without a word.

As William handed over the money he grabbed William by the wrist and pulled him over the counter, the muscles in his temples bulging with hate.

"Keep away from Josie if you know what's good for you, Willie boy. I'll not ask again."

"Let go, sir. You've no right to threaten me."

"I hope you keep it that way, Johnston. Stay away from her and we'll all be happy."

William came out of the shop shaking with rage. Who the hell did the O'Neils they think they were?

An urgent whisper focused his attention. He saw Josie crouching behind the entry to the back of the post office.

"Your oul Uncle is after threatening me. What's happened? Are you alright...?" she stopped him before he could say anymore.

"Don't meet me in the village again. Someone saw us together, then I came home upset and they were putting two and two together. I'm sorry, William."

"You didn't say anything about my plans did you?"

"No, I did not. Is that all you can think about? I have to go. Meet me tomorrow after milkin' at the foot stick."

"I'll do my best. I have things to do. Wait for me."

Tomorrow was Saturday. He had other plans.

WAR DECLARED
Military Movements at Omagh Depot
Recruits still Rushing to the Colours
200 recruits have joined the colours at Omagh.
The majority of whom were sent to the 3rd Battalion
Royal Inniskillen Fusiliers

Tyrone Constitution, 30th July 1914

Chapter 13

William and Paul met at the hut at nine o'clock on Saturday morning. They had fixed up an oul bike and had ridden it over the fields and lanes all summer. The tyre on the front was solid rubber but the back tyre was made of wood with a metal rim. They called it the gut wrencher.

"Do you think it'll get us there?" Paul asked.

He was the lighter of the two boys and always rode on the bar. They had strapped a meal bag stuffed with straw over the bar to pad it out, but this did little for the comfort of the ride.

"We will have to take our time. Ma gave me bread and a can of milk, but the can is too hard to carry so we may drink it now and have the bread later."

"Where did you say you were going?"

"I said we were going up to Cranagh to look for birds' nests. What did you say?"

"Jez, William, I niver thought of that. I said we were going fishing and me Da gave me an odd look. He said he hoped I wasn't poachin' down at Huston's water."

"Did he believe you?"

"I think so? He's away to the mart in Strabane."

They headed off to Omagh through Gortin Glen. William rode in the saddle while Paul sat astride the bar. It was a tough uphill struggle. Potholes and piles of dung from the many horses that used the road made them swerve and fall into the ruts along the ditch. They laughed and sang songs they had learned at school. The road was busy and more than once they were cussed by passing carts when the horses shied from the noise they were making.

At the top of the glen they stopped and ate the bread, drinking from the fresh stream of water running over the mossy banks.

"Do you think it will be like this over in France, William?"

"It'll be better, Paul. I can't wait to be there. This place will be here when we get home again, but the war won't last long. We need to be in on it now before it's too late."

"We need to get a move on then. Good job it's downhill all the way. My arse is numb."

They took off like bats out of hell, their screams of fear and sheer panic echoing back through the glen. The wind cut into their eyes making big sissy tears run down their faces as they charged over potholes and stones. They were almost in the ditch a few times before they got to the bottom. The tyre was shredded to bits on the rim. They didn't care. They were still all in one piece as they rattled their way down into Omagh. It was a great to be alive.

As they came nearer to the barracks, the road was lined with people, queues of men coming and going through the gates.

"My God, William, half the country must be joining up! Where do they all come from?"

"We thought the fair had big crowds, but they wouldn't hold a candle to this and the best of it is I've yet to see anyone I know."

Soldiers were marshalling the crowds of men and boys into three lines which snaked away out in front and around a tall building in the middle of a square.

"Keep close to me, Paul, so we don't get separated." William spoke in a half whisper, his eyes darting around the sea of faces surrounding them.

"Look lively there lads, keep the line moving." A burly man in uniform with a baton under one arm paraded up and down the line.

They couldn't believe the crowds that were standing around the recruiting office. There were hundreds in the three long queues. William ducked down low pulling at Paul's sleeve.

"What's wrong, William?"

"Keep your head down, Paul, I think I just seen the minister's son. Don't want any nosey parker takin' the news back home."

It took over two hours for them to get to the big table to sign up and answer all the questions, like what age you were. William said he was born in 1896 and they never batted an eye. He was lying by two years, but they didn't question it. Paul told them the same. At the end of another queue a red faced man with a white coat over his uniform stuck a stick in their mouths, looked down their throats, asked them to breathe in and out, poked their ribs a couple of times and that was that. They signed the paper and the sergeant gave them a shilling each and told them they were soldiers.

David stood in the long line of men being herded like cattle into more lines. He was keeping an eye out for any familiar faces or anyone who might recognise him. It was unlikely given that he had spent the nine years incarcerated in that hell hole called a school. His last two years at Trinity had been good. He had found himself finally coming to a veiled understanding about his faith and his place in the great scheme of things yet he was still dogged by doubt about his future and what his part in it would be. As his mind wandered, he thought he had caught sight of two young lads from the village but dismissed it as they disappeared into the throng of bodies. They would be no more than fifteen and this was no place for children.

The line shifted and he was confronted with a tall man in uniform staring at him his eyes bulging.

"Name."

David stared back at him.

"You lost your tongue boy, what's your name, haven't got all day."

"David Faulkner," he blurted out aware of the suppressed laughter of the men around him.

"Age, address and occupation, quick as you can boy."

"Twenty-one, 105 Gortin Road, reporter," David had it out before he had time to think about it.

"You're a reporter are you? Well, I'm Lord Kitchener at your service. Move up to the red line boy."

David suddenly became aware for the first time that any decisions he made from now on would be crucial. He turned and walked away from the recruiting line ignoring the side long looks he was getting from some of the men he had been standing with.

He left Saint Lucia and walked up Castle Street towards the Court House. He met the Dray man coming down the steep hill, the horse pulling its head to the side uncomfortable at the weight in the cart on its downward journey.

The town seemed to be a hive of activity yet it wasn't a fair day. Groups of men and boys were standing around the hill talking and laughing and passing clay pipes around. There was a carnival atmosphere without the carnival.

He walked on up towards the Fair Green heading for Blacks Solicitors who had offices near Trinity church.

It had been a while since he had seen Donald Black and, when he had, it had always been in the company of his father. He liked Black mainly because he treated him well and had always listened to his point of view, something his father had never been guilty of. He also trusted his judgment and was confident that any business he discussed with him would remain a matter between them and them alone.

At the front door he met two men who clapped him on the back with an air of familiarity. He didn't know who they were but assumed they were parishioners of his father's. There was no such thing as privacy in a town the size of Omagh. He knocked the door and a tall lady ushered him into the once familiar office of his childhood.

Black was sitting behind a rather large desk which was piled high with papers. He rose immediately and greeted David with a warm smile and a firm handshake.

"David, my boy, what an unexpected pleasure, I heard you were home." He frowned, "nothing wrong, I hope, your father in good health?"

"Oh yes, indeed, father is well. I do apologise for dropping in without an appointment but I was in town and took a chance that I might be able to have a word with you in private."

"Certainly, David. As it happens I am between appointments at the moment. Have a seat and I will see if I can scramble up a cup of tea, Mrs Kelly should be around somewhere." And with that he left the room and following a conversation presumably with Mrs Kelly, Black returned.

"Now, David, you have my undivided attention. What can I do for you?"

"Firstly, I want to be reassured that our conversation will be a private matter between you and me and that what I tell you today will not be related back to my father. If this is not possible I would appreciate it if you would say so now and I will leave and this conversation will never be mentioned again"

If Black was surprised at David's request he did not show it.

"I can see that whatever you wish to discuss with me is of a serious nature. Let me reassure you that unless you have broken the law, David, and I trust you have not, I will help to the best of my ability. I assure you that whatever is discussed today will be treated with the utmost respect and I will not discuss it with anyone unless you give me permission to do so."

Reassured, David outlined his plans.

"I want to join the army, but to be more specific, I want to write about the war. I want to be a news reporter, a war correspondent. I have done well in my studies especially English. I can write well, my reports have all been consistently good and writing is all I want to do."

David flushed as he realised he was stammering like a schoolboy who had been sent to the headmaster.

"I am aware you are a busy man but I believe you would be sympathetic to my plans, I..."

Black sat forward in his seat and interrupted.

"David, my boy, I do fully understand what you are saying and the very sound reasons you have for saying them, but let us not get too expeditious. Have you discussed this with your father?"

David stood pushing his chair back the flush fading as his anger took hold.

"I am my own man, Mr Black. I have reached my majority and can make my own decisions. Will you help me or not?"

"Please do sit down, David. You must forgive me if I have given you the wrong impression but if I am to assist you I must ask these pertinent questions. I believe I will go and look for Mrs Kelly perhaps a whiskey would be of more benefit. These are trying times, excuse me," he left, closing the door behind him.

David bowed his head. He knew his behaviour was erratic but his longing to take his future into his own hands had become urgent and his resolve had hardened. He stood up again as Black returned with the woman who he presumed was Mrs Kelly, carrying a tray of glasses and a large decanter of whiskey.

"Please do sit down. You must try to relax and I believe this is just the remedy for that and then we can settle down to business."

He accepted the glass saluting his host and sipping his drink "I appreciate your patience, sir, and your hospitality."

"Now, David, let us begin. What age are you now?"

"I will be 22 on my next birthday in three months' time."

An hour later, mellowed by the whiskey and Black's reassurances, David made his way down the courthouse hill and home to face his father.

Mr Black watched the young man depart towards the town reflecting on the numbers of young men who were setting their store on this war. He turned and lifted the phone.

CHANNEL SERVICES DISRUPTED
Liverpool route closing
due to requisitioning of vessels:
The SS Donegal, one of the steamers running
between Belfast and Heysham is under
orders to act as a store ship. The Donegal
arrived in Belfast on Wednesday morning
and her cargo was hurriedly discharged

Ulster Herald, September 1914

Chapter 14

Padraig was working the top field, laying hedges and mending fences. He saw young Mullan from Cranagh climb the ditch at the bottom of the field coming in his direction. He watched his progress, mulling over what news he brought today. Mullan was one of a team of field runners working for the Brotherhood. They carried intelligence from around the area and reported on movements in and out of Omagh Army camp. He was breathless when he reached Padraig and stood for a moment leaning on the fence.

"Jez Padraig, how do you climb up here every day, I'm busted. Here's a message for ye," and he pulled out an envelope from his back pocket.

"Yer soft, young Mullan, try runnin' up and down the mountain every day, that'll put muscle on ye. There's tae in yon bag over by the gate help yerself while I see what's in the message."

Padraig opened the letter and read its contents. When he had finished he pulled out a box of matches and burned it, the black ash blowing away on the wind. He went to the gate and sat down beside Mullan pouring tea for himself into the jar.

"There's no reply."

"Right then, I'll be away home. Thanks for the tae."

"Yer welcome. Remember to get that exercise. Ye niver know when ye need it."

He watched him disappear down into the valley. He threw the remains of the tae at the ditch. He packed his up and headed home trying to control the anger that was coursing through him.

His son was the talk of the country and for all the wrong reasons. It was time to put a stop to it. He had been too soft on Paul, young Mullan could teach them all how to serve the cause.

He did as he was told, kept his mouth shut and didn't draw attention to himself. He would remember him when the time came to stand up and be counted.

The house was quiet when he arrived back. He found Mary and Paul in the turf shed bent over filling the turf baskets. They hadn't noticed him and their laughter stopped him in his tracks. He loved them so much and yet they had become strangers to him, his world now revolved around his politics, secret meetings and now spying on his family. Mary and Paul turned and saw him. "Padraig I didn't think you would be back at this time, have you eaten yet?"

"Naw, I'll get it later"

"Is there something wrong Da?"

"Aye, there is. What were you and Johnston doin' on Saturday in Omagh?" Paul stared at him knowing, he had found out but not knowing how. "Well, where were you?"

"Padraig, what's this about? Mary put her hand on Paul's arm and felt him trembling. She could sense the tension in Paul. Neither of them spoke. "What is going on?" she was on the verge of tears afraid now of what the answer would be.

Paul broke the silence never takin' his eyes of his Da.

"I have joined the army. That's what me and William were doin' on Saturday. We have signed up. We have to report to the camp on the 7th of September at eight in the morning. I'm sorry Ma."

Mary cried out, her knees giving way beneath her. She would have fallen if they had not caught her.

"I hope this makes you happy, Paul, seein' your mother in such a state. We had better get her in to the fire."

"Who told ye?"

"Niver mind that. Help me to get yer Ma into the house."

Mary sat by the fire, a cup of tea in her hand, her eyes glazed over from crying. Padraig and Paul had left to carry on their argument in the barn. She took her shawl from the hook on the door and left the house following a short cut to the road through a path in the back garden ignoring the loud voices in the barn. She needed to see William.

The milking was almost over. William's head was pushed against the soft furry underbelly of the cow as his hands forced the milk from her udder into the pail on the floor when Mrs McGovern burst into the milking parlour and began shouting at him.

"I'll never forgive you for this William Johnston. How could you do this to us? We always treated you like part of the family and this is how you pay us back! If anything happens to him you'll be the one to blame. You had no business putting such thoughts in his head. What got into you?"

His Ma stood up from the corner of the parlour and looked at him and then back at Mrs McGovern.

"What are you talking about, Mary?" she asked.

William's heart sank. He had still not told his Ma his plans. He couldn't seem to get the right time. All day he had rehearsed it in his head but, when the time came to tell her, his mouth dried up and he found some excuse to avoid her. Now, it was too late.

"You know fine well what I'm talking about. Don't pretend you don't know your brave boy is joining up and going to war and he's talked our Paul into going with him."

"No, Mary, I don't know. Is this true, William?"

Before William could answer, his Da had limped across the parlour and gripped his hand.

"Good for you, boy! If I was your age and I still had me health I would be away as fast as my legs could carry me."

Mrs McGovern slumped down on a stool, her head in her hands. Ma just stood there, her hands limp at her side. He looked away from her, wishing it could be different for her sake.

"Answer me, William; is this true?"

He looked up, "Yes. I was going to tell you when we had finished the milking."

"Have you signed anything?" Her voice was controlled. "Have you signed the papers?"

Mrs McGovern stood up kicking the stool into the pit. She was getting hysterical again.

"It's all signed and sealed. Death warrants at sixteen." She began sobbing again. "What am I going to do without Paul? What got into you, William? Have you not read the papers?"

His Ma stared at him. Then, without a word, she took Mrs McGovern's hand and led her out of the byre.

His Da was smiling from ear to ear and began slapping his back. "Pay no heed to the women, lad. Them McGoverns were born mithering* and complaining. When are you away, lad? Have you a date?"

"Aye, we're to be at the camp in Omagh on Monday at eight o'clock to get kitted out."

"Sure, it will make a man out of you. Come on now. Let's get this milking finished."

He slapped William on the back again and went back to the milking. In an odd sort of a way he felt his Da was on his side for the first time.

Ma had settled Mrs McGovern down and saw her off home by the time they went to the house for their breakfast.

She was quiet, but his Da kept up the questions wanting to know all about the Army camp and who said what and had he seen anyone he knew. It was the longest conversation they had had in years. All that day he had tried to catch time with his Ma but she had managed to avoid him. After supper his Da put on his coat and hat and lifted the latch.

"Well, I'm away to the Plumb to spread the news. I'm as proud as punch, cub, and that's no mistake. I'll see you later, Ann."

William watched him through the window as he made his way out of the gate, his head held high, the smoke from his pipe leaving a trail behind him. Ma went off to settle wee John in the bottom room. She had not spoken a word to him since the row in the byre.

He wanted to go to the river to try and see Paul and find out what had happened, but he couldn't leave the house until he had talked the whole thing over with her.

She came up from the room and he could see she had been crying. "Ma I'm sorry you had to find out like this...."

She turned on him her voice breaking in harsh whispers.

"Sorry is not good enough, William. You made a decision that could end your life and I had to hear it from Mary McGovern. What possessed you, William? What did I do to deserve this?"

"I was going to tell you after milking time. That was what Paul and me had agreed. I don't know why that changed. I'm sorry it happened this way but I'm not sorry I'm going."

"Are things so bad here that you would risk your life for a war that has nothing to do with you?"

"It has everything to do with me. The recruiting sergeant told us that if we don't take a stand against the Germans then they will be on our doorstep next."

"God forgive them for leading weans away from their families to get killed for nothing."

"Look I'm going no matter what you say. I'm away out I need to find out what happened over at McGovern's."

He left her sitting by the fire her head bowed.

Paul didn't turn up at their usual spot at the river. William walked on into the Plumb and found him leaning over the bridge. When he saw William he stuck his hands in his pocket and kicked the dust up on the road in front of him. "I was lookin' for you. What happened, Paul?"

"I'm sorry, William. I couldn't face you I didn't know what to say to you."

William said nothing, trying hard not to lose his temper. The last thing he needed now was a fight.

Paul eventually broke the silence.

"All hell broke out at our house, William. Someone saw us in Omagh. Saw us coming out of the camp and they told my Da. I couldn't lie. I had to tell them. I couldn't stop Ma from going to your house. She was out and away and I didn't see her goin'."

"Aye well, she soon let my ones know the news. I hadn't said a word. I was sticking to the plan. Now Ma's in a state but I've told her I'm going no matter what."

"What did your Da say?"

"Oh, he's alright. He's in the pub celebrating. Now all of a sudden I'm a hero. What about yours?"

"We had a big row. I've niver seen him so angry before. Then all af a sudden he said he would take us to the camp on Monday morning. I don't understand it. I'm really sorry, William, I didn't go to meet you. I didn't know what you would think. That's me. Big coward, and I haven't even left home yet."

"I thought your Da would have gone mad when he heard. Did he say anything else?"

"Naw, that's the funny thing. He said he was going to a meeting in Carrickmore and left shortly after Ma came back from your house. She's still in a state. I'll need to get on home. Will I see you tomorrow?"

"Aye, same place but maybe a bit later."

"Aye, see ya then." The lads parted, each lost in thought of the path they had chosen for their future.

WAR CASUALTIES
Wounded: Officers 57, other ranks 629
Missing: Officers 96, other ranks 4,183
Total 5,127
Many men missing

Tyrone Constitution,1914

Chapter 15

They had to report to the camp in Omagh on Monday 7th September at eight o'clock. William's Ma had laid on a spread and his aunts were all crowded into the kitchen. His Da was handing out nips of poteen in the barn to the uncles and a few of the neighbours. He managed to get Jim Brown to slip him a drop without his Ma seeing.

"It's not fair, Jim. Here I am going to defend king and country and I can't even get a wee shot of poteen to see me on the road."

"Aye, but as long as you don't overdo it you'll be alright for Monday morning" Jim replied pouring another large shot into William's cup.

"How are you getting to Omagh?"

"Paul's Da is taking us on the cart. We're leaving at six o'clock." He drained the cup; the sharpness of the drink making him choke and cough.

"McGovern's taking you? Times have changed then."

"What's that supposed to mean Jim?"

Jim Brown shoved the cork back in the bottle. "Awe, nuthin', you need to concern yourself about lad. Good luck to the both of ye. They say it's rough over there."

"Aye, so they say." William wondered about the remark but let it go. Padraig McGovern's politics were no secret. "I think I'll take a walk up around the top field to clear my head. Thanks for the drink, Jim. If anyone asks, I'll be back in a wee while."

He opened the slap* and climbed the hill behind the house. The grasshoppers were silent now. The fields lying low at the bottom of the mountain were brittle and bare after the harvest. Shadows passed over the top of Mount Sawel as the late sun shifted behind the clouds.

His whole short life had been in the shadow of these mountains. He knew all the best nesting sites for the sparrow hawk. Oul Spud Spratt brewed poteen up there and thought nobody knew about it.

They had watched Spud many a time carrying the spuds up on his back with one eye on the path behind him in case he was being followed.

The whistle blew down in the yard and he retraced his steps, his mind filled with wonder at what the next few months would be like.

His Uncle Jack and Aunt Alison were just leaving when he got back to the house. William had not been able to speak to them earlier. His cousin, Walter, had joined the Irish Rifles in Belfast and had already seen service at the Battle of Mons and the Battle of Le Casteau. Aunt Allison began to cry when she saw William and got down from the trap and put her arms around him.

"God look down on you and keep you from harm, William," her sobbing got worse and William returned the hug, not knowing what to say to her. Uncle Jack came over and gently eased her grip from him and led her back to the trap. He came back and grasped William's hand.

"God go with you, William. Walter sends his greetin's from the front. He says they are givin' the Germans a run for their money and for us not to worry. Write home, lad, it's such a comfort to get the letters." He slapped William on the back, then climbed onto the cart and went off down the lane.

The party went on for a couple of hours till they ran out of drink. More stout was needed so his Da and the other eejits headed off to the Plumb. He was glad to have a bit of quiet with the rest of the family. He helped settle his tired little brother in bed with the promise of a story, but after all the fuss in the house the story wasn't needed and he was soon fast asleep. He tucked him in and kissed him. He was going to miss him. His Ma was putting away the last of the cups. He offered to help. "I'll throw out the dish water and get in some turf so you can put your feet up for a while."

"Don't fuss, William. Let's go for a walk before your Da gets back."

They walked down to the orchard at the front of the house, the bats swooping through the air in their nocturnal flight. They sat down on the stump of an old apple tree and Ann cupped her arm into William's.

He sensed what was coming.

"Will you not change your mind, William? You're not old enough. We could put a stop to it now. I'll talk to the minister at church in the morning. He could go with you and explain..."

He broke the grip she had on his arm and stood up his voice raised in anger.

"No, Ma. If you do that I will never forgive you. I'm going and nothing and nobody is going to stop me. Walter is in the thick of it and I wish I was beside him."

She caught his hand and he sat down beside her again, angry with himself for shouting.

"I'm sorry. I know it's hard for you to accept, but I need to do this and I want to be sure that you will give me your blessing."

Her grip on his hand tightened, her eyes pleading with his.

"Are you sure you know what you're letting yourself in for William? This is a terrible war. Men are getting killed by the thousand." She was trying not to cry, but he could hear the tremble in her voice.

"I know, Ma, but my mind is made up. I need to do this and the money is not bad and I'll be back before you know I'm away. Da's not bothered. He'll be glad to see the back of me."

"Don't judge him too harshly, William. He wasn't..." she broke off her head bowed "I – we were young once. We had our dreams, but hardship changes people. That and his leg takes the edge off things for him...."

"Don't make excuses for him. He doesn't deserve it."

"Don't, William, please don't. You mustn't go away with bad feelings. Your Da has had more trouble than most. He's a good man. Make your peace with him, if not for my sake then for God's sake, but don't leave with hate in your heart. It's all I ask."

He put his arms around her, "I will for your sake. I promise." She pulled him to her. She couldn't hold back the tears any longer.

"I wish you hadn't signed the paper. I wish it was over and done and this wasn't happening, but I know you can't be held back. God bless you, son. God bless you and keep you safe."

They sat there for a long time with her clinging to him, her silent sobs coming in waves as her breast rose and fell against him. He felt as if he could feel her heart breaking.

He had to push her away. It was the hardest thing he ever had to do.

He was supposed to meet Josie but had found a note in the hut. She was housebound again. The priest had been to the house and there had been a big row. She was going to try and slip out of the house on Monday morning at five before anyone was awake.

William had hardly slept. It was Sunday morning and he could hear the clatter of the weans up in the kitchen havin' their breakfast and his ma's quiet voice going over their Sunday school lessons before they went to church. His da had come home drunk again and woke the house. He had been drunk most nights since the party the week before. William had gone to bed early in an attempt to avoid his drunken slabbering. He heard him coming up the road singing the sash. Ma tried to keep him quiet when he came into the house. Then there was a loud crash. William jumped out of bed and reached the kitchen to find her trying to lift his da unto the settle seat. Water from the upturned bucket was everywhere. They managed to get him down to the bedroom.

"Get back to bed, William. I'll fix him up now."

"How do you put up with this Ma?"

"Go back to bed."

She put her finger to her lips and pushed him gently out the door.

Now, as he washed for church, he heard his parents muffled voices, his Da laughing, and then they both came into the kitchen.

"Good morning, son. I hear you had a hand at putting me to my bed last night again."

"Aye, I did. Are you fit for church?"

"Now, William, you should know by now I never have a hangover and if I fall asleep durin' the sermon your Ma will give me a nudge to wake me up. Won't you my darling wife?"

"Come on now, John. Stop all this nonsense. We may never hear the sermon if we don't get a move on." Her eyes held William's. He turned and went to finish dressing.

The three mile trip to church on Sundays had always been a noisy family outing. If the weather was fine they would leave earlier and walk, joining up with other families, the children racing each other along the road. John rested his leg at intervals giving the children an excuse to dawdle and pick flowers. Today even Dan the cart horse seemed to be a reluctant as they climbed up the long bray.

At the church William found himself the centre of attention. His Da had spread the news and men and boys gathered around him to hear the final details of his plans.

Inside Ann prayed as she had never prayed before. The minister began his sermon.

"My sermon today is taken from Matthew Chapter 11 verse 28-30. 'Come unto me all ye who labour and are heavy laden and I will give ye rest. Take my yolk upon you, and learn from me; for I am meek and lowly in heart: and ye shall find rest unto your souls. For my yolk is easy, and my burden is light.'

At this pivotal point in the ministry of Jesus he calls on his followers to 'come unto me all ye who labour and are heavy laden and I will give you rest.' For those of you who prepare to leave your families and fight for the good of your country. For the families you leave behind, take comfort in Christ's words to give you rest from the burdens you carry and to share your load.

Remember, God hears our prayers and that our prayers depends on faith in God; faith that God knows what is in your heart and in that faith, you will be delivered into his loving care. As God's servants here on earth, we depend a great deal on faith and love as we aspire to do God's work safe in the knowledge that he sent his only son Jesus Christ, to die on the cross, for our salvation."

William's mind wandered. The hypnotic sound of the minister's voice washed over him. He felt at peace for the first time since he had made his decision to join the army. Tomorrow he would be a soldier.

The minister's voice broke into his thoughts. "Let us thank God for his word. Amen."

Reverend Bowman stood in the porch shaking hands with the members of the congregation at the end of the service. He held Ann's hand a little longer than usual. "God will keep him safe, Mrs Johnston. I shall have him and all the young men in my daily prayers."

"Thank you, Reverend. We appreciate that." Ann stepped away as John took the minister's hand.

"Aye, Reverend, we are very proud of our boy. It's what we all hope for our children that they honour their country and do their duty. Did I see your lad in the village, Reverend? Is he back from Dublin? I suppose he'll be joining up?"

"Come away, John." Ann caught John's arm. "Begging your pardon, Reverend. We have a lot to do today and we must get back."

The Reverend Bowman watched them passing through the gate. John Johnston's last remark had not been the first of its kind lately. The thought of his own son out in what must be a living hell appalled him. He had no words but God's to comfort the families of the sons who had already fallen in battle. He would try to talk to David at dinner. These past weeks the rift between them had grown. In the past he would have come to church and they would have lunch together. Now he was not a party to his son's comings and goings. He returned to the church to pray again for the dead and wounded and to ask the Lord for guidance in this time of turmoil.

GOVERNMENT PURCHASES HORSES IN TYRONE
The Government bought twenty
horses in Omagh on Thursday last.
There were several classes: Horses for officers, chargers,
cavalry horses, and those suitable for the yeomenry
horses. Also light draught and pack horses.
The purchasing officer will attend Fintona and Trillick on
Friday and Irvinestown and Clogher on Saturday. Prices
range from £35 to £70.

Tyrone Constitution 1914

Chapter 16

Duncan, the butler, announced George Huston. Pre-dinner drinks were being enjoyed in the drawing room. All heads turned to inspect the late arrival. The Duke, a stickler for punctuality, nodded his greeting to Huston, as he hurried across the room to the group of guests gathered around the ornate fireplace.

"Forgive me, your Grace, I was unexpectedly delayed in Omagh and, to top it all, my horse picked up a stone"

"Drink sir?" Duncan asked.

"Thank you, Duncan, gin and soda. I intended to catch the last Londonderry train but I missed it unfortunately."

"It's time you got a motor car, old boy. They say they are guaranteed never to let you down. For myself, I think there is nothing more reliable than a good, well bred filly." Edward Harcourt winked meaningfully and tapped the point of his nose. The Duke frowned.

"Careful, Harcourt. We do not want to offend the ladies."

The small gathering of friends of the Duke and Duchess had been a weekly affair in the past but the war had changed many of the routines and the dinner guest list had grown to include the most senior serving officers who either lived nearby or were billeted within the grounds. Generally, when the ladies retired, the table became a battlefield where the strategy of the camp was discussed in a less formal setting.

Harcourt was a neighbour, a frequent visitor and a great favourite with the ladies.

"Beg your pardon, ladies," Harcourt bowed deeply to the Duchess and the other ladies present.

The Duke moved across to George Huston leaving, Harcourt amusing his audience with one of his wild stories.

"Now, George, what is causing a stir about Omagh to have kept you late this evening?"

"Again, I apologise, your Grace. It was a phone message I received from an old friend, Robert Black. He is a solicitor with a practice in Omagh. He had a visit from a young man you may know. The son of the Incumbent in the parish of Plumbridge and Gortin, the Reverend Albert Bowman."

"Yes, I have met with him on Church matters. His son is at Trinity, following his father into the ministry, I believe."

"Ah now, that is debatable, your Grace. David Bowman is the young man's name and it seems he has other plans and his father will not at all happy when he hears of them."

"Now, George, I will not be dragged into a family dispute."

"If you would bear with me, your Grace, I believe this young man may prove to be just what we have been looking for in terms of propaganda reporting about the war effort here in Tyrone."

"I'm intrigued, George, but I repeat I will not be involved in a family quarrel. I suggest you come back to me with the full story privately and I will look at the matter then. Now, I think Duncan is about to call us into dinner."

David sat on the low wall of the graveyard out of sight of the departing congregation. He missed his mother desperately. In her last years on earth they had been separated by his father's unshakeable conviction that boys should be taught at an early age to be self-reliant and independent of feminine influences. His memories of her devotion to him in his childhood years had faded into a deep longing to return to those times when he felt nurtured by her love.

He had been seven when he had been taken away to boarding school in England. He had cried for a week until the other boys had turned on him giving him a beating, leaving him with bruises on his arms and chest that turned green before they faded. It proved to be a cautionary lesson. He had never cried again until the day they told him his mother had passed away.

He had been nine and in sickbay with mumps when matron had told him the news. He could not attend the funeral. The headmaster had been sympathetic but stern. His tears of grief had been silent and lonely. The following summer, he had gone home for the holidays. The house felt empty without her. He had crept into her room that first night and opened her wardrobe only to find it as empty as the house. Next day, father had taken him to the grave.

"Your mother is in heaven now with the lord. Say your prayers, boy. We must see about tea. Mrs McFadden will not be pleased if we are late. I was fortunate to find her. Good housekeepers are hard to find in a small parish so you must be courteous and obedient. When I am not at home you will be answerable to her."

He had never visited her grave again until last week. The headstone was plain, the message brief: 'With the Lord.'

His tears fell unchecked.

He had spent three years at Trinity College in Dublin studying theology. They had been good years. He had come to value his own God given talent, writing. In his early years at boarding school he had scribbled in jotters, nonsense drivel his English master had called it when in a moment of madness he had proudly produced a poem at lessons. He wrote a journal pouring out all his frustrations.

The wet bed sheets he hid unsuccessfully from matron that first year and his very public humiliation at their very public discovery giving further ammunition to the sixth form bullies who had made his life unbearable. He had been so terrified of the discovery of his pathetic outpourings on paper that before he began his third year he had burned them and had seldom written with such candour again.

Trinity changed all that. He began to write again. First, it was a necessity in order to meet the standard of study expected of him. Then, the passion for the written word insatiable, he devoured Irish writers. Yeats and Wilde opened up a new world of literature that he had not explored before. He had written poetry again which had been well received by his tutor. His writing had matured with a new freedom of expression. He grew in confidence in the debating chamber and made new friends. He was his own man now and he was resolved to stand up for himself in his choice of career. His father would be angry but he would have to accept the inevitable.

He was late for lunch and called out his apology to Mrs McFadden as she came from the kitchen, holding a plate of potatoes.

"We waited, your father is still in the dining room. I will bring you your soup."

"No, I will not have soup. The main course will be ample. After lunch, I would appreciate it if you would ensure we are not disturbed by father's usual stream of Sunday callers. I will take in the potatoes. It all smells very good. Thank you for waiting for me."

He could tell his Father was angry when he entered the dining room. "My apologies, father, I met Mrs Mac in the hall," He placed the potatoes on the table and took his seat in the usual place.

"Where on earth have you been? You have missed the soup."

"Yes, I have apologised to her and told her I would go straight to the main course hence the potatoes."

"You missed morning prayer also."

"Father I ..."

"It is at times like these that the congregation look to us to set examples. God is their only solace. The war comes ever closer and the names of the fatalities are people we know. They need us, David, and I would appreciate your support."

Mrs McFadden knocked and entered and placed a plate of roast beef and vegetables on the table.

"There is a trifle and cream on the sideboard so you can help yourselves. Can I get you anything else, Reverend?"

"No, thank you. I am expecting my usual visit from the Dean at four o'clock and we will have tea in the study. Thank you."

Mrs McFadden removed the soup plate then hesitated, looking at David, then back to the Rector.

"Beg pardon, Reverend, Mr David said you were not to be disturbed after lunch that I was to tell any callers you were not to be disturbed"

"What on earth do you mean? David, what is the reason for cancelling my afternoon guests?"

"Thank you Mrs McFadden. We will ring the bell if we need you," David said. Mrs McFadden waited, never taking her eyes of the Rector.

"Forgive my son's ill manners. You may go for the moment and I will ring when we have finished so you can clear. Thank you."

As the door closed behind her his father stood up pushing his chair back his face contorted with rage.

"What on earth do you mean by this behaviour, David? How dare you embarrass me? Explain yourself this instant."

David stood and placed his hand on his father's arm.

"Please sit down, Father. When we have had our lunch I will explain but you must calm down first. Perhaps I was a little hasty, but I have been home for weeks now and we have not had a single conversation about my future. Can we eat first and not waste this delicious food?"

"What is there to discuss? Your future is in the ministry. Always has been. I was talking it over with the Bishop recently and he has assured me you will soon be attached to a suitable parish within the Derry Diocese?"

"That's just it, father. You have discussed my future with the Bishop. Has it ever occurred to you to ask me what it is that I want to do with my future? I am not going into the ministry. Whatever arrangements you have made on my behalf must be cancelled. I have set in motion a chain of events, which will see me joining the Army as a non-commissioned officer. I am presently awaiting my orders."

He was not prepared for the look of shock on his father's face or the tears that welled up in his eyes. He swayed on his feet and David caught him, lowering him into his chair.

"Father, I'm sorry, I should never have broken it to you this way. It was never my intention to upset you. Can I get you a drink of water?"

"Yes. A drink would be welcome. I think a stronger drink is called for. You will find a bottle of brandy in my desk in the study. I keep it for emergencies and this would appear to be just such a time. On your way will you ask Mrs McFadden to come in and clear the table, I seem to have lost my appetite."

David returned with the brandy and poured a measure from a glass on the sideboard and placed it on the table.

"You must eat something if only to avoid upsetting Mrs Mac."

They ate in silence, his Father pushing the food around the plate. Then, suddenly, he set down his fork.

"This is not over David."

"Yes it is and all I ask for is to have your support in this."

"I need time, David, time to come to terms with it. Can you allow me that much?"

"I'm sorry, Father. That will not be possible. I have an appointment in Omagh tomorrow with Colonel Robinson so perhaps we could have a word this evening after the Dean leaves."

"It's all a bit sudden, David. Surely you are not enlisting straight away?"

"I have. I am now a serving soldier with a commission as a Second Lieutenant in the Royal Inniskilling Fusiliers."

"You surely have not enlisted already? Have you signed anything? Please tell me you have not."

"I signed the papers on Friday. There is nothing you can do to change this, father."

"You have known this all weekend and you chose not to tell me. Why are you so intent on this path, David? You have had the best education anyone could ask for and just when you can now reap the benefits you propose to throw it away in the Army. I won't have it, David. Do you hear me? I will not let you throw away your life in some muddy field in France."

"You cannot stop me. I am over twenty one, I make my own decisions now, Father. I believe I can play my part in this war, not with a gun but with a pen. I am to be assigned as an official war correspondent for the Inniskillens. I report for training at Baronscourt officer training camp on Monday next."

"I shall talk to the Duke. He's a reasonable man. We can postpone this for a while at least. Please, David."

"You will not interfere, father. Should I discover you have attempted to meddle in my business, I will never forgive you. I have some things to do now but I will be back for supper. I hope by then you will be sufficiently recovered to be reasonable about this and give me your blessing."

He left the house and crossed the road to his mother's grave.

"I believe you were with me here today, mother, helping me to stand up for myself. Watch over me now and in the future and may the Lord God watch over father."

He made his way back to his room to begin to pack.

GOVERNMENT ADVERTISEMENT
Fall in and join your chums.
Recruiting barometer of Tyrone Battalion
9th Royal Inniskilling Fusiliers

3rd October
A Company (Mid Tyrone) 155
B Company (North Tyrone) 135
C Company (Southern Tyrone and Cookstown) 175
D Company (Dungannon) 165
Total 630

4th October
A Company 195
B Company 145
C Company 185
D Company 175
Total 700

Tyrone Constitution, September 1914

Chapter 17

On his last night at home, William went down the lane to check on the animals in the lower field. His Da was there, carrying buckets of water from the river to fill the troughs.

"Let me help you with those buckets, Da."

"Thanks, son. We would need some easier way of getting the water up for the animals."

"Aye, we would but until that happens we'll just have to do it with buckets."

"Well, you're off to the army tomorrow. Are you excited?"

"I suppose I am. It'll be a big change for me." he paused "It'll be a big change around here as well. How will you be able to manage when I'm gone?"

"Ach, don't you worry about me, son. I'll manage. The army are buying beef in bulk to help feed the troops so I have a mind to sell of a couple of the heifers at the next fair day and I might get rid of some of the milkers if things get tough."

There was a silence between them as they moved into the next field. William remembered his mother's words about making a peace with between them. They stopped at the next water trough and sat down on the ditch.

"What do you think about this war, Da? Is Carson to be trusted or is it all talk with him?"

John sat down beside him and looked his son in the eye.

"Carson is a great man, an educated man who knows more than the likes of us, William, and we are duty bound to follow him. As loyal Protestants we all signed a 'Solemn League and Covenant' two years ago to stop this Home Rule Bill but they have it now wither we like it or not but this war will prove our worth. We pledged our loyalty to King and country. I would have signed in blood if they had asked me. In fact they say some people did. I have complete faith in Carson. This war is only a distraction and when it's over the government will find out that we will not bow to Home Rule and we will do what is necessary to stop it. This war is being fought for freedom and we will fight for that here at home if we have to.

We are being tested by this war and we need to prove we are true to our vow of allegiance to the crown. The Germans are a mad race of dictators who think they can ride roughshod over the rest of us. Well they have a shock coming to them we're not that easy to beat. The Ulster Volunteers are trained and ready to fight here in Ulster or wherever they are needed. If I was fit I'd be away myself but I'm a cripple and all I have to offer is my trust and faith that Carson and God will lead us all the way to victory."

William had heard these arguments many times from gatherings at the house and at the fairs. He had no interest in the politics, but he understood enough and had learned to keep his opinions to himself.

"Will you make sure Ma is alright when I'm away, Da? I'm worried about her. She tries to hide her feelings but she misses Elsie and now I'll be away. It's going to be a big change for her."

I'll see to her, William, sure haven't I always tried to do my best, maybe not as well as I should have. This bloody injury didn't help. It has left me slow and I can't get used to being so useless at times."

"Do you still have a lot of pain?" William had never talked about what happened to his leg. His Da had always limped and over the years he had not given it much thought.

"Aye, I do. It's a burden I'll have to carry to me grave. I wish I could be back to my old self again, but that's not goin' to happen so I'll have to make the best of it."

"Does the drink help?" As soon as the question was asked William regretted it. "Sorry I didn't mean to..."

"It's alright, son. You have a right to know. You're a man now and to answer your question 'yes' the drink helps. It helps to take the edge off the pain especially at night and it helps me to forget things I wish I hadn't done."

William was startled. "What do you mean? What things?"

"I had my own war. I was a soldier once not much older than you. I fought the Boers in 1890 at a place called the Orange River in South Africa."

William paled and stared open mouthed, his disbelief obvious.

"I know this will come as a shock to you but I have never talked about those times to anyone except your mother. She has kept me sane and I owe her a lot. We put it behind us and over the years you weans have been our most treasured blessin's and the loss of the wee ones our most terrible heartache."

"Is that how you got hurt, is that what happened to you? God, Da, all these years I just thought..."

"I know, William. I should have told you before, but there was never a good time to burden you with this. It was my burden and I have tried to live with it, God knows I tried, but the drink got the better of me. I'm not proud of my weakness. I know there have been times when you were ashamed of me. I'm ashamed of myself and that's the truth of it."

"How come no one has ever told me? Uncle Jack, Aunt Alison - did all of them know?"

"It's well over 20 years ago now. I made it known within the family it was not to be gossiped about. I went away and then I came home again. Not the same man, but a man for all that. I fought for my country and my scars are there to constantly remind me."

William's colour was returning and with it a deep realisation of the truth in what he was hearing. "How did you get injured?"

John bowed his head and was silent.

"Are you all right?" William moved closer putting his hand on his father's outstretched leg."

"My war was a strange war. I was a soldier one minute and a cripple the next."

"Were you in the Inniskillens?"

"Naw, son, I was in the Donegal Artillery, it's now the Eleventh since they joined the Fermanagh Volunteers. We trained in Finnar, which is where you will be going if I know anything. It's a cul spot cub but I loved it. The sea and the mountains of Donegal are beautiful. The place is full o' rabbit warrens and, boys, did we have the great crack huntin' them. I was a fit in those days, could outrun any man in the regiment."

"What was it like to kill people?"

"They're not people when you're in the thick of it, they're your enemy. It's what soldiers are trained to do, kill or be killed. The Boers were ruthless. They were fightin' in their own land that and the heat gave them the upper hand."

"How long were you in Africa for?"

"It was a short war for me. I had no sooner got there till I stopped a bullet with my knee. Dumdums they were called. I was lucky, the fella beside me got one in the head. I spent three weeks in a hospital in Cape Town and another four weeks in Dublin. The knee was shattered. Nothing to be done but come home and get on with it. I tried to re-enlist to do something that didn't need two good legs but they told me point blank my army days were over."

"God, how have you managed all these years?"

"Your mother has been my strength. I thank God for her every day and I was young and strong then. Age is catchin' up with me now and the drink has become a habit. I know I have a battle on my hands to keep that demon at bay."

"I won't go, Da. I'll stay home and do more for you. I am a selfish shit."

William hugged his father, tears welling up as the full story of his hardships became clear.

"Naw, son, I won't have that. You must go. This is your time. I want you to go and take your chance at this. My only regret was it was too short for me. Before I was injured, I was a good soldier. I had great mates and I saw things and places I could never have imagined. I want the same for you. Just dodge the bullets and come home and tell me all about it."

"I'm so sorry, Da."

"Sorry! Sure what have you to be sorry about? It's not your problem. It's something I'll have to sort out myself."

"I'm sorry I didn't understand what you have been through these past years. I could have helped more, made more of an effort now I'm leaving just when I could be of more help to you."

"Look, son, you're going off to war with my blessin'. You could say you're going to fight for your oul cripple of a Da and that's enough for me. We'll manage. The harvest is in and winter's coming so there will be less to do and don't they say this war will be over by Christmas. I promise I'll try and cut down the drink and stay in with her and the wee John a bit more when you're away."

John stood up leaning heavily on his good leg and offered his hand to his son. "Is it a deal, son?"

William took his fathers hand and rose to stand beside him. "It's a deal, Da."

They walked home up the field in the gathering dusk of the evening.

Earlier, Ann had come to look for them stopping, when she heard them talking together. She stood for a moment then turned back leaving them alone.

MOBILISATION OF TROOPS

Last week has been one of the busiest witnessed at Omagh depot since mobilisation took place. Recruits are coming in plentiful, batches arriving on almost every train. So great are the numbers, staff are having considerable trouble finding clothing and equipment.

Tyrone Constitution, October 1914

Chapter 18

Josie stood at the end of the lane shivering. It wasn't a cold morning but lack of sleep was catching up on her. She had got into bed with all her clothes on and as soon as the dawn appeared had pulled on her coat and crept out of the house. Her Da was snoring loudly in the back room. The mantel clock showed twenty-five to five.

William said they were leaving at six o'clock. She hoped he had got her note. It was almost that time now. She pulled the coat tighter round her shoulders watching the lane for a sign of him and wondering what her life was going to be like without him in the months to come.

She didn't regret what they had done that first night.It had been more than she had ever thought it would be. It had felt so natural and William had been so gentle. They had done it again a few times since, both of them surprised at the depth of the passion they were feelin'.

She wished with all her heart that he didn't have to go to this war. She was afraid for him. The newspapers were saying that the casualties were high and that conditions in the trenches were very bad. Hopefully, it would all be over before William got there and then when he was home again they could begin to make plans for their future together.

He arrived out of breath and immediately gathered her up in his arms. "I haven't much time. Ma is up and makin' a big breakfast. She thinks I'm down for one last dander around the river."

They clung to each other, each trying to blot out the inevitable moment when they must say goodbye.

"No matter what happens, Josie, I want you to believe me when I say that I love you and that I will be home again sooner than you think."

Hot tears were flooding her eyes. She couldn't hold them back. She sobbed and clung to him desperate to keep hold of him for as long as she could.

"Please don't cry, Josie. I want to see that smile so I can remember it." He wiped away the tears and smiled down at her.

"I thought of that," she said, pulling an envelope out of her pocket. "It's a picture that was taken of me last year at that wedding I went to." She blushed. "That's if you want it?"

"That's great, Josie. Now I can look at you every night before I go to sleep. I wish I had a photo to give to you."

They kissed, "I have to go now. Ma will start wonderin'. I'll write to you as often as I can and send them to the post office. You will have to check, in case they send them up to the house. Will you write back?"

"Try to stop me!" she smiled up at him and they parted as the sun rose to burn away the morning dew.

The family were all up in the kitchen when he arrived back, wee John hardly awake and rubbing the sleep from his eyes.

"Where did you walk to, cub, I was nearly goin' out to look for ye?"

"Now, John. No givin' the lad a scolding. He just wanted to say his own farewell to the farm. I have packed some bread and jam for you and Paul, but I'm sure his Ma has done the same." Ann's voice was a hoarse whisper as she tried to hold back the tears that had flowed most of the night, leaving her red eyed and pale from lack of sleep.

"Thanks, Ma. I have a feelin' the army hasn't found a cook like you."

"Ach now, the food wasn't that bad as I recall. The cook in our billet always said an army marches on its stomach. I remember a young fella called Toby couldn't be filled. You had to watch your plate or he would have it before you could blink an eye." He took William's hand and held it. "You keep both your eyes open, son, and obey orders and may God keep you safe"

The sound of the cart on the road created a flurry of excitement as the family crowded around William as he lifted wee John up and kissed him. Ann stood by the door, the tears now running unchecked down her face.

"God go with you, son. We will pray for your safe return."

"I'm proud of you, son. Give them hell when you get out there."

He hugged them both, his own tears welling up as their warmth and love flowed over him.

"I'll be home soon on leave and I'll write as often as I can." He left the house and walked down to the waiting cart.

Paul's Da hardly spoke a word all the way into Omagh. William kept his mouth shut, knowing how McGovern felt about the British army. He was surprised when Paul said he was taking them into Omagh. But he had thought nothing more about it until Jim Black had made comment on it at the gathering. He had said nothing to Paul and now they were on their way at last and he couldn't wait to get into the uniform and begin this new adventure in their lives.

As they neared the camp they had to stop a good distance from the gates because of the crowds hanging around the road. Paul's Da got down from the cart and tied up the harness to a tree by the ditch.

"Well, Da, William and me will go on from here. You have no need to bother yourself coming any further with us."

"Naw, Paul. Sure it's no bother. I'll walk down the road a bit and see what's happening. Looks like there's more than wan fool about this fine morning."

There was complete chaos at the gate. Women and weans were crying and the hawkers were out in strength, shouting out their wares, selling anything and everything to the mass of folk standing around the gates.

Paul and William got out their passes. Paul turned to his Da to say his farewells.

"It's time to go now. Sure I'll be back before you know it."

"Thanks for the lift, Mr. McGovern. I'm much obliged to you."

"Well, I have nothing to thank you for Willie Johnston, but I wish you a safe passage. Now, Paul, you are coming with me, we have an appointment at that office over there." And with that he left them standing, their mouths hanging open like dead fish.

"What are you going on about, Da? Wait come back. What appointment?"

McGovern ignored him and walked on. They watched as his tall frame bent and entered the small building to the right of the gates.

"Why is your Da going in there, Paul?"

"Jez, I don't know, William. Sure he knows nobody in this place. Will I go after him?"

"No, we had better wait."

They didn't have to wait long. McGovern came out again accompanied by a sergeant and two other armed soldiers. "Now then, which of you lads is Paul McGovern?"

Paul stared at his Da and then back at the Sergeant.

"I am. I'm here to report for duty." Paul's voice shook.

"Sorry, lad, you are not going anywhere. My name is Sergeant Millford. Do you know this man?"

"Yes. He's my Da."

"According to the papers which I have been shown by your father you are underage. As from now you are relieved of any duty or promise you may have made to the recruiting Sergeant."

He turned to McGovern.

"Thank you for supplying this information, Mr. McGovern. If you have no further business, I would suggest that you take your son home. These men will see you to the gate."

McGovern caught William's eye and held his gaze for a few seconds before he answered.

"No, my business is done here. Come on, Paul. It's time we were on our way."

"I'm not going anywhere. I have joined the army. I signed the paper." Paul's face was as white as a ghost.

The other two soldiers moved closer.

"You had best get on home now with your father. We don't want any trouble. I have my orders. Recruits must be nineteen. Rules are rules."

The sergeant was staring at William now. William felt the sweat break out on the back of his neck. He turned and walked away. McGovern had not told on him and he wanted to get as much distance as he could between himself and the sergeant. He got lost in the crowd afraid to look back, afraid to see the look on Paul's face.

He handed in his papers at the main office.

"Billet 67, soldier. Join the line behind the building on the right to collect your kit. Get a move on, lad. Next."

He moved towards the building and joined the queue at the stores.

It had all gone wrong. Paul and he were supposed to be in this together.

Now Paul was on his way home. It didn't feel right.

He accepted the heavy bundle and followed the others in front of him as they trudged through iron gates to a field. As far as the eye could see the field was filled with a sea of tents. Men walked along muddy paths between the tents the sound of their voices ringing through the clear morning air.

William had never felt so alone in his life.

Paul followed his Da down the road to where they had left the cart. Padraig undid the harness and climbed up unto the cart. They had not spoken since they had emerged from the camp gates, jostling and pushing their way through a tide of men making their way in.

"Get up, Paul. It's time for home."

"Naw, I have other plans and going home isn't one of them. You had no right to do what you did, no right at all. You made a fool out of me." Paul's voice rose in anger, oblivious to sidelong glances of men passing him where he stood on the road.

"I trusted you, but not anymore. I'll niver forgive you for this."

"Do as you're told and get up now, Paul. You'll thank me in the long run."

"I'm niver coming home again. I'm joining the army and you can't stop me. Tell my Ma I'll write when I'm settled."

The lash from the whip across his shoulders took him completely by surprise. He hadn't seen it coming. His Da had never raised a finger to him in his entire life. He stepped away raising his arm to fend off another blow.

"Get up on the cart, Paul, or by God I will whip you here on the road."

For a moment father and son looked at each other. Rage and regret simmering between them. Then the moment was lost.

Paul turned and walked away in the direction of the town.

"Paul, come back, come back, son. I'm sorry, God forgive me, it's for your own good."

Padraig McGovern watched, helpless as his son disappeared into the throng of men on the road.

Nurses Cannot Help at the Front

A letter was received at Castlederg Guardians from a nurse working in the Infirmary stating she had offered her services as a volunteer nurse to the French Red Cross in connection with the present war. In the event she would be called up, she would be very grateful if they would grant her a leave of absence for such time as she would be away. Permission was refused on the grounds that it would set a precedent.

Tyrone Constitution, 1914

Chapter 19

William stood in the middle of long lines of men at six the next morning. It had been an uncomfortable night and he had not slept well. He was sharing a tent with fourteen men with little space between them. At lights out one of the men began to say the Lord's Prayer. Several, including William joined in. Minutes later, all that broke the silence was snoring and loud farts left the air rank in the confined space.

Next morning after breakfast they were lined up on parade. He had missed the usual first sounds of the day at home. His mammy raking up the fire, the smell of the porridge as it stewed on the hot embers of the turf. The rooster calling in the yard as the farm woke up to the day.

He was brought back to reality by orders being barked out by the sergeant. "Attention!"

Men shuffled and straightened up the line. Most of them had been training in the Ulster Volunteer Force training camps around the country and knew what was expected. Others like William followed the actions of the men in front in the hope their ignorance would not be noticed.

"My name is Sergeant Millford and I will be your mother, your father, your granny, your wife for the next six weeks."

This opening announcement caused some whispered remarks and laughter that was soon silenced.

"Silence in the ranks. This is not a game nor a side show at the circus. We are an army at war. You, God help us all, are now soldiers of his most esteemed Majesty King George V and as such will begin by acquainting yourselves with the standards of behaviour befitting a soldier of the British army. Do I make myself clear?" The men were silent.

"Yes, sir' is the response expected of you when addressed by a senior officer. Do I make myself clear?"

"Yes, sir!"

"You are soldiers now. You will be expected to follow orders without question. You will be trained in the skilful art of killing your enemy before he kills you. There is no room for cowards in this army. Cowardice will be punished by death. Countermanding orders is punishable by loss of pay and all privileges.

You will form an orderly line at the medical tent for attestation by the company medical unit. At two o'clock you will assemble in formation on the parade ground at the front of the main building where there will be a briefing by the commanding officer. Do I make myself clear?"

"Yes, sir!"

Following the order to fall out men began to move towards the medical tent in small groups, some lighting up cigarettes.

William fell in beside two of the men from his tent and decided to strike up a conversation with them. "What is attestation? It sounds painful."

"It's just a medical. Nothing to worry about, but by the way somebody was farting last night, they might need medical attention." All three broke out laughing.

"Aye, the air was a bit thick at times. I'm William Johnston. Do you mind if I stick around with you boys?"

"Aye, surely, William. Glad to know you. I'm Mark Long and this wee pile of blubber is Tommy McKeown. It was likely him who was doing most of the ass ripping last night." Mark stepped back to avoid a playful punch from Tommy.

"Have you two just met?" William asked.

"Naw," Tommy replied. "We went to school together. Decided to join up last month and here we are, soldiers about to fight a war. I can't believe it. It's like a dream come true. My da served in Africa. We used to listen to his stories. They had a great time down there. I always thought it would be great to follow in his footsteps, so I could tell my weans all about my war. What about you, William?"

A lump of pride rose in William's throat.

"Aye, my Da was in Africa. He was injured out in '91. Still has a bad leg."

"Was he in the Inniskillens?" Mark asked

"Naw, the Donegal Artillery. It's the Eleventh Inniskillens now. He said it was a great regiment."

"Are you from around here?" Tommy asked.

"Well, might as well be. I live about ten miles away."

"If you're from around here how come you hardly know anybody?"

"Jez Tommy, stop pesterin' the fella."

"I was only askin'."

"That's alright. I don't mind. I'm on my own here. My best friend was to join with me but his oul boy stopped him. My Da wants me to see a bit of the world like he did so here I am, rearin' to go."

"Aye, we're the same. There's no work and too many mouths to be fed on nothing. Mark's brother is going to the hiring fair next week. He wanted to come with us, but he's only sixteen. It's no place for boys. This is a man's job."

William felt the anger rising up in him at this remark but said nothing. He realised that a wrong word now would only draw attention to him.

"I had a hard time keeping him from following me" said Tommy. "My Ma has enough to deal with now I'm away. Have you any brothers, William?" Before William could answer they had reached the medical tent and they were separated each of them directed behind separate canvas screens and told to strip. This examination was more thorough than the last one William had been given. He was red faced by the time it had finished. He dressed and met the others outside.

"My God," Tommy laughed. "That was attestation alright. My testations have niver had such a goin' over before. How did you two get on? Did they find any brains down there, Mark?"

Their laughter joined in the general chorus of men coming away from the medical tent.

The three lads made their way to the mess tent for food. This consisted of a meat stew followed by tapioca pudding doled out into their mess tins.

"It tastes alright," Mark said, scraping the tin, "but I could eat the same again. Do you think all the portions will be as small as this Tommy?"

"You're just a greedy pig, Mark. It's not a bit of wonder your Ma's glad to see the back of you. Sure, you ate the poor woman out of house and home."

The banter between his new friends cheered William up and he was soon telling them stories of home and his friend, Paul.

At two o'clock they were assembled in front of the main building which turned out to be the officers' mess. The Sergeant stood them to attention.

A tall man emerged from the front entrance followed by several other officers.

"I am Colonel Robertson and am proud to have been given command of the 109th Tyrone Brigade of His Majesty's Army. We have a great deal of hard work ahead of us in the coming weeks in order to prepare us for the battlefields of Belgium.

"Each of you has an important part to play in this war. You must be prepared both mentally and physically to play your part in gaining victory over the enemy. Victory comes at a cost, a cost we must all be willing to pay if we are to achieve that victory. Tomorrow you will decamp and travel by train to Ballyshannon in Donegal, then on by road to Finner training camp.

"I have granted you all five hours leave in Omagh town from four until nine this evening in order that you may meet with family and friends. I expect you to behave in a manner which befits a British soldier and that neither the civilians in Omagh nor I will be given cause to regret this decision.

"I will see you in Finner. God save the King."

"The Colonel stepped back and the Sergeant marched forward addressing the men once again. "You have your orders, but remember you must return to camp sober on or before nine o'clock. Lateness and drunkenness will not be tolerated. Stand at ease."

"Three cheers for the colonel!"

The men gave three rousing cheers, filling the quadrangle with a burst of energy and good humour before they were dismissed.

The men, excited now at the prospect of the unexpected leave, made for the tents to prepare for their first sortie as soldiers.

The road into the town teemed with soldiers. William with his two new friends made their way down the street, proudly showing off their newly acquired uniforms.

"Do you know where there's a public house, William? Och, can we call you Willie?" asked Tommy.

"You can call me Willie if you like as long as me Ma doesn't hear you and, no, I don't know anything about public houses in Omagh. I don't drink." William could feel himself redden with embarrassment. "I've tried a drop of poteen but it tasted like paraffin and anyway, I never had the money for it."

"That's not drink, Willie," Tommy said. "I think it's time you were formally introduced to the real stuff."

"We have the money now, boy," Mark said. "I have a feeling if we follow the mob here we'll soon find a good bottle of porter."

The town was packed with soldiers but no one seemed to mind apart from some young lads that turned their backs as they passed by.

In the first pub the publican refused to serve them and William and Mark had to drag Tommy out onto the street to avoid a fight.

In the next place they were welcomed with open arms. The barman shook each man who entered by the hand and thanked them for standing up to the Hun.

After two bottles of porter William began to feel light headed and made his way outside to get a breath of air.

The pub was next to a hardware shop and barrels and baskets of produce blocked the narrow footpath. William was about to turn and go back inside when he saw Paul crossing the street further down. At least he thought it was

Paul because he recognised his way of walking even though the man was wearing an odd felt hat and a ragged topcoat tied in the middle with binder twine.

He crossed the road and followed the man as he walked towards the Courthouse catching up with him at the top of the hill at the junction near the church.

"Paul, Paul!" William shouted in a hoarse whisper worried that he was shouting at a stranger. The figure turned and sure enough it was Paul.

"Jez, William, you're a sight for sore eyes." He resisted grabbing William by the shoulders.

"What's going on? Why are you dressed like that?" William asked.

"Don't stop, William. Keep on walking up the hill past the church. There's an entry there by the stable yard. I'll talk to you there. Don't tell anyone you have seen me."

Paul left William standing on the street and skirted around the courthouse his head down. 'Thank you, God' he muttered to himself.

He had spent the last two nights sleeping in the stables and helping to muck out as payment for his keep. He had found the hat and coat wrapped up in one of the stalls. When the landlord had made no objections he had pulled it on over his own clothes. He trusted no one now; not since he realised he had been spotted at the camp.

He had tried to re-enlist the next day but had been chased by the same soldier his Da had spoken to. He didn't try again for fear he would end up in gaol. He had a little money but not enough to take him to a recruitment station far enough away where no one would know him. He was still angry with his Da. He couldn't believe he had turned him in at the camp. Now he was more determined than ever to join up. He just needed some money to get to Belfast, far enough away not to be recognised.

He was more worried about his Ma. He knew she would be breaking her heart, worried sick about him, but he couldn't go home again. How could his Da have done this to him?

William came into the stable yard and Paul called him over to the stall he had been sharing with a nice grey hunter the night before.

"Paul, what the hell is going on? Are you in trouble? How did you get here?"

"Stop, William. I've not been home since I last saw you."

"What?" William stared at his friend.

"Let me finish! I had no idea he was going to tell on me at the camp. One of his pals from Carrickmore told him. He had been nosing around the camp that weekend trying to get information, I suppose. I don't know but it's done now. I can't join up in Omagh."

"What are you going to do then?"

"I need some cash to get me out of here. I might try Cookstown, I'll join up there, change my name, I will do whatever it takes."

"What about home? Your Ma must be mad with worry."

"I know. I don't know how to get a message to her and let her know I'm alright?" He sat down on a bale of hay bowing his head. "It's a mess, a bloody mess and I don't know what to do."

"I can't help. We're leaving in the morning early. I think you should go home, have it out with your Da. Try and talk to him. Joining up under someone else's name is not a good idea, doing a disappearing act won't help. They will be in a state at home. You can't leave them not knowing what's happened to you. You need to think about this. I have a few shillings but it won't be enough for you to get to Cookstown. Talk to your Da again, Paul. Maybe he will see sense and change his mind."

"I don't think so William. He lashed me right there on the road at the camp. He's niver hit me before."

"I think he's sick to the stomach that you're joining Carson's army more than anything else. You need to talk to him. I'll have to get back to the camp. We were only allowed a couple of hours. Here I have one and sixpence, take it, it might get you a cart ride back home. I wish I could do more, Paul."

Paul clasped William's hand and they embraced then broke apart, embarrassed by their emotions.

"Thanks William, you're a true friend. I will go home even though I know in my heart it will do no good. All I know for sure is I am going to join up and be a part of this war if he likes it or not."

William couldn't find the words to answer him. His throat was tight with emotion as he turned to walk down Castle Hill, trying to look like a soldier but wishing he and Paul were back on the banks of the Glenelly, waiting for the pull of the line on their fishing rods.

RELIEF FOR SOLDIERS' RELATIVES

A meeting of Omagh Committee had been summoned in connection with a statement made by the Urban Council on Monday to the effect that relatives of soldiers on active service were not receiving their separation allowance regularly. The separation allowance granted by the Government for the wife was one shilling and four pence per day and three pence for each child. It was noted there had been a great deal of ignorance about the matter, but it was very satisfactory too know such cases would be attended to promptly.

Ulster Herald, September 1914

Chapter 20

Paul watched William walk away from him down the hill, wondering when they would meet again. The stable man appeared at his side.

"Are you doing any work here today? Couple of stalls there need mucking out and there's harness to clean in the tack room."

"I'm sorry, Mr Heaney. I'm leaving, going back home. There are some things I need to deal with. Would you know the price of a train fare to Newtown?"

"That's short notice, lad. Has something happened at home?"

"No, Mr Heaney. I've just come to a decision. It's a decision I'm not happy with but it's a decision just the same. Thank you for the bed and all your kindness."

"Well lad, these are difficult times. I hope all goes well with you. I don't know the train fare but there is a carrier cart going your way with a delivery to Cranagh, I'll speak to him. He owes me a favour or two.

"Jez, that would be great will he need paid?"

"Slip him a copper or two when he drops you off. He's a decent man. He leaves from the station yard at half seven so be on time or he'll go on without you. His name is Doherty. It'll be on the side of his cart. Tell him I sent you."

"Thanks, Mr Heaney"

"You're welcome, lad. I just hope it all works out for you. Goodbye and good luck to you."

He set off for the station yard, glad to be leaving the coat and hat behind and the smell they emitted. He walked up by the cow common and washed his face and neck in the cattle trough.

There were soldiers in uniform standing about in groups, some with girls laughing and flirting. He moved away down the hill, jealous of their comradeship.

It was almost time to meet the carrier.

The carthorse was a big brown draught and Paul wondered how it had missed the army horse fair. They had sold one of theirs but the price paid didn't make up for the loss of the horse to the working day on the farm.

He met the carter at the station as planned and they set off in good time. He was a man of few words so conversation between them consisted of the weather and him cursing about the deep holes in the road forcing him to navigate the horse and cart around them.

Paul spent most of the journey trying to gather himself together for the meeting with his da. He had worked out what he wanted to say but knew he would be hard to convince.

Padraig was tired. He had not slept for the best part of two nights. The horse had lost a shoe leaving him having to walk. He trudged the roads around Omagh and Newtown, asking anyone who would listen if they knew Paul.

He had visited the nuns at the Sacred Heart in Omagh on the off chance that Paul might have gone there for food or shelter but they had not seen anyone fitting Paul's description. They had sent him to Father Francis.

The priest was sympathetic and listened patiently to Padraig's story.

"You know, my son," said the priest, "we are living in very serious times and young men's imaginations are fired up with thoughts of adventure and there is a great pull for them to experience far away fields. This war unfortunately answers all of their dreams so we cannot fault them for wanting to be a part of it. Political differences are of no concern to them at their age. It is up to you as his father to guide him through the pitfalls of life."

Padraig listened to the priest's advice with a heavy heart. He could still see Paul's face after he had hit him with the whip outside the camp and knew that it would always be between them now, no matter what happened in the future.

"Have you been to the police barracks?" Father Francis asked.

"No. That would be my last resort."

"Do you want me to go for you? I know the sergeant, it can't do any harm."

"Alright, father. I'm at my wits' end now so it's better than nothing."

Padraig left the parochial house and decided to head for home. He had not been fair on Mary. She must be out of her mind with worry by now. He should have thought sooner and sent a message to the house. He stopped to allow a cart to pass him a few miles out of the town and he was tempted to cadge a lift.

As it passed, he could have sworn Paul was sitting in the front with the driver. Any thought of calling for a ride left him as he watched it move on. His weariness must be making him see things. Then the cart stopped and Paul stepped down unto the road.

As the cart had climbed a steep hill they had passed a man standing in the ditch. Paul realised it was his Da.

"Slow down mister, I need to get down."

"What's up, cub? Do you need a pish?"

"Naw, that's my Da we just passed, can you give him a lift as well?"

"Aye, sure there's plenty of room in the back. Whoa boy. Whoa." The horse and cart came to a standstill.

"Could you wait a few minutes, Mister? Me and me Da had words a couple of days ago. I just want to speak to him first if you don't mind."

"Now if it's a fight you're going to have, I'll be on my way. I'm a peaceable man and I've no time for fights."

"No fights, I promise and I only need a minute or two."

"Alright, but if I hear one word of anger, I'll drive off and leave you both to settle your differences on the road. I'm a peaceable man."

"Thanks, mister. You're a gentleman."

Father and son met on the road. Padraig spoke a silent prayer as he caught hold of Paul's hand.

"Hello, Da," Paul bit his bottom lip finding it hard to look his Da in the eye.

"Are you on your way home, son?"

Then all the emotions hit Padraig at once and he took his son in his arms and held him tighter than he had done since he was a wean.

Paul clung to his Da for a moment. Then he pulled away.

"Is Ma alright?"

"She will be now, son, now she knows you're safe." The carter's shout brought them to their senses.

"Are you two ready to get going? I have to be in Cranagh before nightfall?"

They both mounted the cart and set off in silence.

The cockerel crowing outside her window woke Mary out of a fitful sleep. She slid out of the bed, her toes curling as her feet met the cold stone of the floor.

The skin around her eyes was tight and dry. She had cried herself to sleep. She went outside to the water barrel and splashed cold water on her face and neck the water chilled her to the bone but did not compare with the cold chill in her heart. When Paul had left three days ago she had been numb with grief and helpless to stop the madness of his actions. She had spent the morning in a state of shock. The fire had gone out in the grate and the hens had perched on the kitchen table looking for feed before she had been shaken out of her grief to fetch the corn from the barn to feed them.

Padraig had arrived back on Monday afternoon. He lit the fire without a word. Then he had told her what had happened in Omagh. She had attacked him with her fists screaming and cursing him. This new ordeal was worse than she could ever have imagined. Now they had no idea where Paul was and the thought of it pushed her into haze of despair and vexation. Padraig had tried to comfort her but she was beyond his words. They said the prayers and went to bed.

In the bedroom he tried to embrace her but she shook him off and climbed into the bed, her tears running unchecked unto the pillow.

"I'll go into Omagh first thing in the morning. He can't have got far."

She ignored him.

He was gone after milking and had not come home last night at all. She had gone up to Martin's place and John Joe Martin had come down and helped her with the work in the byre.

She was baking bread but she had no idea how long she had been standing kneading the dough. There was a light tap on the door. 'Tinkers', she thought as she cleaned her hands on her apron.

She opened the door. Ann Johnston was standing on the doorstep clutching a small muslin parcel in her hand.

"Hello, Mary, I hope you don't mind my coming over. I've just churned some butter," she held out the parcel. Her awkwardness was obvious.

"I only just heard about Paul."

"What have you heard? I'm at my wits end. Padraig hasn't been home since yesterday," her tears flooded her face again.

"Sorry, I shouldn't have come." Ann turned to walk away.

"No, God no. Please come in. I'm the one who should be sorry for all my carry on. I'm selfish but not knowing what has happened is eating me up inside." She pulled at her apron again, wiping her face, embarrassed at her outburst.

"What did you hear?" she asked again.

Ann followed her into the small kitchen. The table was covered in flour, the fire almost out and a small child lay sleeping on the chair in the corner.

"I only heard that Padraig stopped Paul at the camp."

Ann didn't think now was the best time to mention the talk in the village about the fight on the road. Mary began to cry again and the boy woke at the noise and wailed in sympathy.

Ann lifted him.

"This is Oliver. Say hello to Mrs Johnston, Oliver," the child pushed his head into its mother's breast.

"Hello, Oliver, pleased to meet you." The child smiled then hid his head again. Ann smiled, remembering her lost angels..

"You must try to hold on, Mary, for the sake of the child. Paul is a sensible boy. He'll come home when he gets hungry. You wait and see." Ann put some turf on the dwindling fire and filled the kettle. "I'll make us a cup of tae or have you a wee nip of something in the house to settle your nerves?"

"No. Padraig won't have any liquor in the house since his brother took to the drink. I'm sorry Ann I just can't seem to be able to cope with all this. How are you yourself? Sure haven't you as much trouble as me and all I can do is cry."

"Don't mind me, Mary, I know the sorrow you're feeling. Women seem to have to take all that's coming and still carry on as if nothing has happened and men think they have all the answers. Have you had no word at all from Padraig?"

"No, Padraig thought Paul would come home with his tail between his legs. He has no money. He had to pay back the shilling to the army. Padraig was too heavy handed with the cub. It's his heavy handedness that has left us in the mess we're in now. I think I would have got over this whole army thing in time. He would have been with William and they always look out for each other but now I don't know where he is. I could kill Padraig for pushing him away."

Mary began to sob again and Ann could feel her own tears not far from the surface.

"He'll turn up. Sure if he has no money, where else would he go but home. Is there anything I can do for you? Have you slept at all these past few nights?"

"I can't sleep, I can't eat. All I can do is cry. I'm worse than useless."

"We have a lot to put up with, but our children are becoming people in their own right. They are past doing what we want them to do, past listening to our oul stories about what we had to do at their age. I wanted to go to the minister and get William out of this but he went mad at the very idea, said he would never forgive me. This is what he wants to do and I can't change it no matter how much I want to."

They embraced, the little boy in Mary's arms looking wide eyed between them. The door opened and Padraig walked into the kitchen, followed by Paul. The tiny kitchen was filled with noise and raised voices. Mary clung to Paul in another frenzy of crying and weeping.

Ann slipped out of the door unnoticed and walked down the lane into the gathering dusk. She heard her name being called. Mary must have realised she had left. Ann hurried on up the hill. She had no place there. Paul was home and all was well for Mary.

As she neared home a pain in the pit of her stomach gripped her hard. It wasn't a physical pain. She knew that. It was deeper. The hurt of the past few days seemed to consume her and she was jealous. God forgive her, she was jealous of Mary.

She sat down by the side of the road. A bee was buzzing around the wild flowers beside her, its back legs heavy with pollen. Somewhere, high up in the trees, a blackbird was singing.

Life was going on. She knew she had to go on. She was past crying. William wasn't coming home. She wouldn't be cooking his breakfast in the morning or listening to his voice as he talked over the events of his day. He was no longer a part of her daily existence. She had to accept that. There would be no happy ending for her.

She stood up. The blackbird stopped singing his wings catching the branches as he flew away over her head.

The lamp was lit in the kitchen. She paused at the door and lifted the cup from the hook on the water butt and drank long gulps of water before going into the kitchen.

John was sitting at the table a newspaper spread out in front of him. "Where have you been?"

"I've been over at McGoverns."

"What were you doing over there? It's not our fault their cub joined the army and it's not William's fault either."

"Paul is home again." The tears she had denied earlier now flowed down her anguished face. She sank into the chair by the fire.

"Didn't I tell you that last night? McGovern made a show of himself and he did his cub no favours. The sergeant was saying they were on the look out for Paul, missing in action before the action." John laughed at his own joke then looked up and realised his mockery was lost.

"This isn't funny, John. Paul and his Da came back together while I was there with Mary. I don't know all the details but he's home where he belongs which is more than can be said about our William. He's tied into a death sentence just like Mary McGovern said."

"Now, Ann, you're exaggerating. The Con says the Belgians have re-occupied a town called Louvain. The Germans surrendered with a white flag. Look, it's all here in this week's paper. You worry too much. William will be back before you know he's been away. God, I wish I was with him."

"I hope to God you're right, John. I can't bear the thought of anything happening to him," her sobs coming now in short gasps of despair.

John got up and gently lifted Ann to her feet and wrapped his arms around her and she clung to him.

"Oh John, how can this be right? We work hard to care for our children but that means nothing when disease and war can take them from us."

"Hush now, Ann. Try to see it from William's point of view. He is doing something that he wants to do and he will earn real money doing it. We both know William is too headstrong to be hired out. He would have got into some trouble or other and we all would have paid the price and the shame of it."

Ann pulled away from him, the sadness replaced now by anger.

"Don't you dare say such a thing. William would never do anything which would make us ashamed of him."

"That's not what I meant, Ann. Calm down. I'm only trying to see things as he sees them and for once in our lives him and me agrees on something. I'm as proud as any man could be."

"I read the Con as well John. Did you read the casualty list? There's men, some of them no more than boys like our William, dying out there and for what? The McGoverns got their son back. They know this war is wrong."

"Now you're talking like a Fenian. McGovern and his pals up the mountain and around Carrickmore have their own ideas and it's got nothing to do with anything legal. You can be sure of that."

"I'm not interested in what McGovern or anybody else is doing. I just want William back home where he belongs."

"You can't hide from what's going on around you, Ann. The IRB are bringing in arms and parading in full view up and down the streets of Ulster, just waiting their chance to start another rebellion."

"I'm not hiding. You're all as bad as each other as far as I can see. The Ulster Volunteers are hardly hidin' behind a ditch. In the meantime children like our William are getting killed miles from home. I'm away down to the room to say goodnight to the ony child I have left. Did you give him his supper?"

"I did. Sure there was no one else to do it." He turned again to the open paper on the table. As she left the kitchen, he said, "Look, Ann, William wants to do this. We had a long talk before he left. I told him about my army days. I could see he was proud of me at last. I haven't been the greatest Da to the cub and I'm ashamed of that now, but we made our peace and I'm not going to be the one to stop him."

"You were lucky, wounded or not, you came home again. I hope he has the same luck."

When the door closed, John went to the dresser and lifted out the bottle of Poteen, pouring a large measure into a cup on the table, then sat down by the hearth and lit his pipe.

His leg had been paining him a lot these past months. The harvest had been a busy one and the constant work had made it worse. He found a couple of good measures from the bottle eased it and helped him sleep, but in his heart he knew the solution to his problems were not to be found at the bottom of a bottle.

He thought about William and the problems he would face over there. Ann was right as usual. He had been lucky. He had been given another chance at life he should be thanking God instead of filling his belly with more poison. He set down the pipe and lifted the cup and the bottle from the dresser andwent outside to the street. The moon was bright and the stars hung around it like a necklace. He emptied the contents of the cup and the bottle onto the midden* smelling the pungent aroma of the alcohol as it soaked into the mire at his feet.

He raised his eyes heavenward.

"Dear God, I renounce the devil and all his work. I will not touch another drop of drink again as long as my darling son is kept safe and returns to us in good health. Amen."

The door opened and Ann came to stand by him. "What are you doing John?"

"Something I should have done a long time ago. I will need you more than ever now, Ann."

He kissed her then handed her the empty bottle and went back into the house.

Wounded Inniskillens arrive in Cookstown
Two Cookstown men belonging to the Inniskillen
Fusiliers, who were wounded in the first brush with the
enemy at Mons, returned home on Wednesday night and
received a cordial welcome from the townspeople.
As the train steamed into the station the explosion of
fog signals announced their arrival to the
waiting crowd on the platform.

Tyrone Constitution 1914

Chapter 21

Padraig had finally talked Mary into going to bed and he watched her now as she drifted in and out of sleep. He needed to stop Paul, reason with him to change his mind about this dangerous idea he had of joining the British Army. No good would come of it, the Brotherhood were already asking questions about Paul's loyalty to the cause. He knew he was partly to blame, he had let this friendship with the Johnston boy go too far. It should have been nipped in the bud before now.

He left Mary sleeping and came up to the kitchen. Paul was putting fresh turf on the fire and didn't look up.

They had not spoken directly to each other since arriving home, the silence emphasising the deep rift that lay between them.

"Have you thought about what are you going to do now, Paul?"

"Yes, Da, I have. You're not going to like it or agree with me. I am going to be involved in this war..."

"Paul....."

"No, Da. Let me finish. I need to have my say. I made a promise to William and now, thanks to you, I have broken that promise. That can't be helped now but I will do my best to join him at some stage in this war. I met him in Omagh today and I would be on my way to anywhere but here if he hadn't persuaded me to come home and talk to you. He's my best friend and I have let him down very badly. I'm sorry to bring this on you and Ma. I know how much this is hurting her, but it's my life. I am going to make my own decisions.

"I can't allow you to do this, Paul. Why can't you see that? This war is not our fight. If you want a fight then fight for the cause here at home."

"I'm not asking your permission, Da. I'm going. So unless you are going to lock me up I'll be away as soon as I can."

"You would rather go off with Willie Johnston than listen to your own father's advice. Well, I'll not have it. Do you hear me? I'll not have us talked about around the country, a McGovern following the union flag."

"We're all on the same side, Da. Redmond and the Irish Volunteers have joined up with the Ulsters. They're coming from Dublin, Munster and Cork to fight the Germans. We will all be fighting the same war. It's just one army now."

"That's rubbish. The British are playing games with men's lives, Paul, and Redmond is the fool if he thinks they will hand him Ireland on a plate. If

Redmond had what he wanted the UVF would have his head on a plate. This Home Rule Bill is a British sop to keep Carson and his army sweet.

"Home Rule should mean a free republic of all Ireland, what's on offer is a divided Ireland. And guess who will be left behind when the knife falls? Tyrone!" Padraig stood looking down at his son who sat with his head in his hands staring at the floor. Resigned to listen to a speech he had heard so many times before.

"We need young men like you fighting battles on our own doorstep against the oppression that has gone on for centuries, not fightin' and dying for the enemy in another country. I'm happy you're home where you belong, Paul, I just want you to show solidarity with me and the Brotherhood and all we want to achieve in this country."

"They want me to spy on my friends, Da. I can't do that and you can't make me."

Their angry voices rang around the small kitchen.

Mary woke and lay listening to them arguing. The wee one stirred. She got up and tucked him in, whispering and soothing him back to sleep. There was nothing to be gained if she interfered tonight. She climbed back into the bed. They were shouting now and she cried out and buried her head in the pillow.

Padraig had heard the crying. Thinking it was one of the children, he came into the bedroom and realised it was Mary.

"Are you alright?"

"No, Padraig, I'm not. Why can't you try and listen to Paul? Shouting at him will get nowhere. And it's time you were both in bed." She turned away still crying quietly.

He went up to the kitchen. Paul was hunched over and ignored his presence.

"Would you think about what I've said? We need to stick together to keep the movement alight. I have good contacts that will help you move up the ranks."

Paul gazed at the orange flame in the fire the glow reflecting on his young tired face.

"I'm not going to join the Brotherhood, Da. I am going into the British Army whether you like it or not. I want to be with William, but I doubt that will happen now. He's off to his training depot in Donegal tomorrow and I'm sitting here talking shit."

Padraig pushed the kettle over the flame and stood to lift cups from the shelf. He could sense that his argument was useless. He should have taken Paul under control long before this. Now his loyalty to William Johnston was ingrained and immovable. He cursed inwardly and brewed the tea.

"I don't trust Carson, Paul. None of our people can trust the likes of him. He stands for everything we are fighting against. Can't you see that?"

"No, I can't see that. That's the problem in this bloody country. You're all blinded by the past, blinded by things that happened years ago. You can't let go. You can't move on and look for a better way of living together with our neighbours."

"That's a joke coming from you. You're not going to be living together, you're going to be dying together and for what? This army is made out of pawns in another game of British domination. We have been living under the British for long enough to be able to recognise it for what it is."

"Britain didn't start this war, Da. The Germans did that and we can't sit back and watch them kill women and children in their beds without doing something about it. You read the papers but you ignore what's written down in black and white. You and your cohorts filter it to suit yourselves"

"You're too young to understand all this, Paul. It's not as black and white as the newspapers make out..."

"When did being too young stop you from getting involved in the Brotherhood?" Paul saw his Da's fist clench around the cup and knew he was walking a fine line.

"Who told you I was in Omagh Barracks?"

"That doesn't matter, Paul. You were seen and that's that."

"Were you having me followed?"

Padraig didn't answer and began raking the turf in the grate. Paul stared at him, hoping the answer was no.

"Were you having me followed? Answer me Da?"

"Not followed exactly, I asked some of the lads to keep an eye on you. I was worried. You can see how this has affected your mother."

Paul bowed his head. In all of this his mother was the one person he fretted about the most. He had never seen her so unhappy.

"Please leave Ma out of this. How long have you had me watched, Da? How long has some wee git been reporting my movements to you? Following me like some criminal or is he a full time spy down in the camp reporting back to the Brotherhood?"

Padraig jumped up and caught Paul by his shirt collar his face contorted with rage.

"Keep a civil tongue in your head, Paul, I'm your Father and anything I do with regard to you and this mad idea you have, I do because I care about you. Never forget that. You're an Irishman, Paul, and if you join this army they will make you one of them. You will swear allegiance to their King and the day you do that you will be no son of mine. I will disown you. You will never set foot in this house again. You will be dead to this family forever."

The colour had drained from Paul's face. Padraig released his hold on his son, his eyes hard and full of anger. Paul straightened his collar, his colour returning.

"Thanks, Da, for helping me to make up my mind. Goodnight."

Paul sat on the small bed, his thoughts in a turmoil of regret. He knew that whatever he did now would mean the making or the breaking of him. His Da and him were finished. Before tonight he had his doubts about joining up but his betrayal at the camp had helped him to see things more clearly. He needed to straighten things out with his Ma.

His mind was made up. He would bide his time for a day or so. Then he would leave. He had no money, the King's shilling was still out of his reach. William had promised to keep in touch but he knew he wouldn't be here to read the letters. The next Hiring Fair was three days away in Magherafelt.

He lay down and fell into fitful sleep.

He avoided his Da the next morning at breakfast and later in the morning watched him driving the horse cart off down the road to Strabane, to the mart. His Ma looked up as he came into the kitchen. She was packing eggs into boxes for the egg man. She looked tired but smiled and rose to make him tea.

"Did the talk with your Da last night help at all Paul?"

"No it didn't. It just made things worse."

There was a rumble of a cart turning on the street. The egg man had arrived early. As his Ma rushed, in the flurry of finishing the eggs for the market, Paul slipped out and headed for the Plumb.

He crossed the bridge and met Joe Connolly, a farmer from up the valley. Paul passed the time of day as usual and was surprised when Joe spat at his feet and walked on muttering to himself. This was repeated several times as he walked through the village and people he had known all his life turned away from him whispering as he passed by. It became obvious to Paul that word had got out that he was intending to join the British Army. The reality of the bitterness within his own community was a shock to him. People he knew, school pals, neighbours, all steeped in bitterness he had never noticed before.

He made his way up to Johnston's farm. He had written a short letter to William and he wanted Mrs Johnston to pass it on for him. As luck would have it she was crossing the lane as he approached and came towards him with a warm smile and, to his surprise, put her arms around him.

"Oh, Paul, it's so good to see you. I missed you. Are you well?"

"Aye, I'm well enough, but I would be happier if I was with William."

"I'm so sorry things didn't work out for you, Paul, but your mother was relieved to see you home."

"I know, Mrs Johnston. And it must be even harder for you now William has gone."

"Yes, it is. But I must put my faith in God for his safe return."

Paul could tell by the quiver in her voice that the tears were not far away. He felt selfish and thoughtless at coming and reminding her of William's absence.

"Can I offer you a cup of tea, Paul? I have just made some treacle bread. Your favourite if I remember rightly."

"No thanks, Mrs Johnston. I haven't got time. I was wondering if there was any chance you will see William before he goes to Finnar camp. I met him yesterday in Omagh. It was him who talked me into coming home."

"You saw him yesterday?" Ann's heart seemed to miss a beat. "Was he well? We got a letter from the camp to say he was leaving for Finnar in the morning if we wanted to go in and see him off."

The tears she had been holding back now rolled down her cheeks. "We can't go. The animals need to be seen to..."

"Mrs Johnston, I can help you out tomorrow. I'll come over first thing and you and Mr Johnston can go into Omagh and see William."

"Oh Paul, could you? Are you sure? What about your own work? Will your Da be able to manage without you?"

"You let me worry about that. He will have to get used to it sooner or later. I came over to ask you to give William a letter. I wanted to thank him for yesterday and pay back the money he lent me and to wish him good luck."

"Of course I will give it to him. You're a good lad, Paul. We have been lucky that William has had such a good friend in you. I'm sure he would tell you to keep the money."

"No! I want to pay it back."

"Please keep it for my sake. God bless you, Paul."

"I'll be over at five in the morning. That should give you enough time to get to the station," Paul fished the crumpled envelope out of his pocket.

"You'll not forget to give him this. Tell him good luck and that I'll not be far behind him."

"I know things have been bad between you and your Da but he is only doing what he thinks is best for you, Paul. I hope your kind offer will not make things worse between you?"

"Don't worry yourself, Mrs Johnston. I am glad to be able to help."

"Thank you so much, Paul. I need to get myself sorted out if we are to be ready to leave so early."

"Thank you again from the bottom of my heart."

STIRRING SCENES IN OMAGH

It is safe to say that never in the history of Omagh were such stirring scenes as when drafts of the Army Reserveand Special Reserve of the Royal Inniskilling Fusiliers left the town under war mobilisation Orders. St. Eugene's Brass and Reed Band accompanied them. Shortly afterwards a corps of the Ulster Volunteers with a large number of torchbearers, took up their position at the head of National Volunteers. The parade passed through the streets to the station, the Unionist torchbearers encircling the nationalists band to show light to the players. It was indeed a revelation for those who thought such a thing could not have happened.

Tyrone Constitution, October 1914

Chapter 22

William was jolted awake by the sound of a bugle, a chorus of swearing followed by the sound of muffled farts as the men in the tent woke for roll call.

He was billeted along with Tommy, Mark and nine other men he didn't know yet but who seemed to be cheerful enough.

They were moving to Finner camp in Donegal.

The roll call carrying full battle kit that consisted mostly of stones due to lack of proper kit was hard to get used to. It was heavy and cumbersome but William had carried heavier loads back home on the farm. Some of the other less fit lads were having difficulties and the Sergeant was not impressed by complaints coming from the ranks.

Heavy rain was falling as a silver band playing hymns led the way through the streets of the town on the short march to Omagh railway station. It was the 14th September 1914, just two weeks short of his 17th birthday.

Before the platoon was dismissed outside the station, they were told they had half an hour to say goodbye to any family members who had come to see them off.

William was not expecting anyone from home and began to make his way through the throng of bodies pushing their way to the platform when he heard a familiar voice calling out his name. To his amazement he saw his Da, Ma and the wee John pushing their way through the crowd.

His Ma reached him first and threw her arms around him.

"God, Ma. How did you manage to get here? I wasn't expecting to see you all here. How did you manage it what about the animals?"

"Oh, my dear William, I'm so glad we got here in time. We have been on the road since early and the cart was that slow I was sure we would miss you." The tears were coursing down her face as she pulled him into her arms again.

"Don't cry Ma, don't upset yourself, we haven't got long."

Wee John was curious about his big brother's clothes. He wanted to hold his gun and huffed when he told him it wasn't allowed.

To his surprise, his Da threw his arms around him. This was something that hadn't happened for a long time.

"Well, son, you're off then. You look every inch a soldier and I want you to know I'm a very proud man this day. I wanted to give you this. Happy birthday, lad." He pushed a small package into his hand.

"What's this, Da?"

"Open it. I would have given it to you sooner. I thought I'd lost it but your mother had it all the time."

William opened it and stared in amazement at the medal in his hand. "Is this yours, Da?"

"Aye, it is, cub. I niver thought about it until you enlisted. I nearly threw it away when it came in the post all those years ago. It seemed like an insult. Me crippled and all I had to show for it was that. I feel different now and I wanted you to have it to take with you, maybe it will keep you safe out there. I want you to be proud of me and all those men I knew who niver came home." John stood back and saluted William.

"Thanks, Da, I am proud of you and I will make you proud of me." He returned the salute, their eyes locked in their new understanding of each other. "How did you manage to get away from home? Who's milkin' the cows?"

"Paul came by yesterday. He offered to help so we could get away to see you off and to pay you back the money you lent him." She took an envelope from her pocket and gave it to him.

He took it, recognising Paul's familiar scrawl. "He wanted to pay back the money but I told him to keep it. I hope that is what you would want."

"Yes it is, thanks."

He shoved it into his pocket.

"Are you not going to open it?"

"Naw, I'll read it on the train. Let's sit over on these bales. I think we have five minutes before the whistle blows."

The time seemed to drag. He watched Ma, her fixed smile fighting back the tears that threatened to spill out while his Da talked endlessly about the reports from the front. Wee John raced off to see the band as it played at the edge of the station. The music mixed with laughter and the excited screams of the children filled the air.

He wished they hadn't come. He had said his goodbyes. He was ready for this. Paul's letter was burning a hole in his pocket. Maybe he had managed to get re-enlisted. Hope surged in him.

A loud whistle put an end to the happy atmosphere. Men began to climb aboard the carriages.

The band to play 'Abide with me.'

His mother clung to him, the tears which she had held back, now ran freely as she held on to him forcing him to pull away from her.

"I must go, Ma, I'll be home before you know I'm away."

His shook his Da's hand.

"Look after Ma, and remember our promises." Then he turned and climbed on board the carriage. Once inside, men began pushing and shoving to get to a window. He put his kit on the rack and sat down. The black smoke caught by the wind and back draught clouded the platform as the train pulled away.

The noise inside the carriage became subdued for a while as the men stowed away their kitbags and settled in for the journey to Ballyshannon.

William took out the letter. It was short.

Dear William,

You must know how sorry I am not to be sitting beside you now on the way to the camp. My Da was having us watched for a long time. That's how he knew so much. I am biding my time just now but as soon as I get a chance I'll be away and will enlist in the Inniskillens if I can.

Take care of yourself and don't grab all the best lookin cutties for yourself put a word in for me.

Your friend Paul

William was shocked. They had been followed and spied on. It was unbelievable. He pushed the letter into his pocket. They were on the same journey. He told himself this separation was just a distraction. Given time they would meet again.

The train reached Ballyshannon by early afternoon and the troops marched on to Finner camp in formation. Local people watched them on the road, viewing them with mixed emotions. Some cheered while others ignored them. By the time they reached the perimeter of the camp, there was a line of young boys marching in step alongside them, much to the annoyance of the sergeant.

"ROBBERY UNDER ARMS"
Alleged Raid of Volunteer Rifles in Dublin.

A sensational affair occurred in Dublin on
Saturday night. A cart laden with a consignment of
ninety rifles, in charge of a Captain of the
National Volunteers, was held up by a party
of fifty men on the banks of the Grand Canal.
One of the crowd held a revolver to the Captain's head,
and demanded the surrender of the rifles.
The police are investigating the affair.

The Ulster Herald, November 1914

Chapter 23

Paul arrived at the fair early. He had hidden his food bag in the hay shed. There was bread from his supper the night before and he had boiled eggs with the pratties* Ma had cooking for the pigs in the pot in the yard.

He was glad he had been able to help the Johnston's with the milking so William's folks could see him off at the station in Omagh. It was the least he could do for William after letting him down so badly. He didn't know how he was going to tell his ma he was leaving again but he would have to deal with it when the time came.

The village was quiet apart from the usual noise from the cattle and sheep in the pens beside the river.

He was on the look out for a hawker called Johnny Robinson who came on fair days to sell second hand clothes.

Johnny lived in Cookstown and if he could get a lift with him tonight he could go to the recruiting office there and hope no one knew him.

He spotted Johnny and his sister unpacking the cart at their usual place beside the bridge.

"Mornin', Johnny."

Johnny looked up but barely halted his task.

"Mornin'. You're here early. Are you up for hiring?"

"Naw, Johnny. I'm on the look out for a lift to Cookstown tonight an' was wondern' if you could help me out."

Johnny stopped, removed his cap and squinted at Paul. "Now, what would you be doing down that part of the world, cub?"

"I've heard there's a hiring for good wages down in Cookstown with better prospects."

"Aye, well, you don't want to believe all you hear in these time, lad. Hard work is hard work no matter where you find it."

"Could you give me a lift, Johnny? I'm eager to get away tonight."

"Now, that's the thing, cub, Maggie is a bit cautious about givin' lifts. Our oul nag has bother haulin' her and me and the goods home. It's her withers that can't stand the weight any more so I can't help you. Now I can put you on the track of a lift but it will mean a bit o' work on your part."

"I don't mind a bit of work, Johnny. What was it you were thinkin'?"

"Do you know oul Joe Farmer? He has a make shift of a stall up beyond the bridge. He buys and sells pots and pans?"

"Aye, I do, but I thought somebody tul me da he had died from the drink."

"Well, that's another story. But he's here today. I heard and seen him comin' in the Gortin road earlier. I'll walk over with you. He's a bit of an oul cod if he disn't know you. Mind you, he might not remember you at tae time if he's true to form."

They made their way over the bridge. Johnny was a popular man and they were stopped often by other stall holder's shanachin* and passin' the time of day.

Joe Farmer was a grizzle of a man, his beard and hair clung lank on his head and face, giving him a bearlike appearance until he opened his mouth and you were confronted with a toothless mass of fleshy gums.

"Mornin' Joe. Are you well this fine morning?"

"Not well at all. Would ye have a wee drop of mountain dew on ya be any chance?"

Johnny laughed, "A bit early for the hard stuff, Joe. Maggie has tae with her if ye want to drop over later." Johnny winked at Paul.

"Ach, tae, me arse! A body needs something to warm the guts."

"This lad here is after a lift to Cookstown, I told him you and him might come to an arrangement if you're not feeling the best at home time. He could see you right to the dour, what do you say Joe?"

Joe eyed Paul up, "Have you a drop of the craythur* on ye?"

"If I can get a lift on your cart later I might be able to get you what yer after but I can't promise."

"Dam to hell! I'm not interested in a half turned bargain. Can you get a drop or not, if ye can I'll do my bit."

"What is it you drink Joe? Is it stout?"

"Ach, it's no matter what you bring, it'll all do the same. When can you get it? I'm pure thirsty at the minute."

"I'll be back in an hour or so, Joe, and we can seal the deal then if that suits you?"

"Aye well, I suppose beggars can't be choosers. But if you get nabbed by the police I'll deny havin' anything to do with you."

With that, Joe turned away from them and began clattering pots and pans onto the shaky table at the side of the cart.

"Now, where would I be able to get poteen? Sure I never even tasted the stuff."

"Well lad," said Johnny, "I heard about an oul fella called Spud Spratt up Cranagh way who deals in the hard stuff. But you never heard it from me. Mind what you're about now, an keep on the right side of the law. I've heard

146

tell the cells in the barracks are cul and they're not keen on home brew. I'd better get back to me work. Good luck."

"Thanks Johnny and could I ask ye not to mention seeing me if me Da comes into the village?"

Johnny paused in his stride and looked Paul in the eye. "I make it a rule niver to get mixed up in family differences and by the same token I expect ye to keep my name out of anything you do from here on." And with that he strode away into the gathering throng of the busy market.

Paul made his way out of the village on the Cranagh road. It was a long trek uphill through the Glenelly valley. He remembered walks he and William had taken through Barnes Gap, the wildness of the mountains and the freedom they enjoyed growing up here. Halfway up, he stopped to talk to Arthur McCall who was working along a ditch in one of his fields. Arthur knew spud Spratt and his skill at poteen making and, after getting directions and a bit of advice he was on his way to do the deal.

McCall had told him to hold to his price for Spratt was known to be crafty if he thought his customer had more money to spend and to say it was for a sickness cure as he was never known to refuse a sick man.

The house stood in a small valley down a long overgrown lane. The buildings surrounding the small cottage were in dire need of repairs. A large dog growled, straining at the end of a frayed rope.

Smoke snaking out of the chimney was the only clue that the house was lived in. Paul knocked loudly, the noise sending the dog into a frenzy of barking. A second knock prompted a man's voice coughing and swearing before the latch was lifted and Spratt appeared on the step.

"What the hell do you want, wakin' up a man at his rest?"

Paul stepped back. The smell of rank tobacco and spirits hit him. The thought of drinking anything made at the hands of the man in front of him made his stomach turn and it took him a minute or to swallow back the bile rising into his throat.

"Well, speak up, cub, has the cat got your tongue?"

"Sorry Sir. Are you Mr Spratt?"

"Who's askin? What do you want?"

"I'm after a drop of poteen, me uncle's not well and he's after a wee drop to see if it will help his complaint."

Spratt scratched his chin, "How much do you want?"

"It depends on the price, sir, I don't have much money. How much would a naggin be?"

"Spratt blinked several times as if considering the deal. "A naggin will cost ye three shillings."

"My God, sir, that's more than I could pay. Could ye come down a bit? I'm needin to get back before dark, my uncle is not in a good way."

"One and sixpence is my final price. Take it or leave it. It's all the same to me." Paul was relieved to be at the tail of the bargain, it was all the money he had. Spratt handed over the naggin bottle. Paul uncorked it to smell the contents. Then Spratt spat on his hand holding it out to Paul.

"Deal, lad deal," his eyes blinking rapidly as Paul gingerly took his hand to seal the bargain. Half way up the lane Paul stopped and ran his hand over the long grass.

He headed for home, happy his plans were going well. He had almost reached the village when he thought he heard something or someone on the other side of the ditch. The field was empty and the slap lay open. He had only gone a yard or two when he was pushed to the ground from behind.

"Aw jez, sorry, sir I didn't see ye there."

Paul scrambled to his feet and came face to face with Fergal O'Neil. "What the hell are ye playin' at?"

"Oh, I'm not playin', McGovern. I'm deadly serious. I thought you might like a bit of practice for when ye git out to France. The Germans are a deadly bunch af fightin' men so I thought I could help yer training." The sudden punch in his stomach winded him and he fell on his knees. He saw the next blow coming and caught O'Neil's leg pulling him to the ground where they rolled across the road together grappling for purchase. A woman's voice broke through their grunts and with a quick turn O'Neil twisted away and leapt the ditch. He turned back his voice in a low guttural whisper "I'll be back some day to finish the job." Then he ran off, leaving Paul stunned on the road. An old woman came puffing up the hill and leaned over him..

"Are ye alright, cub?" "Aye, missus.Thanks"

"Did ye have a fallin' out with your friend?"

"No friend o'mine, missus."

He checked the bottle in his pocket, it wasn't broken.

"Do ye not know him then?"

"Naw, I don't. Thanks missus." He walked on leaving her looking after him. He was shaking like a leaf and stopped again. He took the bottle out of his pocket pulled the cork and drank a mouthful. He choked as the acrid liquid hit the back of his throat. He retched and spat it out. Then his breakfast followed it onto the road.

Chaplin Of Irish Brigade
the Rev. M.O'Connell, addressing the
military at their mass on Sunday in Fermoy,
informed them that he had been appointed
Chaplin of their portion of the Irish Brigade
now stationed in Fermoy, and that he would go with
them , whwerever they might be sent,
even to the post of danger. Referring to the Belfast
Volunteers, Father O'Connell said that their
friends from the North received a grand
reception from their friends from the South.

Ulster Herald, November 1914

Chapter 24

Mary had thanked God and the Holy Mother for Paul's safe return. She had tried to put it all behind her but she knew in her heart that Paul was not the same since his return home. He had long moments of silence and he clung to Oliver more than usual, taking him to his favourite spots at the river. She knew he was hankering for his friend and the good times they had shared.

She had watched him slip eggs in with the spuds boiling in the pot on the street and last night he had put bread in his pocket when he thought no one was watching. She knew then that he was planning to leave. It hurt her to realise that she could not stop him. Ann Johnston's words kept coming to mind. She knelt down and asked the holy mother to give her Ann's courage and fortitude.

When she had finished her prayers, she pulled out the tin she kept hidden under the bed. It held all the small things she treasured most in the world. Three small teeth, one of them Paul's, wrapped in a hankie. Her mother's wedding band, thin and worn down by hard work. The two half crowns lay at the bottom. She took them out and wrapped them in a poke of paper and pushed them deep into her apron pocket. She had to be strong now. This was Paul's time. Right or wrong she must make the best of it.

Paul came up the lane, his head full of how he was going to leave without making it any worse for Ma. He had decided not to tell about his run in with O'Neil. The less she knew the better. He could hear her busy in the milking parlour, washing pails in the cold water that ran along the narrow channel in the floor. She was singing one of her favourite tunes, happy in the knowledge that he was home, but he knew her happiness was short lived.

He cursed his Da for making this harder on her. If he had gone with William she would be over the worst of it now or at least getting used to the idea. Now she had to go through it all again.

She looked up smiling. "I have been thinking about you. Wondering where you had got to."

"Do you need me for anything?"

"No, son, just glad you're home with us. Your Da has gone to look at sheep up the mountain. He took the Oliver with him for a dander so, if you wait a while, I'll make us some tea."

Paul couldn't meet her gaze. "I haven't time now, Ma. I'm going down to the bottom field to cut more turnips and then Tony Donaghy is comin' to service the sow. I'll be back in an hour or so."

"I will bring the tae down to you. I could do with a walk."

"Thanks, Ma."

He lifted the slap post, aware she was standing in the yard watching him as he crossed the low ditch to the turnip field.

He loved this spot on the farm in the shadow of the Sperrin Mountains. He and William called it th the sparrow hawks' dining room. They had often watched the bird swoop in for the kill on an unsuspecting rabbit plucked from the green moss or small finch caught in midflight.

He would miss all this but he knew there was no turning back now.

She came down as he was filling the last bag. He could smell fresh baked soda bread as she poured the warm tae from the bottle and passed him his cup. They sat without speaking and listened to the rooster crowing his loud territorial anthem from the hen coop. The cows across the far side of the river their heads bowed in their endless communion with the grass.

"When are you leaving, Paul?"

He turned startled, a flush rising on his neck. "What do you mean?"

"I know you're leaving, son. I know you can't hold back. It's something you have to do and, even though it's taking you away from me, I know there is nothing I can do but watch. I just want to know how long I will have you...."

She began to weep, her hand reaching out across the space between them.

He moved over beside her, his tears falling as fast as hers. They sat close on the soft moss.

Time seemed to pause, wrapping them in a grey fog of inevitability. "How did you know?" he asked finally. "Did Mrs Johnston say somethin'?"

"No, son, don't blame her. She told me you wrote a letter to William. She didn't read it. She just thought I should know. She has been kind to me."

"Then how did you know?"

"Call it a mother's instinct, call it what you will but since you came home you have not been yourself. The child that was you has gone somewhere else and then I saw you hiding the food yesterday. I know how much this means to you. If you don't go you will regret it and blame us for holding you back. You must go, Paul, and I must find the strength to give you my blessing."

He suddenly felt lighter, as if the weight of the past weeks had been lifted away from him, but looking at her he was aware of how much it took for her to give him her blessing.

"I don't want to hurt you. I love you so much but you're right. I need to do this. Da tried to push the whole Irish thing at me but he doesn't understand. He wanted me to go to Dublin. I'm not a part of that. I'm part of this place and this place is a part of me. Going to Dublin or Cork is not for me. I want to be with William. I have let him down."

"William doesn't think that, Paul. He knows all this wasn't your fault and as for your Da, I'll deal with him. Make your plan and trust me it will all work out." She took a poke of paper from her pocket and held it out to him.

"I had this bit put by for a rainy day and I think this day has come. God bless you, son and may God and Mary, the blessed mother of Christ, watch over you."

Paul threw his arms around her. "Thank you. I hope I'll make you proud of me."

"I will always be proud of you, Paul."

They heard the sound of the horse and cart on the road above.

"That will be your da back from the mountain. Say nothing to him about this. I'll talk to you later."

Paul watched her walk away. He opened the poke of paper and found two half crowns. Five shillings. It was a fortune. How had she been able to save so much?

When Mary got back to the house, Padraig was stacking turf on the fire. He looked round at her. "Where have you been? The fire is nearly out."

"I took tae down to Paul. He's down cutting turnips. Is the kettle filled?" She fussed over the water pail at the edge of the dresser, filling it with the tin cup.

"What happened to you? You're eyes are very red. Have you been crying?"

"What do you mean?" She turned to the mirror on the wall, lifting her apron to rub her eyes.

"Ach, I was spreadin' straw in the chicken run earlier. It blew back in my face." She went outside and down to the lip of the well and splashed water on her face. Padraig was standing on the step as she came up the street.

"Are you makin' tae or have I got time to go down to speak to Paul? Seamus Martin said he saw him up beyond Cranagh this morning early. Have you any idea what took him up there?"

Mary lifted the towel to dry her face.

"That couldn't be. Paul was cutting turnips all morning. Seamus must be seeing things." The lie tumbled off her tongue. She blessed herself inwardly.

"It's not like Seamus to make a mistake. Are you sure, Mary?"

"What's this, Padraig, an interrogation? Is my word not good enough anymore? How many spies have you got up in the mountain? It's no wonder

Paul wanted away when he heard half the county is following him around."

"That's bullshit, Mary. I was only askin'. What's got into you? Has Paul said something?"

"No, he hasn't. But you would need to stop listening to them that think they have the right to interfere with this family."

Paul came in, but it was too late for Mary to warn him.

"What's all the noise about I heard you shoutin' out on the road. Is everything alright?"

"It's nothing, Paul, just your Ma putting me in my place as usual. I'm away into the Plumb. I have lambs up for sale at three. Wish me luck. We could be doin' with the money." He pulled on his coat then turned back.

"Do you want to come with me, Paul? It'll be a change for you after all them turnips."

"No, Da, I've not finished yet. I have to see Tony Donaghy about the sow. Is there tae on the go?"

"Naw, the fire's out. I'm away. See ye later."

They stood together, watching as Padraig disappeared down the road. "What's goin on, Ma?"

"Someone saw you up the mountain at Cranagh this morning. I said it couldn't have been you because you had been here all day cutting turnips. I think he believed me."

"God, Ma. I'm so sorry. This is my bloody fault. He'll go mad with you now."

"It's done now, Paul. You will have to be more careful. What time are you meetin' that man?"

"At half past five. Da should be back by then."

"Go over the footbridge, Paul, and take the upper road. That way you have less chance of runnin' into him."

"What about you, Ma? What are you going to tell him? What if he finds out you lied to him?"

"I'll tell him what he wants to hear and in my own good time. I have some bread in a cloth on the table for you. It's treacle, your favourite."

Her voice was calm yet she was screaming inside her head. She could not watch him go.

Paul lifted the parcel from the table. He took the poke of money out of his pocket.

"Ma, I can't take all this money. It's too much. You must have had other plans for it?"

"My plans are easily changed, son. It's you who needs it now. Be sure and spend it wisely. Keep it safe from thieves and tinkers. You had best hide it and not in your shoe" she smiled.

"Ach, Ma. Where will I hide it then? In my pocket?"

"Well, they do say that's the first place a thief will look." She took his hand, the smile fixed on him. "Say your prayers as you should and remember us all. Trust no one, son, and keep yourself to yourself."

"Are you saying goodbye now?" He saw the smile waver. "Go, Paul. No looking back."

He pulled her into his arms but she stiffened and pulled away.

"Don't, Paul, please don't say goodbye to me. If you do I will have to run after him and tell him the truth, God forgive me."

She went to the bedroom and closed the door. After a moment the front door closed and she heard him striding away from her.

Omagh Journalist in Lord Kitchener's Army

Sergeant Finnegan, 7th Battallion Inniskillen Fusiliers,
Tipperary, untill a few weeks ago on the staff
Of the 'Ulster Herald' and Allied Newspapers,
is proceeding to Aldershot to undergo a month's
training in Aviation School before receiving
his commission in the royal flying Corps.
Sergeant Finnegan 's abilities as a journalist
Should enable him in the future to write some
very interesting articles on military life.

Ulster Herald, November 1914

Chapter 25

David waited for his meeting with the Camp Adjutant. He had arrived yesterday and had spent an enjoyable evening in the mess getting aquainted with his fellow officers. His billet was in a row of converted cottages which were shared by three others. He was happy and excited about his posting. All the hopes he had carried throughout his life had now been realised and he was ready to meet this new challenge.

The interview had been relaxed and informative, the Adjutant Captain Russell giving him a brief explanation of his duties.

"This post is a new one specifically designed to deal with the large amounts of reports coming from the battlefields and their affect on the public at large, the serving soldiers and the ongoing recruitment drive throughout the country," the Colonel explained. "It will be your responsibility to write and report on all matters pertaining to propaganda, both within the camp and in the local press. We must keep misinformation to a minimum and create good communications between all battalions, both here in Ireland and at the front. This may seem like an enormous amount to take in, Lieutenant Bowman, but given you come highly recommended and with excellent credentials I have no doubt you will fulfil your duties with the utmost diligence. Have you any questions?"

"No sir."

"You will receive your written orders and your Programme of Instruction from our chief instructor and there will be a formal briefing tomorrow. In the interim, I suggest you familiarise yourself with the camp and your fellow officers. At ease, Lieutenant."

He had been assigned a small office space next to the main house and returned there to organise his paperwork and filing system. There was a large manila file on his desk sealed and stamped Confidential with his name underneath. His orders had indeed arrived.

The days that followed were filled with field defences, musketry, scouting and street fighting, leaving David little time to acquaint himself with the task he had come to carry out. He pondered over this problem and finally decided to ask the sergeant major for his advice when they met in the mess.

"You are a serving officer in an army currently at war and not a scribe who expects to sit behind a desk all day writing about the bravery of the rank and file soldiers in that army. Your training in field operations is of paramount importance. When you go to France you will be in the thick of battle and you must be equipped to defend yourself and react to the enemy whose sole purpose is to kill you. Have I answered your question? Do you fully understand your place in this war?"

"Yes, Sir."

"Excellent. Now I think it's your shout, Bowman."

The camp was a hive of activity and more men were arriving on a daily basis. There was very little time for relaxation but he made time to walk along the lake in the evening to take in the peace and tranquility.

It was on one such stroll that he met Elsie Johnston.

"Good evening. How nice to see a familiar face. You are from my father's parish? Do you work here?"

She blushed.

"Oh, forgive my bad manners but I never forget a face. I'm David Bowman."

"Yes, I remember you from church, but it's been a while since I've been home. I work in the main house."

"I have only just arrived to do my training. It's a beautiful place."

"Yes it is. Nice to see you again."

Before he could reply, she walked on leaving him to watch her disappear into the trees.

In the days that followed, David found himself thinking about Elsie. She always seemed so distant when he tried to engage her in conversation.

The opportunity to meet her formally came when he had to interview trainees in the first aid class for an article in the camp newsletter. Elsie was there and after the meeting they walked across the quadrangle together. They found they had a lot in common and were comfortable in each other's company. Unfortunately the housekeeper had something to say about their friendship, calling it inappropriate and made it clear their walks were to stop.

In the third week at Baronscourt, his training was interrupted when he was called to the Captain's office.

The Captain stood him at ease.

"I have new orders for you, Lieutenant, and don't look so worried. You have been promoted to the rank of Captain and are to report for duty at Aldershot in three days time. Congratulations, Captain."

David was shocked "I don't understand sir."

"It seems your work to date has been recognised as a means of boosting morale at home and at the front. This is a big step up for you I wish you every success."

He would be moving to Aldershot to begin training and would be part of the Royal Air Force Volunteer Force. He had been granted two days' leave to visit home before his departure to England on the Steamship Devonshire leaving Belfast docks on Monday. Before he left the camp he wrote a short message to Elsie, telling her of his change of plans and was surprised when on the morning of his departure in the jeep, she was waiting for him at the main gate.

"I just wanted to wish you good luck before you left" she blushed and began to walk away.

"Don't go, Elsie."

He got out and walked towards her. "I am glad to see you, I have very little time but I wanted to ask if you would mind if I wrote to you?"

"Yes, I would like that David, I must go back to the house, nobody knows I'm here."

He bent over and kissed her on the cheek.

"I will write as soon as I get to my posting and give you the address. Look after yourself."

He climbed back into his seat and the jeep roared up the steep drive, leaving her trembling and close to tears.

OMAGH WAR CASUALTIES

Amongst those mentioned in a casualty
list received by the military authorities in Omagh is
Private Andrew Nixon, whose parents reside near
Omagh. He was killed in action and he was one
of five brthers who were serving with the colours.
A sad coincidence was that almost at the same
Time Mrs Nixon (deceased's mother) received
a letter from the King congratulating her on having
five sons in the army.

Ulster Herald 1914

Chapter 26

The cart jolted in and out of the potholes in the road. They were crossing the bog, the only light coming from the full moon and the battered lamp swaying on the bar of the cart. The stars hung like a diamond necklace in the sky above him and every now and then he would catch the silver tail of one speeding across the black wilderness of space. He opened the parcel of food his ma had made for him. He was going to miss her and Oliver. He crossed himself and prayed a silent prayer to Mary, the Mother of Jesus, to intercede and watch over them. He ate only half of the food, leaving what remained for the next morning then sat back to gaze at the sky again.

Spratt's snores had got louder and Paul aimed an odd poke with a stick in an attempt to silence him. This intervention only made matters worse, rousing Spratt into a chorus of oaths. Paul gave up. It would be a long night.

A man suddenly stepped out onto the road in front of the cart. Paul pulled the reins sharply and realised that there was more than one figure on the road. He looked behind him. Three more men were standing behind the low ditch.

In the light from the lamp he could see the man nearest to him had his face masked. The hairs on his neck stood up.

"Can I help you?" His voice was shrill in the stillness of the night, waking Spratt out of his drunken sleep.

"What have you stopped for, boy?" Then his eyes focused on the man standing silently in front of the cart. Spratt pulled a shotgun from under his blanket.

"Who the hell are you and what do you want? We have no money so you're wasting your time. Now move out of the way or I'll give you both barrels."

The man stepped forward and, in one swift movement, the gun was pulled from Spratt's hand.

"Never point a gun, oul man, unless you intend to use it. Now, get down the both of you and move away from the cart." He broke the gun and laughed. "An empty gun will get you killed someday."

Paul stepped down unto the road. Spratt tried to scramble after him fully awake now and in urgent need of a drink.

"Where are you going at this time of night?"

"Who are you to ask?" Paul was angry. This was just another of his Da's pals poking their nose in to his business.

"Are you from around here?"

"Who are you?" Paul asked again defiantly. "You have no right to stop us on the public road."

"We are on the King's business. Answer the question."

Paul felt the blood drain from his face. Maybe he was wrong. He had heard about the vigilantes roaming the country but never thought much about it.

He turned to help Spratt who was shaking uncontrollably now.

"Search them!"

The order came from one of the men behind the cart.

"Please, sir. I'm an oul man just finishin' a hard day at the fair. I don't know this boy. Niver met him before today. I'll be on me way, now. He's nothing to do with me."

Spratt attempted to climb back on the cart but before he could he was hoisted by one of the men into the air and dropped into the ditch.

"Ye were told to get down. Now stay down."

Spratt began to moan loudly. His attacker responded with another kick.

Paul reacted, swinging his fist at the man bending over Spratt, hitting him hard in the gut.

The last thing he remembered was the sky spinning out of control as his head hit the road.

He was brought to his senses by a snorting close to his ear. His head hurt. He opened his eyes to find Spratt's donkey standing over him. He tried to rise to his feet but fell over. His legs were bound by thick twine, his left hand attached to the halter of the donkey. His right hand lay two feet away from him.

He passed out again.

Use of Bayonets.
Ulster Soldiers at Training.
Recently a representitive from the
'Constitution' had the privilage of
witnessing a batch of 54 selected
'non-coms' from all the brigades of
the Ulster Division at battle practice
with bayonets. They are for the most
part Ulster Volunteers – keen as a
razor's edge to serve their country.

Tyrone Constitution, November 1914

Chapter 27

Four real guns had appeared. Not many. But enough to give the men assembled a feeling of the reality of it all. This was serious. The time for playacting was over.

Alan Scott had been a corporal with the Donegal Artillery in the Boer war and had remained in the army until 1909.

He had been drilling the men for eighteen months and they had come to respect him and out of that respect had emerged a fierce loyalty and obedience to his orders.

They were lined up in double ranks. Farmers, labourers, creamery men and Orangemen from all around the district who had answered the call and now stood under the banner of The Ulster Volunteer Force. Their biggest problem was the shortage of guns and the men were getting restless.

"Don't have any bullets, boys. I didn't want to chance it yet just in case I become the target."

The men laughed and some wisecracks were exchanged as they stood at ease in their drill lines in the open barn.

"How many of yous have fired a gun before? If you have, stay in line. If you haven't, step to the left and fallout."

There was silence in the ranks. Someone coughed and feet shuffled on the straw strewn floor of the barn.

"Come on now, boys. There must be some of ye who have held a gun before."

A voice from the middle of the ranks spoke up.

"Well, sir, nobody here that has any sense is going to own up to shootin' practice. Beggin your pardon sir, the Duke niver took too kindly to poachers in these parts."

There was more laughter and then one or two stepped forward.

"I thank you for your honesty, but the Duke is not interested in petty poaching. He wants to ensure that the men in the Ulster Volunteers are trained in all aspects of military matters or, to put it simple, good shots when the time comes to defend ourselves."

"I can shoot."

John Johnston limped up to the front of the ranks and was acknowledged by most of the men around him.

Alan Scott shook his hand.

"How are you, John? I was not expecting you here. What can I do for you?"

"A quick word if you can spare me a minute or two."

"Alright, men. Fall out for a break. I haven't much time, John. What's the trouble?"

"No trouble, Alan. I came to make you an offer. You know I have been under the weather for a while but apart from the leg I'm alright. I'm a good shot and I was thinkin' you could do with my help with these boys, pass on some of my tips."

"To be honest, John, it will soon be out of my control. These men are all being signed up and will be soldiers very soon. If anything changes, I'll get in touch, now I must get back."

John was disappointed. He had been a good soldier and he was angry at the way people of his own kind were treating him. He had given up the drink. It had been hard at first but he had made a promise to God on William's life and he would keep that vow no matter what. As he made his way out of the field he heard his name called. Alan Scott was coming towards him.

"John, I've been thinkin'. I might have a wee job for you. I have to distribute some parcels to a few locations. I have a driver but I need someone to ride along as a lookout."

"Sounds like my kind of job. Where and when?"

"We have a large consignment to be moved in the next week and the more hands on deck the better. I need to do a run up to Dungannon for a collection but I need the backup. Are you sure you're able for it?"

"What's in the parcels or need I ask?"

"Oh, I think you know the answer to that question, John."

"Aye, I think I do. It will be a pleasure to be doing something useful for a change. When are we goin?"

"I will be in touch the day after tomorrow, around mid morning. Say eleven o'clock here. You will be gone for about 24 hours. Be ready and tell no one."

"I would need to tell Ann something. If I'm away that long she's likely to call the police thinkin' I'm in the hedge somewhere."

"Tell her as little as possible. We need to be careful. The police aren't the only ones interested in these parcels. I'm relying on you, John, so don't let me down."

"Leave it to me, Alan. I'm yer man."

They parted company and John whistled his way down the road a happy man. All he needed to do now was convince Ann and that had its own drawbacks. He knew she could be trusted but he didn't think she would be happy about it so the least said the soonest mended. He would tell her he was helpin' an old friend and that was no lie.

John was quivering with excitement. At last he was doing something useful. He was playing his part in defence of his country. In the end he had not told Ann the truth of what he was doing, but a half truth that he was helping a farmer from Gortin to move cattle in Donegal and they might possibly stay the night depending on the weather.

He was one of three men chosen to go as far as Dungannon to receive the last part of a shipment of guns that had landed in Larne in April. The cart was empty, apart from a rifle lying at their feet. They were taking no chances. Fenian vigilantes were known to patrol the roads around Ballygawley and the RIC had mounted patrols under orders to confiscate illegal guns. But Alan had told John that many of the RIC were turning a blind eye to the guns and in some cases actively helping to have them dispersed around the country. Passwords had been exchanged and they were warned that if they were discovered and arrested they were to disclose nothing to the authorities.

The sky was still bright as they reached the outskirts of Dungannon and found their way to their destination, an Orange hall south of the town.

There was a concert in full swing when they arrived. Pony traps and carts were lined along the road and, as they drew up, two men stepped out in front of them and motioned them to pull over.

"Remember men. Leave the talkin' to me. I know the password," John pushed his cap back on his head and smiled down at the strangers.

"Is it too late for the dancin'?"

"The first reel is over but the second is about to begin." "Have ye space at the back?"

"Aye, plenty af space at the back follow me."

A cart to the right of them pulled out revealing a path at the side of the hall. They turned in and followed the man along a lane and into a small barn at the back. The door rattled closed behind them. Three men stood silently in the dim interior of the barn. There were no introductions. John and his men stepped down and removed the tarpaulin from their cart, then fed and watered the horse while the others began moving bales of hay that were built high up to the roof of the barn. Finally, long boxes were exposed in the middle of the hay. The men formed a line passing them from hand to hand loading them onto the middle of the cart. Once the tarpaulin was replaced bales of hay surrounded and covered the precious load. Then the bales were strapped down with baler twine. The entire operation had taken less than thirty minutes.

The music had stopped and, as they trundled their way up the lane, they could hear the voices and laughter of the people leaving the hall. No one paid any attention to them as they came out unto the road and headed for home.

It was quiet on the way back and the cart slower due to the increase in weight. Conversation was kept to a mimimum and carried on in whispers. They stopped outside Ballygawley, driving the cart into a small field protected by a high hawthorn hedge. They ate the bread and milk from the store box at their feet and, after giving the horse a drink and having a much needed pish, they prepared to move on.

John heard the patrol first and put up a warning finger to his lips, catching the horse's bridle and stroking its head gently to keep it quiet. The patrol was on foot walking at a leisurely pace passing the gate to the field they were in. Suddenly, one of the men at the tail of the line called out,

"I'm in need of a pish, there's an open gate here. I'll be quick."

"We've no time, oul woman. Houl on! We're nearly at the crossroads. Ye can pull down yer knickers then."

This brought gales of laughter from the men on the road and relief for John and his fellow smugglers as the footsteps moved on up the road.

It had been a close call.

Sanitary Advice
As an immediate consequence of the war
there will be a deal of sick nursing throughout the
country for a long time to come, and it may
therefore be as well to remind our readers of the
benefits and comfort to sufferers to be derived
from spraying the room with 'Sanitas Fluid';
It is one of the best preparations for washing
the sick and dressing wounds.

Ulster Herald, November 1914

Chapter 28

Ann had been cleaning and baking for days, in preparation for Elsie coming home for a holiday. She could hardly breathe with excitement when the cart turned into the street. It had been months since they had seen her and the young girl who had left them all those months ago had grown into a beautiful young woman and, in that instant, Ann felt an unexplained fear of shame that the house, for all her cleaning, would not be good enough for the young woman who smiled at her now. Her fears disappeared when Elsie threw her arms around her and they were as they had always been – a mother and her blessed daughter. Elsie went round the small kitchen, touching the familiar objects, the hat pins stuck in the cork on the window ledge, the buttons in a jar glinting through the glass and the family Bible by the chair. "Ach, Ma, I have missed home so much. When I was lonely for you all I thought about you sitting here by the fire reading the Bible to us before we went to bed. Where's Da?"

"He had to go away for the night to help a neighbour move cattle. He'll be back in the morning."

"How is he? Is he still drinkin?"

"No, thank God he is trying and it has been hard, his leg is worse and now he has to suffer the pain without the porter. Anyway, we have a whole night to ourselves and I want to hear all the news from the big house."

After the dinner she listened as Elsie talked about all that had happened since she had left home.

"The family are away in London. The Duke is meeting with the King because of Home Rule. The outhouses are all being fixed up for the officers of the Ulster Volunteers and Mr Carson came down and stayed. We all stood out in the drive to welcome him. We are going to get our own Post Office and a canteen to feed the men and all the staff in the house are having first aid lessons so we know what to do if there is trouble. I think I might like to be a nurse. The army nurse said I was a natural. I'm so excited."

Ann's heart missed a beat. She had thanked God many times that Elsie was safe at the big house and now another threat was looming over her small family.

Elsie had seen her mother's reaction to her talk of becoming a nurse and knew that this was not the time to go into more detail, but her plans were made and if she was able to cancel her indenture as a maid she could join the Royal

Army Nursing Corps. It was all in the hands of Mrs Harbinson and Mr Billings, the estate manager.

John returned early the next morning and, much to Elsie's disappointment, was asleep when she got up. She roamed around the farm, wanting to help but Ann had other plans. She had made up a picnic basket, left a note for John and went down to their favourite spot at the river. They settled under the Chestnut tree and Ann listened again to the stories of the people Elsie worked with in the big house.

"Mrs Harbinson is really nice, even though she tries to make believe she is strict. She likes to do embroidery and has been teaching us new stitches in the evening before we go to bed. She was very impressed with my pin cushion."

"When do you get time for all this, Elsie?"

"We are up at six in the morning to get fires lit, have our porridge and then help in the laundry. Mrs Harbinson says I might get moved on to kitchen duties when I go back as we are getting another new maid."

"Are you happy, Elsie?"

"I'm happy now." She bowed her head hesitating. "I wasn't at the beginning."

"Why, did something happen when you went there?" Ann laid her hand on Elsie's arm, "Did someone hurt you?"

"No. Ma. It was nothing like that. It was just so final, like I was niver goin' home again and Da had signed the papers. Three years seemed so long, but I'm alright now and everyone is very good to me. Mrs Harbinson says I'm her best girl and I will go far."

Ann dismissed the twinge of jealousy that rose in her throat, happy and proud that her child had so impressed the people she worked with.

Elsie saw her Da coming down the field and ran into his arms, nearly knocking him off his feet.

"Ach, Elsie, my lovely girl! You're more beautiful now than when you left. I hope those lads at the big house are behaving themselves. Did ye miss us when you were dinin' high with all the gentry of the county?"

"I don't dine with them, Da. Far from it and yes, I do miss ye all, especially at night time."

"Have ye left me any food or have you two ate the lot."

Ann poured more tae and listened again as Elsie told her Da all her news. She had changed so much. She had a new confidence about her leaving, in no doubt that their child had become a woman.

The goodbyes were just as painful as the first time she had left, except this time there were less tears shed as they both had come to accept the reality of their parting.

Tyrone Battalion Royal Inniskillen Fusiliers

Q. What is the best way to enlist in the Tyrone Battalion?
A. Obtain from his UVF Company Officer a railway voucher
to Ballyshannon. Proceed to Finner Camp, and report to me
at the first camp on the right hand side of the road.

BRING YOUR CHUMS

A. Ricardo

Commanding the Tyrone Battalion

(Recruiting literature 1914)

Chapter 29

The parade came up the short hill onto the parade ground and ordered to about turn and stand to attention by the Sergeant. They were facing the sea and the spectacular mountains. The march had been longer than William had expected and breakfast seemed very far away.

The Colonel came forward from the colour party.

"Welcome to Finner Training Camp, men. You are no longer civilians but men of the newly formed 36th Ulster Division. You will follow in the footsteps of those heroic men who have gone before you. We are comrades in what is a tough and bloody war and each man here today will be expected to do his duty in the service of his country.

"The Sergeant will give you your orders presently. Your endurance will be tested to the limit of anything you have experienced before. You will be expected to lay down your life in our efforts to achieve victory over the enemy and you will need the stamina and the trust of the men around you to avoid defeat in that aim. No quarter will be given and none taken. God save the King."

The sergeant saluted the Colonel and called out: "Three cheers for the Colonel."

The men were stood at ease as the sergeant laid out the orders of the day. "Your training begins immediately. Reveille will be at 0600 hours for physical training before breakfast. After breakfast there will be route marches and trench exercises. There will be no room for shirkers or malingerers. Any breach of orders will result in severe punishment and loss of privileges. When you are dismissed you will follow Corporal Hagan who will escort you to your quarters. When you have unpacked your kit and made your bed you will be shown to the mess for your supper. That is all. Attention! Fall out."

"Jesus, my feet are killin' me, Willie." Mark and Tommy fell in beside William as the parade of men followed the Corporal to the bell tents that stood on flat land beyond the parade ground.

"You'll need some meths to harden them off, Tommy, and not just for your feet. Looks like we're in for it, boys."

"Have you got some meths, Mark?"

"Naw, you silly bastard, the army give us enough to carry."

"I was trying to picture me da and his mates comin' here all those years ago and wonderin' how it was for them."

"Aye, well, we'll know soon enough, Willie boy. My Da said the route marches were tough. I think we have our work cut out for us."

That evening, William wrote letters to his Ma and Josie.

Finner Camp,
Ballyshannon Road
Donegal

Dear Ma,
We have settled in well her. The food is not as good as yours but I expected that. There are great views of the mountain and the sea.
    Your son, William

Finner Camp,
Ballyshannon Road
Donegal

Dear Josie
This is a lovely spot. I wish you were here so we could lie together in the sand. I miss you every day.
    Write soon William x

They had been given leave to go into Bundoran and small groups of men left the barracks, excited at the prospect of seeing the sea for the first time. Most of the lads came from the landlocked County Tyrone and had never been near the sea before. They had been warned by Sergeant Milford that fights and drunkeness would mean loss of leave for four weeks and money deducted from their wages.

William was now firm friends with Mark and Tommy and, as they made their way into the town, he wished Paul could be with them to complete the foursome.

Bundoran was busy with crowds of people walking on the paths to and from the beach. The men were completely amazed by the high waves breaking on the rocks. Seagulls swooped and called out their high pitched cry. Then there was the smell.

"What the hell is that smell?" shouted Tommy. "It stinks like rotten eggs! How are we gonta stick that for the next three months?"

"I think it's the sea. Sure it's no worse than pigswill." William laughed at the faces the other two were making. "Townies, the pair of ye."

The sound of laughter echoing across the sand dunes caught their attention. Then suddenly, a gang of girls rushed past them and ran at full pelt into the sea wearing nothing but long bloomers and vests. The sight of them left all the lads standing and staring speechless after them. Mark was the first to speak. "Holy God, lads, the war is over! We have died and gone to heaven. Luck at that wan with the black hair. She's beautiful."

"Aye," was all the other two could say as they watched the girls duck and dive through the waves.

William's thoughts turned to Josie and he wished she could be one of those girls and they could walk on over the dunes and be together. Her letters came twice a week and he was glad to get them. She was very explicit in her longing for him, making his dreams all the more lucid.

Mark had been meeting the dark haired girl called Maeve he had first seen on the beach. He was in love, he had announced and once this war was over he was going to ask her to marry him. The others laughed at his antics each night as he preened himself in front of the small shaving mirror in the tent.

"Be careful, Mark," Tommy had warned him. "These local boyos won't take too kindly to you comin' in and stealin' the best looker in Bundoran."

"Aye and her oul boy is not goin' to like it either" William said.

Later that week, Mark came back early. Maeve had stood him up. He had waited for her at the usual spot for the next two nights but she had not turned up. He continued to go to town hoping against hope that she would be there but she seemed to have disappeared from the town altogether.

William and Tommy decided that enough was enough. The time had come to solve the mystery.

"We're all goin' into the town tonight together," William told Mark. "Someone is bound to know about her. Are you game, Tommy?"

"Aye, and we can go for a few stouts. I'm fed up playin' darts at that community house. Let's make a night of it."

They wandered round the town. Mark began stopping complete strangers asking them if they knew Maeve, which did not go down well with a few of the locals who spat on the road and glared at them.

"I think it's time for a drink, lads. There's a pub we haven't been in yet." William led them into the pub called the Tin Whistle. As they entered the drinkers at the bar stopped talking and turned to stare at them. They sat down near the door, the scraping of the chair's on the stone floor the only noise that broke the silence.

"Can yous not read?" the barman put down the cloth and pointed to the sign above the bar.

The sign was one they had seen before in other public houses in the town. The Army had ordered that no drink should be served to soldiers after 8.30 in the evening but this sign had been altered to read:

NO SOLDIERS OF THE BRITISH ARMY WILL BE SERVED DRINK BETWEEN 0800 HRS AND 0800 HRS.

"Aw, that's a good one," Tommy laughed.

Within seconds they were surrounded.

"Well, lads good of yous to welcome us here." Tommy smiled up at them. "Is it your round? I fancy a stout and my friends here will have the same."

A big man pushed past the others and stood looking down at them. "Which one of you feckers is consortin' with my daughter and goin' round the town broadcastin' it?" Mark spoke up.

"Is her name Maeve? Are you her Da? I've met with your daughter a few times, sir. We went for walks along the front." His eyes were getting wider and the sweat broke on him. "I mean her no harm, sir. We love each other."

Before he could say another word the man yanked him up on his feet and without much effort carried him to the door, throwing him out onto the street. He turned to William and Tommy.

"Get out, or both of yis will join him in the gutter and if I ever see yis luckin' at me or mine again, I'll leave some scars for yis to show the Hun."

They helped Mark up, aware that a small crowd had gathered at the door of the pub and people were walkin' to the other side of the road to avoid them.

The three pals were shaken by the ferocity of the warning. It brought home to them the undercurrent of hostility towards the soldiers in parts of the community.

"Are you alright, Mark?" William asked.

"Aye, nothing to worry about. They can't hide her away forever." He cleaned off the muck on his uniform then turned to look back.

"Come away, Mark. There are plenty more fish in the sea." Tommy laughed and slapped him on the shoulder.

"Let's get that drink now we are here."

As the weeks passed the lads soon forgot the incident. They never went back to the Tin Whistle again.

Cookstown Notes
The half-yearly fair hiring fair in Cookstown
On Saturday was made an occasion for a
recruitment rally, and a large number of young
men listened to urgent appeals to their
Patriotism. The fine band of the 3rd Inniskillings led the
paraded through the streets to the assembly point.

Tyrone Constitution, November 1915

Chapter 30

Paul opened his eyes but closed them again to stop the bright light. He lay unmoving, trying to understand where he was. He had vague memories of faces close to him calling his name and then pain hitting him followed by the darkness. His hand hurt. He opened his eyes, squinting to cut out the glare of the lights. He was in a bed and his Ma was sitting on the chair beside him, her eyes closed. He tried to speak but his voice sounded like a whisper to him.

"Ma, where am I?" She jumped up and crossed herself.

"Oh, Thank God, Paul. You're awake. Thank the Holy Mother for bringing you back to me."

"Where am I, Ma?"

"You're in hospital, Paul. I need to call the nurse and tell her you're awake. I won't be a minute."

He watched her go and tried to get up but then realised his right arm was in a long sling suspended to a pulley on the back of his bed.

His Ma came back, followed by a nurse and a man in a white coat who smiled and spoke to him.

"Welcome back, young man. I am Doctor Anderson. You have been giving us some cause for concern. First we need to check your blood pressure, then I need to ask you a few questions, just to establish your memory of what occurred so I can rule out any brain injury or concussion. Are you happy to do that?"

"Yes I suppose so. But I can't remember anything."

"Are you happy that your Mother stays here with you while we do that?"

"Yes." His Ma came forward and gripped his hand.

"After my examination the police would like to talk to you..."

"The police? What the hell have they got to do with me?" He was shouting his face, flushed in anger. His Ma's grip on his hand tightened.

"Paul, please be calm. They just want to find out what happened to you."

"Did I do something wrong, Ma? Is that why they want to talk to me?"

The doctor sat down on the bed.

"Can we first establish what you remember about the night this happened to you?"

"I don't remember anything."

"You remember your mother, so your memory has not suffered any long term damage. Does your head hurt?"

"No, just some dullness behind my eyes."

"I am going to move your head from side to side, Paul, and I want you to tell me if this is uncomfortable in any way."

"No, but my right hand is painful. My thumb is throbbin'. Why is there a bandage on my arm? It looks funny. Where's my hand? I can't see it." He looked at the doctor and then at his Ma.

"Where is my hand, Ma?" Panic rose up in his chest so he could hardly breathe. "Where is my hand? I can feel it but I can't see it."

Mary had tried to stay calm and hold back the tears but they now ran unchecked as she watched Paul discover the extent of his injury.

"Ma, what's goin' on? For God's sake tell me!" he pleaded, looking again at the doctor.

"I am sorry to have to tell you that you were attacked by persons unknown and, as a result of that attack, you have lost your right hand. We could not save it."

"That can't be. I can feel it I can wriggle my fingers." He was staring at his arm, watching for the movement of his fingers.

"I'm sorry, Paul. Your right hand has been severed from your arm. It is not unusual for people to feel such pain. They are what is known as phantom pains and you could have this sensation for some time."

Paul struggled to speak as the doctor continued.

"You are lucky to be alive. The man who found you had the foresight to bind your arm tightly to stem the flow of blood. You have had several blood transfusions over the last few days but your condition seems to be stabilised. Your memory loss is as a direct result of the shock and trauma you have suffered, but I am confident that, with patience and good care, this will return in time."

Padraig McGovern came into the room. He was pale and dishevelled. He came to Mary's side and grasped his son's hand.

"Da, where were you? Did you know about this? What happened to me, Da?"

"I've been at the barracks." He turned to the doctor. "They are sending round a sergeant to question Paul. Is he fit for all that, doctor?"

"Da. Who did this to me? I can't remember anything." Paul began to breathe heavily, the colour draining from his face, his eyes fixed on his arm.

"Try and be calm Paul." The doctor pulled out his stethoscope. "I need to examine Paul, could you both wait outside."

"No. Don't leave me, Da. I'm scared."

The doctor spoke: "Your parents can stay, Paul but you must try to keep calm. I am going to sound your heart. Perhaps, nurse, you could get Paul a drink of water."

Paul clung to his Da's hand, his breathing becoming more regular.

"Mr McGovern, in answer to your question regarding the interview with the police, I am going to advise them that Paul is not yet in a fit condition to answer their questions. I will review his condition in the morning. Your son now needs to rest so I am going to prescribe an injection to be administered to help with this. You may both stay with Paul for a short time until he is asleep. As for you, young man, you have nothing to be frightened of and what you need now most of all is to relax and try not to worry."

When they were alone, Paul began to sob. Mary ran her hand over his head, her own tears falling silently.

"Paul, listen to me, son." Padraig was on his knees in front of Paul. "All you need to fret about now is getting well again. You need all your strength now to get over this. I know it's going to be hard but we will do all that we can to make this right. I promise you."

Mary knelt beside him and began to say the rosary and both father and son joined in. The nurse came to administer the injection but withdrew to allow the family their time together.

The police sergeant was waiting for her in the small office down the corridor.

"I've come to question a patient called Paul McGovern, nurse."

"Yes sergeant. I have been expecting you. Unfortunately, the doctor has ordered complete rest and Mr McGovern is not to be disturbed tonight. If you ring in the morning we will let you know when he will be well enough to be questioned."

Ann had been writing to William when John came back from the mart.

"Jez, Ann, I have bad news. An awful thing has happened." Her heart seemed to miss a beat. Bad news these days could only mean one thing.

"William, something has happened to William. Oh please God, tell me what it is."

"Naw, it's not William, thank God. It's young Paul McGovern. He was attacked the other night outside Draperstown. He's in hospital. They are saying down at the mart he had his hand cut off, cut off at the wrist."

"No, John. That can't be true. Sure, who would do such a thing to the cub? Are you sure?"

"Aye, I'm sure. It's the talk of the country."

"I must go and see Mary. She will be out of her wits if this is true."

"Don't waste your time, Ann. She's at the hospital sittin' with him. Seems he almost died. A milkman found him on the side of the road and brought him into the hospital. If he had lain any longer he would have bled to death. An oul tinker from the other side of Cookstown was lying under the cart sleepin'."

"William must be told. I'm in the middle of a letter to him now. How do I tell him such news?"

"Don't tell him. William has enough on his plate. Let the hare sit, Ann. Wait till we know more about it, then we can decide to tell him. They say his Da is being questioned by the police."

"No, John. That must be gossip, Paul's Da doted on him, he wouldn't hurt a hair on his head. Dear God, I pray he'll be alright. William will be at his wit's end when he hears this."

"Listen to me Ann. Don't tell him, not yet. He's training mornin', noon and night. He needs to keep himself together."

"He needs to be told John, no matter what you say"

"Ach, niver mind what I think. You'll do what you want anyway." Later that night, Ann wrote a new letter to William:

Dear William

I am sorry to tell you some bad news. Paul has had some sort of accident on the road to Draperstown. It seems he has lost his hand at the wrist. He was found on the road by a milkman. He's in hospital. I will try and find out more and let you know. There is not much you can do but pray for him.

Take care of yourself

Love from us all Mammy xxx

Ann left the envelope for the postman and lifted down the Bible.

John was up early as usual to do the milkin'. He lifted the envelope down as Ann came into the kitchen. "Did you tell him?"

"Yes, I did. He needs to know. Will you give the letter to the postman if he comes when I'm down feedin the hens?"

John was on the street when the postman came along the road. "Morning, John. I've nothing for you today. Has the missus anything for William? That woman of yours is a great letter writer. Your lad must get wan every other day."

"Naw, she has nothing for ye today Micky. Good luck till ye."

John walked up into the house. He lifted the letter down from the mantel shelf and set on the dying embers of the fire. He carefully filled the grate with fresh turf, sending orange sparks up the broad chimney.

Josie had gone to the chapel before work for morning mass. Normally, she tried to avoid going every day, but for the past two weeks she had been praying morning, noon and night. She was feeling sick every morning. Her Ma had caught her retching her breakfast up at the side of the house yesterday and had threatened her with castor oil, her ma's cure for everything from a sore toe to toothache, but she had a notion that caster oil wouldn't work this time.

Her monthly cycle was late and she was terrified about what that meant. Being pregnant before marriage was a mortal sin, but being pregnant to a protestant was a far greater sin in the eyes of her family and the priest. A girl in the senior class had got caught out. She disappeared from April last year and had come back after Christmas looking awful. She never smiled or joined in with the girls in the playground and wasn't allowed to go anywhere without her big brother. Mary Kelly said she heard she'd had a wean in a convent in Donegal and they took it away from her. She was sent to the hiring fair the following summer and hadn't been seen since.

In her last letter to William she had tried to comfort him about Paul's attack. He would be in an awful way. The two of them had always been so close when they were at school and there had been times when she had felt jealous about their friendship. Paul had always been there when she had wanted William to herself and there was an undercurrent between her and Paul that she didn't understand. Often she had caught him looking at her then turning away when she caught him looking.

She had decided not to tell William about her sickness. It would be better to speak to him when he was home on leave and by that time it might be nothing more than her imagination and mixed up dates. She crossed herself. As she made her way across the village she met William's Ma. Mrs Johnston stopped her and Josie felt herself blushing.

"Hello, Josie. How are you, I have missed you in the shop. Are you well?"

"I'm fine, Mrs Johnston. Have you heard from William lately?"

The question was out before she could stop herself. She bit her tongue and felt her face redden again. "Why yes, Josie. He writes faithfully every week. In fact I am just going to post him a letter to him now. He likes to keep up with the latest news in the village."

"Has he heard about Paul McGovern?"

"Yes. I wrote and told him. I'm surprised I haven't heard from him since. He and Paul were very good friends as you know. I have been up to see Paul's mother. They are taking it all very badly."

"Is Paul home then?" Josie asked

"No. He has to stay for another week, but we are all praying for him. I must get on and catch the post. It has been nice to talk to you again."

Josie watched her go into the post office. Her letter would likely be in the same postbag as the one she had just posted. If only she knew.

Letters:
The Ulster Herald shall be pleased to publish
letters received by relatives and friends from
soldiers serving with the military forces.
They should be forwarded to:
The Editor,
The Ulster Herald

Chapter 31

William's platoon had been out on twenty-four hour manoeuvres. The real kit had arrived a few days ago and it seemed a lot heavier than the stones they had been used to at the beginning. Tommy and Mark had gone into the town. Mark still had a notion he might meet up with Maeve again although he didn't talk as much about her as he had done, which was a relief to them all.

William walked down to the post office to check his mail and found two letters from home. He had one from Josie and one from his Ma. He loved the letters from home. He was looking forward to his first leave in three week's time. He opened his ma's letter first. Her letters were the usual mix of news about the children and the work about the farm. He was so proud to hear that his da was still off the drink and was doing some work down at Baronscourt with his old army buddy. He opened Josie's letter and the smile that had been on his face disappeared was replaced by one of horror as he read her letter.

Dear William,

I hope this finds you well. I miss you so much, William and can't wait until you come home on leave. The beach sounds so romantic. I wish I could be there with you. I am sure you must be so worried about Paul. It came as an awful shock to everyone here. He has come round again but they say the doctors couldn't save his hand. God take care of him it must be terrible for his Ma and Da.

You take care of yourself and come home soon. I miss and love you so much. Josie xxxxxxx

William was stunned. His legs refused to move. The letter fell at his feet. He picked it up his hand, trembling as he read the words again 'the doctors couldn't save his hand'. He reread his Ma's letter, thinking he had missed a page but there was no mention of this news in her letter. Maybe there was another letter and he had missed it.

He ran back to the post office but the door was locked for the day. He went to the sergeant's mess to look for Jock the postmaster and found him drinking a pint at the bar.

"What are you doin' here, Willie boy? Ye will get into trouble if anyone finds you in here."

"I think there was another letter from my Ma, Jock. One dated before this one. Would you have missed it do ye think?"

"Now, Willie boy, you should know better than askin' me a question like that. Every letter that comes into my bag is sorted and resorted before they are placed into the owner's box. You had two letters. One from your mother and one from that nice girl you have up at home. They both came yesterday when you were out on manoeuvres and none today. Now, if you're wise, you will get out of here sharpish."

William crossed to the officer's mess and asked to see the sergeant. The corporal at the desk was dismissive.

"Put your request in writing, Private Johnston, using the appropriate special request form and it will be dealt with in due time." He pushed the pale green form across the desk.

"This can't wait, Corporal. It's a private family matter. I need it dealt with as soon as possible."

"All I can do is inform the sergeant when he comes on duty, but it must go through the proper channels."

William saw red, thumping the desk hard with his fist.

"I don't give a fuck about channels. I need to get home, my friend may be dead and all you can talk about is channels."

The door to the colonel's office swung open. The Corporal immediately stood to attention.

"What on earth is going on here, corporal?"

"Sorry, sir, Private Johnston is looking for Sergeant Milford. He was just leaving, sir."

"I think Private Johnston had better explain this outburst himself, Corporal, and I sincerely hope for his sake it's a good one. Well, Johnston, what have you to say for yourself?"

William stood to attention.

"I'm sorry, sir, but I've had very bad news from home. I want to request compassionate leave to go home, sir."

"On what grounds are you making your request?"

"My best friend has been attacked and is badly injured in the hospital. I need to get home to see him, sir...."

"I'm sorry to hear that, Private Johnston, but compassionate leave cannot be granted unless to attend a funeral of a close family relative. Rules are rules."

William's voice was now a whisper, his distress very evident.

"He's lost his hand, sir. He's the only friend I have ever had, sir. He needs me and now I'm lettin' him down. Beggin' your pardon, sir. I meant no disrespect."

"You have used threatening behaviour towards a superior officer. Such behaviour will not be tolerated in this camp, no matter what the excuse. You are in the Army now, an Army that is currently at war. You are confined to barracks until further orders. Corporal, you will issue Private Johnston with the necessary paperwork with copies to Sergeant Milford. I expect to have your report on this matter on my desk before 1700 hours today."

The colonel returned to his office and closed the door. "I only want to get home, Corporal."

The Corporal turned to a file behind him and brought out a set of duplicate forms.

"Give me your full name rank and serial number."

"Please, Corporal."

"There is no getting out of this now, soldier. Name, rank and serial number and make it quick before the Colonel goes off duty."

He answered in a hoarse whisper the number recited so many times in drill came to his tongue with no difficulty.

"This is a formal notification that you are confined to barracks until such times as the Colonel sees fit to drop any charges levied at you as a result of your behaviour. You will not leave the perimeter of the camp for any reason unless ordered to do so by a superior officer. You will not consume nor be in possession of hard liquor. You will report to the sergeant three times each day for orders until such times as this matter has been dealt with. Do you understand, Private?"

"I'm sorry, Corporal. I'm at my wits end about this."

"Do you understand the charge, Private Johnston?"

"Yes, corporal."

"Please sign or make your mark in the box of this declaration."

He bent over the desk his eyes refusing to focus on the page in front of him. The pen seemed to move automatically in his hand a blob of black ink forming beside his name. The corporal blotted the signature and handed William the yellow top sheet.

"This is a copy for your information. You will be notified of any charges that may result. You are dismissed."

The door of the office swung closed behind him and he walked across the parade ground, unaware of those around him.

As he approached his billet he could hear loud voices and laughter from inside the tent. Another card game was in full flow. The boys were back and Mark's voice was protesting loudly as usual that he was not a cheat, the others breaking into a chant of cheat, cheat, cheat. He walked on, following the path up to the shooting range, empty of men and shooting at this time of the evening. He sank down on a sand dune, the yellow form still clutched in his hand. Rabbits were hopping a few feet away from him, unconcerned with his presence. He read the charge sheet again, bile rising in his throat. He vomited, spit and saliva running down his chin. The paper slipped to the ground. He tried to imagine Paul without his hand and he balled his hands into fists, his knuckles white to the bone with anger. The rabbits had disappeared. He swiped his sleeve over his mouth and picked up the page. The ink was smudged. He tore it up and dropped it again, some of the yellow tatters catching in the vomit while others were caught by the wind and blown over the dunes. He stood watching them float in the breeze. In that moment he made up his mind. He turned and walked back towards his billet. He was going home no matter what.

The next morning, he left his kit bag under the tent flap and reported as ordered to the Sergeant.

"Private William Johnston reporting as ordered, sir."

The Sergeant raised his head and glared at him, then stood and walked around the desk, stopping immediately in front of William.

"Private Johnston, I have been looking forward to seeing you this morning to tell you what a lucky man you are." He stepped closer until his face was only inches from William's, making him blink and swallow hard.

"Have you lost your voice since yesterday? Don't you want to know why you are a lucky man Johnston?"

"Sergeant, I am sorry..."

"No, I'm sorry Private, sorry I was not there when you decided to abuse and threaten my Corporal because, Private Johnston, that is when you got lucky. If I had been within earshot of your rant you would have spent the night in the lock-up on dry rations and I would have ensured that your behaviour would have resulted in a much more serious charge involving a court martial and imprisonment at his majesty's service. As it is, Johnston, the Colonel through his great mercy and kindness has taken pity on you and has granted you a three day furlough to go and visit your sick friend. Do you understand, Johnston, just how lucky you are?"

William stood transfixed his head reeling as he tried to take in what the Sergeant was telling him.

"The response I am waiting for, Johnston is 'Yes, sir. Thank you, Sergeant.'"

"Yes, Sir, thank you Sergeant."

William repeated the words but could not believe what he was hearing. The sergeant returned to his desk then swung round his jaw set in a hard line.

"Your furlough begins at 1200 hours today and will end at 1200 hours on Thursday. Report to the office to collect your leave pass and I warn you, Private Johnston. If in future your behaviour is brought to my attention for any reason you will feel the full effect of military discipline. You are dismissed."

William walked up the long hill home. He had not told them he was coming. There had been no time. He could see his Ma carting buckets of water from the well at the bottom of the lane, her shoulders bowed under the weight. She turned, hearing his step at the gate, she turned dropping the buckets, water splashed around her feet. She threw her arms around him.

"What are you doing here? You're not due leave yet. Are you alright?" The questions tumbled from her as she clung to him, laughing.

"Hello, Ma. Let go now before ye have me off me feet. Come on into the house, I haven't much time." He pushed her away and went into the kitchen. She came in after him, the laughter gone from her.

"What's wrong, William? What's happened to bring you home? Are you in trouble?"

"Why didn't you tell me about Paul, Ma? I've been wonderin' all the way here on the train why you didn't tell me that Paul had been attacked?"

"I did tell you. I wrote a letter to you as soon as your Da told me. It was given to the postman the next morning."

"The last letter I got from you was last Friday. I checked with the postmaster in the camp. I got no letter since then."

"I'll ask the postman in the morning. I know I told you about Paul as soon as I heard. Sit down now and I will get you some food you must be hungry."

"I need to get to McGovern's before dark."

"How did you hear then?"

"Josie wrote and told me"

"Josie O'Neil. Why would she be writing to you?"

"We're friends, Ma. She thought I should know about Paul."

Ann took the side of smoked ham from the hook in the corner and carved thick slices onto a plate.

"Don't mention this to your Da. You know how he is about the O'Neils."

The door from the bedroom opened and John came into the kitchen. "Well! Look who's here. You're a sight for sore eyes."

John Johnston embraced his son, his face beaming with pride.

"My God, cub! It's good to see ye. We didn't expect ye till next month."
"Do you want some of this ham, John?" Ann asked, wondering if he had heard anything. He ignored her.

"Well, William, my lad. How is army life? You look as fit as a fiddle."
"It's hard work, but I'm in with a nice bunch of lads. We get on well."
"How come you're home on leave early? Are you shipping out to England already?"
"Naw, I'm here to go and see Paul."
"You shouldn't be wastin' your leave on young McGovern after the way things turned out."
"Seems it wasn't Paul's fault 'the way things turned out' as ye put it. Anyway, I'm here now. Have you heard anything today?"
"Well, as far as I hear, he is still in hospital. The oul fella who was with him is still drunk," John laughed.

William dropped the fork onto his plate with a clatter and stood up, his hands clenched into fists.

"Do you find it funny, Da? My best friend is attacked and loses his hand and you think it's funny."
"Now, William, please don't take offence. Your Da means no harm. We're very sorry about Paul. I have been over to the house and his family are just glad he wasn't killed."
"Sorry, cub. My sense of humour is no better than iver it was, don't let us get on the wrong foot and you only home. Did you get leave, cub? You haven't done anything foolish?"
"No, Da. I have a pass. I have to be back on Thursday. I need to get to the hospital in the morning. Can I borrow the cart?"
"You can. But you won't get far. We have no horse. It went to the army sale two weeks ago. How did you find out about Paul anyway?"
"A friend wrote me."
"I did write to tell you, William. You remember, John. I left it with you to pass on to the postman."
"What day was that now? Sure you write every day. The postman never leaves the street. Even he can't keep track on all your letters."
"I wrote the night you told me the news and asked you to give it to the postman."
"I can't remember, Ann. Honest to God it must have got lost in the post."
"Well, I will be askin' the postman tomorrow. He's a careful man and he might remember."

"Don't upset yourself now, Ma, and thanks for the feed. I've missed your cookin'. I'm away up to McGoverns to speak to Paul's Ma and see about a lift to the hospital. I won't be late, so don't put wee John to bed before I see him."

"He will be so excited to see you, William. I will have a special supper ready for you when you get home."

"You'll not get a great welcome up there, wearin' that uniform. Oul McGovern and his kind haven't changed since you left. Be careful on the road."

Wounded Soldiers Arrive in Ireland
The wounded soldiers who came to
Omagh recently are progressing favourably,
and they are indebted to those who take them
for motor drives, etc.

Ulster Herald, November 1914

Chapter 32

William walked over the familiar fields and along the river to McGoverns, every step a memory of Paul and their friendship and the happy days they had spent in each other's company. The horror of what had happened to Paul and how he was dealing with it hung around his every waking moment. If he could get the bastard he would make him pay.

There was a light in the kitchen. The dog barked at his approach then stopped and came to welcome him. He knocked and Mary McGovern's voice shouted, "Come on in," William stepped into the kitchen. Mary stood up, putting her hand to her mouth.

"William, you're the last person I thought to see today."

"I came as soon as I could. How is Paul?"

"You can ask him yourself. He's coming home today. Padraig went to collect him a few hours ago. Come in and sit down with me by the fire, William."

"How is he?" William sat down beside her, his hand reaching out to comfort her.

"Awe, William. It's an awful thing they have done to him. He is so full of anger I hardly recognise him." Her sobs caught in her throat and she lifted her apron to dry her tears. He put his arm around her, not sure what to do or say.

A cart was pulling into the street.

"That's them now. Will you stay a while? Paul will be glad to see you."

"Maybe I should go and leave him to settle in?"

The door opened and Paul came into the kitchen. He stared at William for a long moment, not speaking.

Padraig followed and saw William. "Where the hell did you come from?"

"Padraig, that's no way to speak to a friend and neighbour. William has come a long way to see how Paul is."

"It's alright, Mrs McGovern. This is a bad time. I'll come back later, that is if Paul feels like he is up to a visit."

William looked Paul in the eye and for a split second didn't recognise his friend.

"Aye, best come another day. I'm tired," he said, then turned away, his left hand holding his bandaged arm.

William was walking away from the house when Paul's Da came out of the door and called to him. William waited.

"I blame you for what has happened to Paul and I'd be obliged if you kept your distance from him."

"Did Paul tell you to say that?"

"Get off my farm, Johnston, and don't come back!"

"You can't blame me for all this. If you had left us alone, Paul would be in Finner camp with me now."

Padraig McGovern let out a roar and lunged at William and they fell together unto the mud of the street. The dog began to bark as the two men wrestled and punched at each other.

The cold water that drenched them came as a surprise and they broke apart rubbing the water from their eyes.

Mary stood over them, holding the empty bucket, her anger plain to see. "Is this your answer to everything, Padraig? Get up and apologise to William." She leaned forward and took William by the hand, helping him to stand. Blood was gushing from his mouth and there was a deep cut above his eye.

"Come inside, William. I need to clean your face."

"Naw Mrs. McGovern. I'm alright. I'll get on home."

"Padraig, just don't stand there! Apologise."

"If ye think I'm goin' to apologise ye can think again..."

Paul called out from the door

"Come on in, William let Ma fix ye up." Padraig looked from one to the other, wiped his face on his sleeve and walked off down the lane.

"Come on in, William," Mary said "Niver mind Padraig. He'll soon cool off. Are you dizzy or anything?"

William followed her into the kitchen. She pulled out a chair and he sat down, his eyes never leaving Paul who was standing by the fire. Mary poured water from the kettle into a basin. "I need a bit of muslin. I'll be back in a minute."

"How are you, Paul?"

"Not good. I'm a cripple now, neither good for man nor beast."

"What happened? Who did this?"

"I don't know. I can't remember anything. They say I was nearly dead when I was found. My hand was cut off and layin' beside me." He broke off, "I'm niver goin' to get it back, William. I'm niver goin' to be able to fish again."

He broke off. Not able to speak. William rose from the chair and embraced him. They were both crying when Mary walked back into the kitchen. She embraced them both, her tears mingling with theirs.

Later, when she had patched William up and made them tae, she put on her shawl and, leaving them to talk, went out to look for Padraig.

She lit the Tilly lamp and went down the lane. It was cold and she pulled her shawl tighter around herself. She had been glad to see William. The two boys had been so close over the years of their childhood and she had always sensed a strong bond between them. Paul had hardly spoken since the attack. He had been moved to a big ward full of other patients and she had hoped that might help him but it had the opposite effect. He had lain on his side facing the wall and only sat up when the nurse insisted or when food was put on his tray and even then he had to be cajoled to eat it. He had lost weight, more noticeable now that he was wearing his own clothes. This unexpected visit from William was just what he needed. Maybe he would talk about the attack now.

She swung the lamp into the dark corners of the hedge, afraid that Padraig might have fallen in the ditch. She knew he would be angry with her. She had crossed a fine line tonight. It was the first time she had ever contradicted him. In the past she had listened in silence when he had ridiculed protestant neighbours and over the past year there had been nights when he had not come home until the early hours, shivering as he got into bed beside her. In the morning, when she would ask him where he had been, he would laugh and plant a kiss on her cheek and tell her he had another wee wife up the mountain. Since Paul's attack, his republican friends had been feeding him a poisonous mix of hate and relentless bigotry which was spinning him out of control. At times it was as if he was in another place and his long absences till the middle of the night had become more frequent. Even when Paul was in hospital he had gone out on his own late at night to ceilidh* he said but she had asked no questions.

She heard him cough further down the lane.

He had seen her coming, swinging the lamp into the dark corners of the hedge as she walked. At times her face was illuminated and she looked more beautiful than ever. She was the love of his life but they had never agreed on politics and his republican views. She had never turned on him before until tonight and he was angry with her. She had spoken against him in front of that wee shit all dressed up in his British army khaki, stickin' his nose into their business as if he had the right to. He had near shit himself to see Johnston standing there in the kitchen. He had asked Colum to come in for tae when he had dropped them home in his cart. Thank Christ he had said no, he didn't want the boyos to hear he had a British soldier sitting in his house.

199

He coughed and the lamp swung in his direction. "Are you going to sit down here all night?"

"I will if I have to. Don't expect me to go into the house when that Protestant bastard is in it."

"Padraig, that's enough of such talk. Has it ever occurred to you that William is just what Paul needs? A good friend that he can talk to and maybe help him to come to terms with what has happened to him."

"He needs his family, not some know it all in a uniform. He wouldn't be in this trouble if that wee git hadn't led him on in the first place. He shouldn't be here sittin' at my fireside as if he owned the place and that's your doin'. I won't have it, Mary. Go up and get rid of him before anybody else turns up and sees him."

"Are you out of your mind Padraig? I will not tell him to leave and it's my fireside as well or am I just a hired help you picked up at the fair one day?" She turned to leave then swung back to face him again.

"Who are you expectin' to turn up tonight, Padraig? I hope you are not bringin' them boys you call friends into my kitchen. They will get a short welcome from me if they come anywhere near Paul in his trouble." She left him and went back to the house, afraid that the visitors he was expecting had turned up already.

As soon as his Ma left the house, Paul stood up and lifted his coat from the hook on the door, struggling with the awkwardness of the sling on his right arm. William tried to take the coat.

"Here, let me help ye."

"Don't ye start treatin' me like an invalid as well. Ye can leave a note for me Ma. There's a pencil an' paper on the shelf."

William wrote the note. He felt awkward as Paul struggled with his coat. "Where are we going, Paul. It's pitch black and your ma took the lamp."

"When did the dark ever stop us, William?"

They left the house and stood for a few moments to allow their eyes to become accustomed to the darkness. They walked in silence, the only noise from their breathing as they cut across the upper field behind the house and down the far side of the hill. They could hear the river bubbling over the stones at the foot stick. A bat flew past and the clouds shifted to cast a luminous light on the water.

The outline of the hut was just visible as they followed the familiar swathes of boggy ground to the place where they had spent so many happy hours of their childhood. They sat down on a log, allowing the silence to wrap around them as they both came to terms with the shift their lives had taken in such a short space of time.

"How's army life?"

"It's alright"

"Is that it? 'It's alright.' I'm not missin' anything then."

"Sorry Paul." William paused for a minute. "Luk, I don't know what to say that won't make you more unhappy than you are about the way things turned out. There hasn't been a day since I left when I have done something new or heard a yarn and I didn't think of how ye would have enjoyed the crack. I miss ye. It's just not the same without you."

"How could things have gone so wrong, William? If Da had left me alone and let me join the army I wouldn't be sitting here a cripple."

"Luk, Paul. You can't be batin' yerself up. Ye're alive, it could have been worse. Ye could be dead. Have the police found anything that would say who done this? What about Spratt? Has anybody spoke to him ta see what he remembers? Will I go and have a word with him?"

"Naw, William. Spratt has no idea when he shit last, niver mind rememberin' stuff that happened two weeks ago. The police said they would keep the file open, whatever that means, and Da has his boys on the case, which will be of no help at all. Bastards!"

"Have you thought much about which hand ye lost?"

"What do you mean, which hand?"

"It's yer right hand."

Paul crossed his left hand over to the bandaged stump.

"Aye, so what are ye sayin'?" He frowned at William. "Are you sayin' they took me right hand deliberately?"

"I don't know what to say, I'm just tryin to make some sense of it."

A silence settled again between them.

"Have ye seen Josie since you've been home?"

"Not yit"

"Are you goin to see her?"

"Aye, I'll try the morra. We have been writin' to each other, it was her that tul me about what happened to you."

"Josie's a nice girl."

"Aye. I've missed her since I've been away." Paul stood up suddenly.

"I think I'll go home. It's getting cold an' Ma will start to worry." "Are you sure ye don't remember anything, Paul?"

"Naw, I don't, so don't keep askin', William. Da has my head turned askin' questions I can't answer. I'll go now."

"Aye, you're right. I'll walk with you to the road."

"Naw, no need. I'll be alright."

"Can I come and see ye before I go back? Or ye could come to my house. Ma would be happy to see ya."

"Aye, what time?"

"Say about six. Ye could have yer tae with us."

"Naw, no tae, Tell her my appetite's not good. I'll see you then. Goodnight, William."

"Goodnight, Paul."

The kitchen was empty when she got back. The fire had burnt down. The tea she had made earlier was untouched and cold in the cups. There was a note 'Away for a walk. Don't worry. William.'

It only struck her then that Paul would have to learn to write again, she couldn't bear to think about all the things he would have to cope with now.

She was washing the cups when Padraig came in. He lifted the note, read it, then screwed it into a ball and threw it on the fire. He came to stand behind her and slipped his arms around her waist.

"Can we not fall out again about this. I can't change the way I'm committed to the cause. I want this country to be free and to come out of slavery to the British."

She swung around her face, white with anger.

"Your longin' for Ireland to be free is what has left this family and our son in the state we're in. If you had put as much effort into this family and less on the boyos up the mountain we wouldn't be in this sorry state."

"Ye can't be blamin' me for everthing, Mary. I did what I thought was best for the cub. The Germans are slaughterin' Irish men over in Belgium all for a lie put out by the British and our own demented fools in Dublin. I wish ta God ye could see it my way fir a change. Your Da was an Irishman true, an' faithful. Why can't ye forget about the mistakes made years ago an stand beside me on this?"

"Don't drag all that up again, Padraig. You know how I feel about the politics. I grew up believing in something honest and worthy. What happened to my father was neither. Now you want to drag our son into it and expect me to approve. This latest shambles is typical of how you have been sucked in. There was a better way to deal with this, Padraig, and havin' them boyos spyin' on your own son wasn't the way to do it. Paul will never trust you again. I hope you can live with that." She knelt on the floor by the chair and began to say the evening rosary.

"Jaysus and the saints forgive ye', Mary. I can't listen to this. I'm away to me bed. I'll say my own prayers tonight."

The light was still on and Paul stood for a moment listening to the raised voices coming from the kitchen. It had started to rain, big heavy drops spilling through the light, then melting into the darkness at his feet. He turned and headed for the barn. The dog hadn't barked, but came and sniffed his hand in welcome, following him as he sat down in the corner of the hay and empty sacks. His arm was sore and he felt light headed. He pulled a sack around himself and drfted into sleep.

The nightmare came unbidden. He was back on the mountain watching his right hand falling and the dark shadow of a man holding a hatchet about to cut off the other one. He screamed and woke up, the sweat pouring over his body. The dog was awake and panting beside him. He couldn't get up. His legs buckled and then darkness engulfed him.

Mary found him lying unconscious, the bandage on his hand soaked with fresh blood. She screamed for Padraig, afraid if she tried to move him she would make things worse. She took off her apron and tied it around his wrist in the hope it would stem the flow of blood. She screamed Padraig's name again and then she heard him running from the house.

"What the hell has happened, Mary?" he knelt down and tried to lift Paul's head.

"No, Padraig. Don't move him, hold the apron tight. We need to stop the bleeding. I'll go into the house and get a blanket and a sheet and then you have to go and get Doctor Nabney."

Padraig was kneeling, holding on to the apron when she came back carrying Oliver and the bedding. The boy was fast asleep. She put him down gently on the hay and threw a blanket over him.

"He was a bit unsettled. Go you on to the doctor and tell him to hurry."

"My God, Mary! He's in a bad way. I'm afraid to leave him."

"Pray, Padraig, as you go. But go now. I will do my best to look after him." Padraig crossed himself and hurried out of the barn. The dog usually followed him but it was nowhere to be seen. He would have to walk two miles to Nabney's surgery. He prayed the doctor was available and not out on some other errand of mercy.

Over the next hour, Paul drifted in and out of consciousness. But the bleeding had stopped. Mary left him long enough to get water from the can in the house and washed his face and wetting his dry lips. He had no fever and she thanked God for his mercy. Memories of the influenza epidemic in 1908 came back to her. The loss of life at that time had been more than could be borne for many in the parish.

The fever that came with it had been ferocious, her poor mother and uncle had perished. The Johnstons were the worst hit losing three small children within hours of each other. Mary crossed herself and began a decade of the rosary.

She heard the horse and trap on the lane. Doctor Nabney came into the barn nodding to her. Then he knelt down beside Paul.

"Has he stirred at all, Mrs McGovern?"

"He came round a few times but seemed to drift off again. Will he be alright?"

"There's no fever but he has lost a lot of blood by the looks of it. You have done a good job here, Mrs McGovern. Have you some knowledge of nursing?"

"I have read a lot of books doctor and I nursed my dear mother during the epidemic. She and my uncle passed at that time."

"I remember your mother well. It was a sad time for the country. I lost many of my patients and members of my own family. Padraig has told me Paul was only discharged yesterday from the hospital after his recent attack. Perhaps he was sent home a little too early. Was he in good spirits Padraig?"

"He was very quiet on the way home and then he went out with a friend for a walk last night. I waited up but he didn't come home. Then Mary found him in here this morning."

"I missed him when I went to the boys' room. I thought he had just gone out to the back to relieve himself. He didn't come in after ten minutes and that's when I went to look for him."

"Had he been drinking?"

"Not at all!" Padraig reacted angrily. "Paul has niver even tasted strong spirits. He's been a Pioneer since his confirmation."

"I am sorry, I only ask, Padraig, because alcohol can thin the blood. We must get him to the hospital. Can we carry him between us, Padraig, out to my trap. It has a hatch at the back and some blankets."

"I can carry him myself if you open the trap dur'."

"Right then, I'll go out first."

"Can I go with him, Doctor?" Ann asked.

"Indeed, I will insist you do, Mrs McGovern. You will be immensely helpful when they ask for information. Did he get a letter home with him from the hospital?"

"Yes. It's on the mantelshelf. I'll fetch it for you when I collect my shawl. Padraig, will you take Oliver in to the house with you when we go. He has slept through it all."

"You would be best to take the letter with you, Mrs McGovern, to give to the doctor at the hospital."

Mary carried the lamp outside while the doctor let down the step at the back allowing Padraig to lay his son on the soft leather of the seat and cover him up. He crossed himself and laid his hand on Paul's brow. Paul moaned but then was silent.

"God go with you, son." Padraig turned to the doctor. "Thank you, doctor. I'm sorry for me temper."

He embraced Mary and they clung to each other in despair. "We must hurry, Mrs McGovern."

Mary stepped up into the trap and the cart disappeared down the lane.

Government Notice

We wish to draw attention to the dependents
of unmarried soldiers to the regulations published
in another column regarding the granting of
allowance to them. The rules should be read
carefully so that dependants will obtain
what they are justly entitled to.

Tyrone Constitution, December 1914

Chapter 33

Josie was trembling with anger and disappointment. William was home and she was the last person to know about it. Cormac had come home from work in the dairy in Newtownstewart and said he had seen William getting off the train when he was collecting creamery cans. She had hardly slept all night and made an excuse of a sore head to her uncle in the shop saying she had to go home. She couldn't settle and decided to go over to the hut at the river where she normally met William but he wasn't there. On her way back home she saw him at the bridge talking to the Reverend Bowman. He saw her and turned away as she was about to pass them. She felt sick. Was he ignoring her on purpose? She fought off the urge to turn and speak to him but she kept on up the hill towards home.

She stopped at a four bar gate and tried to think what to do next when she saw him running up the hill towards her.

"Josie, God, I'm glad to see you. I have been hanging around the village this past half hour waitin' for you. Come on. Give me a hug." She pushed him away.

"No William. Not here in full view of the whole county. You need to answer a few questions first. What are you doin here? Your leave is weeks away, and how come the whole village knows you're home before I do? What happened to your face?"

"Ach, Josie, don't be cross. I came to find you as soon as I could. I got special leave to come home and see Paul. I only arrived yesterday, and this was the first chance I got. Can we go somewhere?"

Josie reached up to his face. "What happened to you? Your face is all cut. Have you been in a fight?"

"I was on an exercise and I fell down a shugh. It's nothing serious. Are you goin' home?"

"Aye I am. I went down to the oul hut at the river. I thought you would come there."

"Well, I'm here now. But you're right, it's not a great place."

"I need to go back home. Mammy is going to Strabane later. Can you come to the hut at two?"

"Right, I'll be there. I'd better get out of here before anyone sees us. I can't wait to kiss you." he left her and went striding away down the hill.

The tears came unchecked, and she wiped her face on her hankie and headed for home. She knew she had to tell him and wondered how he would take it.

He was late and she cursed him, then crossed herself and repeated another Hail Mary to add to the mountain of Hail Marys she had recited these past weeks. He finally arrived running along the river bank, his face flushed.

"I'm sorry, Josie. I got waylaid by my Da. He was goin' to a pig sale and I had to help him load the cart. He pulled her gently into his arms and all her anger melted away.

"Is your lip sore?" she whispered in his ear. "Why?"

"Because I want to kiss it better."

The kiss was long and more passionate than any they had experienced before.

"Let's go in the shed," William said. "My lips need more of your medicine."

She pulled back pushing him away. "No. Not yet. I need to talk to you first."

"We can talk later. I'm here till tmorrow." He took her hand again but she pulled it away. He was startled by the sudden change in her.

"What's wrong, Josie?

"Nothing.Well, there is something. Just don't be mad at me when I tell you." Her mouth was dry, and she couldn't swallow.

"What in God's name would I be mad at you for. I love ye."

"I'm goin' to have a baby." She blurted it out, watching his face. He stepped back his eyes bulging, shocked at what he was hearing.

"What? How?" He stuttered, running his hand through his hair.

"I'm so sorry, William"

They stood there for what seemed an eternity to Josie. "Are you sure?" he asked.

"I haven't seen a doctor yet, but I'm sure. I don't know what to do. I'll get killed at home. I'll be sent away." She crossed herself again, tears running down her face. He lifted her off her feet and swung her around, shouting at the top of his voice.

"I'm going to be a Da. Holy Moses, Josie, what are you cryin about?" He set her down and kissed her on the lips then swung her off her feet again.

"Stop, William." She was laughing, "Stop or I'll be sick all over you."

He stopped and they clung to each other, laughing.

"What are we goin to do, William? I'm so scared."

"I should go and see your Da and Ma when I come home on leave next time. There will be more time so we will do it right. First of all, Josie O'Neil, will you marry me?"

"No, William. You just don't know what you're sayin'. My Da and my brothers would shoot you dead on the spot if you came near our house lookin' to marry me. You're a Protestant, so it just won't happen like that."

"But I'm willin' to do right by you, Josie."

"I would be tarred and feathered before they would let me marry a Protestant."

"There must be a way, Josie. We love each other and I'm happy about the wean. I want to shout and tell everyone about it."

"It's not as simple as that, William."

"What's not simple about it, Josie?"

"I can't marry you, William."

"Do you love me, Josie?"

"Would you be a Roman Catholic and go to mass every Sunday, and have this wean christened in the chapel to be a Roman Catholic?"

The smile that had been playing on his face faded. He stared at her as if he was seeing her for the first time.

"It won't come to that, Josie."

"What do you mean, it won't come to that?" She was glaring at him. "We'll get married in my church. No need for a big crowd or anything. Rev Bowman will help us."

"So, that's your answer. I become a Protestant and pray in your church. Is that what you're sayin? "

"Aye, you'll be a Protestant. That's what wives do, follow their man, and that wean will be a Protestant and after that an Orangeman" he grabbed her again laughing loudly. "Imagine oul O'Neil will have a grandson wearin' a sash."

"Let go of me, William Johnston." As he left her down she slapped him across the face and he staggered back, shocked.

"You think this is a laughin' matter. No wean of mine will ever be an Orangeman, not while I have breath in me. I'd marry the divel before I'd marry you, William Johnston, and don't go talkin' about this to anyone. Not if you don't want to fall into another shugh. This time you might not be so able to climb out of it." She walked away then turned back.

"By the way, your wee lapdog, McGovern, is back in hospital. Seems he was taken bad last night. Maybe he fell into the same shugh as you did."

He balled his fist. Hot rage blinded him. She stood her ground, daring him. "Aye. Go on, William. Hit me."

"Naw, Josie, you're not worth getting into trouble for. God forgive ye for bringing Paul into this because I won't."

Then it was his turn to walk away.

His whole world seemed to be coming apart, first Paul and now this. He hadn't meant to rile her, the Orangeman jibe was meant to be a joke. He could still feel her slap on his face and he was shocked at her biting tongue.

He would have to go to McGovern's again and risk another fight. He didn't have much time left before he had to catch the train and go back to camp. Wee John would have to wait and anyway he didn't want to go home. Last night had been enough for him. When he had arrived in with the cuts and bruises on his face his Da had told him off.

"Well, well! Luk at you. Didn't I tell you to watch yourself if you went up there. McGovern is not interested in how you feel about his son. His focus is on that uniform and how many of the men wearin' it will be in the ground with a bullet in their heads," he lifted the Tyrone Constitution newspaper and disappeared behind it.

"Are you alright, William? Will I get a cloth and clean it?"

"Naw Ma. Mrs McGovern cleaned it. It's only a scratch. It'll be gone by the morning. Would it be alright if Paul came over tomorrow night just for a chat Ma. I said it would be alright with you. He'll be here about six o'clock."

"You didn't ask if it was alright with me." John spoke out from behind the newspaper. "Have I no say in this house anymore? You've been home for hours now and you haven't as much as said hello to your brother. He waited up till his eyes wouldn't stay open and your Ma had to carry him down to bed."

"I'm sorry. I'll make time for him after school tomorrow."

"Will Paul have tae with us?"

"Naw, Ma. He he said not to go to any trouble. He hasn't much of an appetite these days."

"I suppose not, God love him. Will you fill the water can for me, William?"

He went out to the well, and watched the can filling up. He stooped and cupped his hands to drink from the spring in the same way he had since he was a child. His Ma came down the street to stand beside him.

"What happened at McGovern's?"

"Paul's Da didn't like me standin' in his kitchen wearin' a British Army uniform. He followed me outside and there was a fight. Paul's Ma brought me in and cleaned my face and then Paul and I went for a walk."

"How was Paul?"

"It's hard to tell. He's not sayin much and his Da is not helpin'."

"I'm glad you asked Paul down here but you need to be careful, William. Maybe you shouldn't wear the uniform when you are at home."

"Naw, I am a soldier of the King's now and I am proud to wear his uniform and them as doesn't like it can look the other way."

Now he was on the road up to McGovern's again. The row with Josie kept playing over in his mind. Where did she get the idea he would be a turncoat, get married in the Chapel, crossing himself and eating a piece of paper. He wouldn't ever be able to live here again if that happened. His family would disown him. His mother would never be able to cope with losing him. She had lost enough years ago. It wasn't worth it. Josie was right. They could never get married. There was nothing to be done.

He was in old working clothes. His Mother was trying to clean his tunic. It was covered in muck and dried blood from the fight and he needed to be spick and span for his return to duty.

At McGovern's there was a pony and trap on the street. It looked like Father Murphy. He knocked on the door and McGovern opened it.

"You again. Did I not make it clear enough that you're not welcome here?" He made to close the door.

"Will you just tell me is Paul alright? I heard he was back in hospital. Just tell me is he alright?"

McGovern leaned out of the doorway, his jaw brittle, veins on his neck standing out. William stood back, afraid he was going to hit him again. The older man bowed his head then spoke in a guttural whisper.

"He's back in the hospital. He nearly bled to death. He didn't come to his bed an Mary went lookin' for him and found him in the barn. There was blood everywhere comin from his stump," he stammered then looked up again. "What happened last night when you both left here? If I thought for one minute you and yours had anything to do with this, I would do gaol for it."

"I wouldn't hurt Paul and you damned well should know that."

Father Murphy came out to the door..

"Shush now, Padraig. Let us keep calm.What happened when you left here last night, William?"

"Nothing happened. We went down to the river. We talked for a while about the attack and then he went home, said he was tired. I offered to walk him home but he wouldn't hear tell of it."

"You should have come with him anyway." Padraig gritted his teeth. "He didn't want me to. He's too proud. He didn't want to look like an invalid. Honest to God, he was alright when he left me."

"He could have died in the barn."

McGovern was looking into the far distance. "I went to bed in a rage. I was sleepin' and he was bleedin to death."

"But he didn't, Padraig, thanks be to God," the Priest crossed himself and McGovern did the same.

"They took him away to the hospital. I don't know what's happening. Father Murphy is takin' me to the hospital. Wan of the neighbours was to take Oliver but her wean tuck sick so we're takin' him with us."

"Luk, Mr McGovern, I know how you feel about me but I want to help. Let me take Oliver over to Ma. She would be happy to help out."

"Thank you, William it is a sound idea. I'm sure you will agree, Padraig. The wee fella would be better with Mrs Johnston. The authorities in the County Hospital won't let young children into the ward."

McGovern bowed his head then looked up at William.

"Aye, you'd best come in. I need get a few things together."

William made a fuss of Oliver.

"Our Paul told me you were a soldier now. Do you have a gun? My dada has a gun. He said he was going to shoot the bad men who hurt Paul."

William and the priest exchanged looks. "How would you like to come to my house and play with wee John?" Oliver beamed a big smile and wriggled out of William's arms and ran to tell his Da.

"It is a very good of you to help, William. Padraig has taken this very badly. I know you and Paul have been good friends over the years.We all need friends at times like these."

McGovern came into the kitchen pulling on his coat. "Thank you for this. I will try and get back when I can."

"Don't worry about Oliver. he can be tucked in with wee John if you can't get back. Tell Paul I was askin' after him. I have to be back at Finner the morrow so I won't be able see him until my next leave."

"Aye, I'd best get on." He picked Oliver up, hugged him and handed him to William.

"Be a good boy, Oliver. I'll see you later."

Prisoners – But Not For Long

Three soldiers from the Royal Inniskilling Fusiliers,
who arrived in Omagh Depot, related the
interesting story of their capture and subsequent
escape from the Germans after the Battle of Mons.

Tyrone Constitution, November 1914

Chapter 34

William arrived home as the tea was being put on the table. "One more wee mouth to feed, Ma," and he set Oliver in at the table. Wee John stared at Oliver then came running into his big brother's arms.

"William. Have you got your gun with you?" he asked.

"No John, I had to leave it behind."

"I told Ma I was goin' to join the army and she got cross. Did she get cross with you when you joined the army, William?"

"You're too young." Oliver said, "Da said our Paul was too young. So Da brought him home."

"Did your Paul git hit by bad men?"

"Aye, my da's goin to shoot them."

"That's enough talk, boys. I have apple cake for good boys but you have to eat up the bread first. William, can you help me lift something down in the back room?" William followed her. "Close the door over. What's going on, William?" she whispered.

"Paul collapsed. He was found unconscious in the barn this morning."

Ann gasped, "Dear God, William. Is he alright?"

"He's in the County Hospital. Mrs McGovern went with him and the doctor. I went up to see how he was and his Da was at his wits end not knowing how he was. The priest was there. He's takin' Mr McGovern to the hospital, so I offered to take Oliver. I don't know when they will be back so he might have to spend the night here, if that's alright with you. I didn't know what else to do."

"I'm proud of you." She stood on her tiptoes and kissed him.

"What will Da say? I don't want any arguments in front of the weans. They know too much already."

"You just leave your Da to me. Now go and get something to eat. He's in the byre milkin'. I'll go over and tell him. Better out there so he can shout all he wants."

John was washing out the pails when she came into the milking parlour. "William's back, but Paul didn't come." Before she could finish he interrupted her.

"Good job. I didn't want us to get involved. People would talk. Best keepin' McGovern and his trouble as far away as possible." He looked up from his task and saw she was standing with her arms folded.

215

"What?" he asked. Puzzled, "Why are you luckin' at me like that?" "Young Paul has been taken bad. He's in the hospital again and we are lookin' after their youngest. I don't want you to be startin' any argument with William about this, John. The wean will likely have to stay the night and it is our duty as good neighbours to do what we can to help."

"How did William know? I hope he gets no blame for this, Ann. Didn't he come home last night with a bloody nose?"

"That's nonsense, John. The McGovern's know William wouldn't harm Paul. William heard it in the village and went up there. He has brought their wee lad Oliver down to us until his Da can go to the hospital."

"Aye what are you wantin' with me then? It seems to me my opinion doesn't count anymore. I'm just the hired hand."

"Ach, John. Don't take on so much. I'm proud of William and so should you be." She came and took him by the hand.

"The wee wean is here now and we don't want to upset him with raised voices.William will be goin' back tomorrow so we should make the best of the time we have with him now and wee John will have a playmate for a while."

He put his arms around her. "You're a wonderful woman, Ann. God knows how you put up with me."

"I'm proud of you, John. I know the pain is bad without the drink and it makes you crabbit at times but you have beaten the habit and it's a testament to your will how you have managed to do without it and still be in pain."

"I couldn't have done it without you."

"We did it with God's help and prayer. Come on, let's get finished here and go into the fireside. They will be missin' us and you need your tae."

Ann was out on the street when Mary McGovern called to collect Oliver. They embraced.

"Come in. Have you news of Paul?"

"Aye Ann. He's home again. They gave him a tonic bottle and he has to go back to see another doctor on Monday.I came as soon as we got him settled, Padraig is waitin' till I get back."

"The boys are still asleep. I thought it better to keep them away from school. I hope that is alright with you, Mary. Have you had any sleep yourself?"

"I nodded off for a while but we are afraid to leave him on his own so I won't stay long. Padraig has his work to do."

William came up from his room, tucking his shirt into his trousers. "Have you news about Paul?"

"I was just telling your Ma. He got home but he must stay in bed. No walkin' to the river for a day or two. He wants to see you if you have time before you go for the train."

"I'll go as soon as I get dressed. My train leaves at twelve o'clock." He hesitated. "I will be wearin' my uniform, Mrs McGovern. I know Paul's Da tuck umbrage at me wearin' it in your house the last time."

"Padraig is grateful for your help, William. We both are."

"I wish I could do more to help Paul, but I have to get back to Finner today."

"I know, William. You will always be in our prayers."

"Thanks, Mrs McGovern. I'll go and get dressed now and get the boys up. I had to call a stop to them chitterin' last night. Will ye wait for me?"

"No, William. I have to go to see the doctor later about dressings for Paul's arm. So I'll get on as soon as Oliver is dressed"

"Sure leave Oliver here, Mary. William can take him over when he's goin' can't you William?"

"Aye surely. But I had better get goin'. I will see you after a while, Mrs McGovern." He went down to the bedroom and they herd the hulabaloo as he began to pull the blankets from the squealing boys.

"I cannot thank you enough for all for your help, Ann. William is a fine young man. You must be very proud of him"

"I am, but I wish he wasn't in the army. He is just seventeen and there is not a day when I don't think of tryin' to get him out of it and home again but I know he would not want that so I have to bide by it."

"I wish things could have been different but we must make do with what we have."

The two women embraced again. The boys came into the kitchen, Oliver was excited to tell his Ma about his adventure.Then he happily waved to her as she left him with his new friend. Later, William said goodbye to his Ma.

"I think your Da is goin down the lane with you, William, I'll let you both have some time together. God bless you and watch over you and come home safe to us."

"Thanks, Ma, for all you have done these past days. Write to me when ye can. I love you dearly."

John and the boys walked down the lane with him, the boys lingering behind poking sticks in the stream that ran along the ditch.

"Are you sure it's wise to go over there after what happened the last time?"

"Luk, Da. I'm goin to see Paul. It's why I got this leave and he will need every friend he can get after what's happened to him."

"Have the police found anyone to answer for it yit?"

"Naw, but if I could get whoever it was they would be sorry."

"Best you're getting away, cub. Ye don't want to get mixed up in this, them boyos up the mountain are best avoided."

"What's it got to do with them? Have you heard somethin', Da?"

"Keep your voice down, William. Them weans have big ears"

"Have ye heard somethin Da?"

"I heard a rumour that the boyos decided to teach young McGovern a lesson for darin' to join the British army and things got carried away. That's all I've heard, Wlliam, but you're not to go accusing up at McGoverns. It's only a rumour."

"Jez, Da. If it's true it's enough to drive McGovern mad. Who told ye this?"

"Aw naw, cub. I'll not be spillin' the beans. What I heard was men talkin' in huddles at the mart, no names and ye must keep it under your hat for now."

William was silent, staring ahead, his jaw clenched in defiance. John stopped, looking back to where the boys sat hunched over the shugh.

He caught William by the sleeve, his voice a hoarse whisper.

"William, you must promise me to keep quiet about this. Let it sit for the time being. It's still a rumour, keep out of it."

"You know more than you're sayin Da. What's the truth of this?"

"Luk, keep yer mouth shut and get on that train. I will keep my ear to the ground in the meantime and if I hear anything more I'll keep ye posted. I'm sorry I spoke about it. The best thing for you to do is to say nothing. Promise me, William."

"Aye, I know you're right. There's enough goin' on with Paul now. Tellin' him about this wudn't help but I will be home again before we move out and I'll keep ye till your word to let me know if you hear anything more. I had best get over there now or I'll be late for the train. Come on, Oliver! Yer ma is luckin' for ye."

John put his arm on William's shoulder and pulled him into an embrace.

"God bless ye, son. I will pray fer ye."

"Thanks, Da, and I'm proud of ye for stayin' af the drink. Ma is more settled now than I've seen her for a long time"

John watched him striding out onto the road, McGovern's wean hanging onto his hand. God alone knew how this would end when the truth finally came out about the attack and he was thankful William would be well away by then.

Mr Bonar Law and Sir E. Carson.
Relations between Mr Bonar Law and
Sir Edward Carson appear to be on the wane as
has been reported in the English press. Nothing has been
seen of Sir E. Carson for the last week or two and
speculation has grown that relations between the two
gentlemen have been strained for some time.

Ulster Herald, December 1915

Chapter 35

Oliver raced the last part of the lane up to the house and was caught in his Ma's arms before he got inside the door.

"Go on in, William. Oliver is goin' to help me feed the hens and check for eggs. Just because he's not at school won't mean he gets out of his jobs. There's tae in the pot and bread if ye feel like a bite. Padraig has gone to the lower field so you have the place to yourselves. I'll see you before ye go."

Paul was lying in the settle bed by the fire. He was white faced with dark circles under his eyes. He smiled and tried to sit up.

"Don't try to get up, Paul. How are ye? Jez I'm so sorry, I shuld have walked ye home. How's the arm now?"

"Will ye sit down, man, and give over with the questions. I'm sick, sore and tired af questions. I want ye to tell me all the crack about the camp. Tell me about the trainin', anything that will lift me for a while."

"Aye, I'm sorry. Ye must be ready tae go mad."

"Did ye see Josie while ye were home?"

William had not thought about Josie since he had left her at the hut earlier. "Aye, I saw her today, much good it did me."

"What do ye mean?"

"She brought me 'great tidings of joy'. I'm goin' to be a dada."

"Holy shit, William."

"Well, I don't know about 'holy' shit but I'm in it up to my eyes."

"What are ye goin to do? Will ye marry hur?"

"Naw. She turned me down. Said she wuld't marry a Protestant even if he was the last man standin'."

"What will she do? Does her wans know about it?"

"I woudn't think so or I wouldn't be sittin here."

"Holy shit, It's as well you're not livin' within a hundred miles of here when this gets out. Poor Josie! Is there nothing you can do?"

"Poor, Josie, my arse! You should've heard the things she said to me. I was ready to marry her and she turned me down. Now she can do what she likes."

"What about the child?"

"Now, who's askin' too many questions? Anything else you want to know?"

"Sorry, I should know better."

William poked the fire and stacked more turf on it.

"Thanks for helpin' out with Oliver and everything, William. Especially after getting a punch the other night. Me Da can't help it. His bitterness runs deep about the Brits. I must be a big disappointment on that front. I'm a disappointment on all sides I..." he bowed his head and and let out a loud wail of grief. William jumped up, frightened at the despair on Paul's face.

"God, Paul. I wish I could do more." He sat on the side of the bed and held Paul's hand, his eyes never leaving the bandaged stump.

"I'm sorry, Paul, sorry for all this mess. If I hadn't talked ye into joinin' up all this wouldn't have happened."

"Christ, William. Don't go blamin' yerself. Ye weren't to know. I made my own decisions. Nobody forced me to do anything I didn't want to. My Da tried and this is where it got me. I'm a cripple and that changes everything."

"The attack on you has taken a lot out af your people. I know your Da and me will niver see eye to eye on anything but we both care about you, Paul."

Oliver calling the dog broke the tension. William stood up.

"I must go and catch the train. I'm under orders not to miss it."

"How did you get leave so early? I thought you wouldn't be home for another six weeks?"

"I put in for special leave as soon as I heard about your attack. The Sergeant wanted to court martial me for cheek but the Colonel was on my side."

"Trust ye to get uppity. The Master at school could vouch for your cheek." They both laughed at the memories of those shared days in the schoolhouse.

William leaned over and shook Paul's hand.

"It's good to hear you laugh. Ye need to look after yerself now, Paul. I will write to ye now I have no need to write to Josie."

"I wish I was goin' with you."

"Aye, me too."

The goodbyes were left unsaid.

William came out of the house and young Oliver came running to greet him. "Are you goin' to get your gun now, William?" he asked. Mary McGovern caught up with him.

"Come on now, cub,you're all muddy and William needs to keep his uniform clean." She leaned up to him and kissed him on the cheek. "Thanks, William, for all your help. You will be in our prayers.

"I've told Paul I will write and Ma said to tell you to come over anytime you feel the need."

"I will. Goodbye and God bless you"

Paul was up and able to go outside. It had been a week since William had left for Finner. His arm was healing slowly but the pain niver seemed to go away. There were times when he found himself flexin' the ghost hand and if he closed his eyes he could imagine it was still there attached to his arm. The reality was very hard to stomach. His left hand was useless. He couldn't write his own name and even cleaning his arse with his left hand was hard, the first time he had messed up his trousers and he couldn't look at his ma for days after.

He was going to mass in the morning, his first time since the attack. Father Murphy had been up to the house most days and he had urged Paul to come to Chapel. People were asking after him and prayers had been said for him every Sunday since the attack. He wasn't looking forward to it but he might see Josie. He couldn't get her out of his thoughts. She was in his dreams. She was in his arms. He was holding her in his arms, his hands exploring the soft curves of her body. He wanted to stay there always in that place where he had two strong hands and arms. He remembered William asking him if he had odd dreams and he had not understood until now. Now dreams were all he had. Josie would never want a cripple?

The Chapel was bursting at the seams when they went in. Then the noisy chittering stopped and people stared, crossing themselves as he passed down the aisle. Paul could feel all eyes on him as they took their usual seats. He had hoped praying would be easier in the chapel but it wasn't. The mass droned on. He tried to pray but the anger always got the better of him. He wanted to stand up and shout at the altar, 'why me?'

He saw Josie as he came back to his seat after he received the host and stared at her but she looked away. At the end of mass several of the younger children crowded around him curious and asking questions like 'will you grow another arm?' and 'is your other hand in your pocket?' Padraig chased them. "You would think their Ma's would teach them a bit af manners, wee brats.

Are ye alright cub?"

"Aye, sure they're only weans. Our Oliver loves his new rise to fame. None of the other cubs has a one-handed big brother."

"Paul, don't say that."

"Sorry, Ma."

Josie came over as they were leaving. She looked different. Her lovely hair was tied up in a tight bun.

"Hello, Paul."

"Hello, Josie, How are ye?"

"No better than yourself, I'm thinkin. How's your arm?"

"Better than it was."

"Have ye been to the hut?"

"Naw. Not for a while, but I might get a walk over later."

"Aye, well, must get home. Luk after yerself."

Paul's heart raced all the way home. He was sure Josie wanted to meet him at the hut. His Ma caught him smiling, making him blush.

It rained. Great swathes of rain fell all afternoon blocking out the mountains. Paul watched from the window, hoping it would stop and he could get down to the hut but darkness came early. His obvious disappointment was not lost on his Ma.

"Were ye hopin' to go out, Paul?"

"Aye I thought I would go for a walk but maybe tomorrow."

"Were you meetin' Josie O'Neil?"

"What makes you ask that?"

"Ach, I thought I heard her mention the hut when she was talkin' to ye earlier. She writes to William, it was her that told him about the attack."

"Aye, Ma, I know. William told me"

Padraig looked up from the paper he was reading.

"Was she curtin' him? Hur oul boy wouldn't need to hear that."

"How anything's a secret around here beggars belief, I'm away to me bed."

"What's wrong with him?"

"Too many questions, Padraig. Leave him be."

The sun had broken through the dark clouds the following day as Paul headed down to the river.

He didn't expect Josie to be there but still he hoped that she might turn up.

The hut was in bad shape, the roof had caved and grass and moss covered the trough they had used for a seat.He sat down, yesterday's rain seeping through his trousers. It was cold. The river hadn't changed. The deep pool opposite the hut reflected the circles on the still water and the plop of trout feeding on the fly. A heron rose up in front of him, its wings flapping like windmills as it disappeared over his head.

He hadn't heard her coming until she was standing next to him. He jumped up.

"Josie!"

"Sorry, Paul. Did I make you jump?"

"I wasn't expectin ye. Well I hoped ye would come but..." he was stammering, suddenly nervous.

"I knew you wouldn't get out yesterday. It was so wet all day but I hoped ye would make it today."

She was going to sit down and he stopped her.

"Don't sit down unless ye want a wet arse." They both laughed.

"We could walk over to the bridge. There are some big stones over there. She followed him. He paused. There was a steep bank and he was self-concious of his poor balance, afraid he might fall. She held out her hand and he took it aware that his palm was wet and clammy despite the cold. They settled on a flat rock near the edge of the water.

"Did ye see William when he was home?" Paul asked.

"Aye, I did. He suits the uniform."

"Aye, It was made for him...the army I mean. Do you miss him?"

"No, he's not worth the trouble."

"What do you mean?"

"We fell out. He's away to war and I'm here."

"I thought you loved each other?"

"Aye, I thought I loved him and I thought he loved me but the soldier in him won that war. I niver want to see him again."

"Jez, Josie, that's a bit harsh."

"Not harsh at all if you knew how he's left me?"

"Did he hit you?"

"Naw, he might be a lot of things but he wouldn't hit me." She turned away from him.

"I'm in big trouble, Paul" she whispered. "Didn't he tell you?"

Paul didn't answer, afraid to lie, not wanting to let on what William had told him.

"Luk, Paul, I know you know what I'm talkin' about. You and him can't help yourselves. Always heads together at school. No one good enough to be in the gang of two." She got up. "Well, here's the news, just in case he didn't tell you. I'm expectin' a wean and it's his. I'm away home."

"Josie, please don't go. I like you. Stay, you can trust me. Honest." She sat down again.

"I'm at me wits end. I don't know what to do."

She burst into tears, "I will have to go away to a convent and they will take the baby away and I'll niver see it again."

She sat down again, sobbing into her hands." I'm sorry, Paul, I shouldn't be complainin'. You have your own trouble. How's your...arm?" She nearly said hand.

"Ach, it will heal in time. But I need to teach my left hand to do what my right hand can't do anymore"

Paul moved over beside her, his sling making it awkward to get closer. "Do your wans' know?"

"God, no, but I will soon not be able to hide it. Mammy thinks I'm eatin' the profits in the shop."

"Do you love William?"

"I thought I did but now I'm not sure. I'm not sure about anything anymore except that I can't marry him."

"What will you do?"

"I thought of runnin' away to Dublin, but sure I don't know anybody in Dublin or anywhere else. Who wants the likes of me anyway?" She began to sob again.

"I want ye."

For a moment they both stared at one another. Then she laughed, her face blotched from the crying. "Don't be daft, Paul."

"I mean it, Josie. I have always liked you, but you only had eyes for William and I gave up, but I won't give up on you again. Will you marry me?"

"Are ye serious?"

"Yes I love you, Josie and I know William asked you. I'm glad you turned him down. It would'nt have worked but we can make it work. I'm a one-armed man but I will do my best for you if ye will let me."

"God, Paul. I don't know what to say. I niver knew you felt like this about me. I thought you hated me for takin' William away from ye."

"It was the other way around. Not that I hated William. But you niver seen me. You treated me like I wasn't there half the time and I was afraid to speak. William is my friend but I was jealous, God forgive me, and then this happened."

He moved his right arm. The stump showed clearly now from under the sling. He watched her reaction. She blinked away another tear, staring at him.

"I nearly died. For a while I thought I was in hell that I deserved this for goin' agin me Da about the army."

His voice dropped to a hoarse whisper. "I love you, Josie O'Neil, but if ye say no I'll not blame ye."

"I can't believe this is happening, Paul, do yu know what you're sayin'?"

"Aye, I do. It's all I've thought about in the last week. We can get married and I'll be a father to the wean. You have no need to be shamed. William and ye would niver have worked out, but we can, Josie."

"How will we tell them?"

"I'll come with ye. We'll tell the families and then go to the priest.

Just say when you're ready and that's what we'll do"

As they walked back to the hut, Paul put his arm around her and they kissed for the first time.

Her Ma was in the kitchen, stirring the porridge, when Josie came in.

"Mornin', Ma. Is there tae brewin'?"

"Aye, what has ye up at this time af day. Are ye goin' early to the shop?"

"Naw, I just cudn't sleep." Her Ma turned from the stove and staredcat her.

"When is it due?"

The question hit her like a slap on the face. She couldn't think what to say. "What do ye mean?"

"Ye know well what I mean, Josie, so don't be tryin to deny it."

All the weeks she had been hiding it slipped away in a mixture of relief and fear.

"How did ye know?"

"I'm yer Mother Josie. Did ye really think I wouldn't notice. Whose is it and if ye say that cub Johnston ye can get yer coat and get out now before yer Da hears about it. Who is it, Josie? Who's the Da?"

"Paul McGovern," his name came to her lips in her desperation.

"Holy Mother of God." Bridget O'Neil crossed herself and came to sit next to her sobbing youngest wean. "How far on are ye?"

"I don't know, Ma"

"How can ye not know, Josie? Think! When was yer last monthly? Was it before young Paul's attack?"

"I think so."

"Ye think so. What in under God happened? Did he force ye?"

"Naw, Ma. Paul wouldn't do that. I think I've missed twice and I was sick a lot at the start."

"Have ye told him?"

"Aye, he asked me to wed him but I didn't know what to say"

"No wuld have been a good start. In the first place, Josie, you're only fifteen.

We'll have to go to the priest."

"What about Da?"

"What about him? He'll find out soon enough. We tell Father Murphy first. We'll go this morning after mass. Go and get dressed before they all get up and wash yer face. Tears are too late now."

"Ach, Ma, I'm scared," she felt she was going to choke she sucked in deep breaths but coudn't stop the hysteria that she felt building up in her chest.

"Come on now! Stop that. I hear yer Da gettin' up. Get on ta yer room and get yer clothes on. Stay down there till he gets away ta work."

She sat for a long time on her bed running her hand around her belly. She would marry Paul now. It was better that than goin' to a convent and them taking the child from her.

"You're mine," she whispered. "Nobody is goin' to take ye away."

After mass, they waited until the chapel was empty and Father Murphy came from the vestry. He was surprised to see them.

"Bridget, Josie. What can I do for you ladies? Is everything alright?"

"Can we have a private word, Father?"

"Of course I'm just going to the parochial house for breakfast. You can join me if you care to."

"I would rather we talked here, Father. I need your advice." Bridget didn't trust the housekeeper. She was no priest. She made it her business to listen at doors to catch any gossip that was going.

They spent an hour in the vestry. Josie had willed herself not to cry but her tears flowed when the priest began to ask questions.

"How long were you and Paul McGovern fornicating? Did he force himself on you?"

"Why haven't you confessed your sin?"

Before they left the chapel Josie had given her confession with a punishment of twelve daily decades of the Rosary for four weeks and a weekly confession. She was to have no further contact with Paul until Father Murphy had seen him and his parents. He would be calling back to discuss the matter with her father later in the day.

They walked across the bridge in silence, Josie's tears dry on her flushed skin.

As they got nearer home, her Ma muttered: "Now the hard part, girl, and don't expect sympathy from yer Da and the boys. It's time te face the music." Josie didn't answer. She wanted to run up the mountain and die in a bog hole.

Father Murphy climbed down from the trap and was tethering the horse when Mary came around from the back of the house.

"Good day, Father. We didn't expect you today. I think Paul is in inside."

"Good day to you, Mrs McGovern. Would it be possible to speak to him privately?"

"Of course, Father. Go on in and I'll finish my jobs.There is nothing wrong, is there, Father?"

"Give me a moment with Paul first. Is Padraig about at all?"

"Aye, He's down at the far field layin' a hedge. Will I blow the whistle for him tae come home?"

"Yes, that'd be helpful and I will talk with you both shortly."

Father Murphy came into the kitchen as the blast of three high pitched whistles pierced the air. Paul stood up and went to the window.

"Hello, Father. Why has ma blown the whistle? It's not dinner time."

"Good day, Paul. I asked her to call your father. All in good time, I need to talk to you first."

"Is there something wrong, Father?"

"Well, that depends on you Paul." The priest sat down and motioned him to take the seat opposite "Would you have any knowledge about the subject of the visit I have had from Josie O'Neil and her mother this morning after mass?"

Paul was silent. He felt his stomach turning and he thought he was going to throw up right in front of the priest.

"Am I to take your silence as a sign you do not know or that you know but cannot speak about it to me? Which is it Paul?"

"She told me yesterday she was goin'to have a wean and she was going to tell her Ma and Da."

"Did she tell you who the father was?"

Paul dropped his head, sure that eye contact with the priest would make the truth harder to mask.

"Have you been fornicating with Josie O'Neil?"

"Yes, Father."

"I'm disappointed with you, Paul. Disappointed you have not seen fit to confess this flagrant sinful union with a girl at your confessions. God cannot be expected to overlook the sinner if he is not contrite and sorry for such actions. I take it you accept that this child is yours?"

"Yes, Father."

"Do your parents know you were involved with Josie O'Neil?" Paul raised his head and looked the priest in the eye.

"No, Father. They do not know and I would be obliged if you would allow me to tell them in my own time."

"You have had more than enough time to tell them. Now it is out of your hands. I will speak to them as soon as your Father comes in from his work. The O'Neil family will also have to be told and arrangements will have to be made for a wedding."

Padraig came into the kitchen, pulling his cap off as he greeted the priest, Mary close behind him.

"Is there something going on, Father? Have you heard something about the attack on our Paul?"

"Calm yourself, Padraig. I was just going to call you." He turned to Paul. "Do you want to explain what has happened or will I?"

"What's this all about, Paul?" Mary came and sat down beside him. He squeezed her arm trying to reassure her. Then he stood up, determined to prove he was his own man and prepared to take responsibility.

"Josie O'Neil and me are getting married. She is expectin' my wean." Father Murphy interrupted, "I have just come from..."

"Please, Father Murphy. I want to explain in my own way. I had been seeing Josie before my attack and again since. We love each other and we want to be married, not just because she's goin to have a wean but because we want to be together." The silence in the kitchen stopped him. His Da and Ma were looking at him as if he was a stranger, their shocked faces pale and disbelieving. Padraig was the first to speak.

"Thank you, Father Murphy, for your help, but Mary and me would be obliged if you could leave us now. We will come and see you later at the parochial house."

"You realise that this is a matter of urgency now, Padraig. I am going to the O'Neil house now and it is not a meeting that holds any pleasure for me." Padraig turned on the priest, his face white with anger.

"This is not about you, Father. This is a family matter. We will deal with it in our own way."

"Padraig, please! Father Murphy is only trying to help." Mary moved between them. "Thank you Father. We will come to the parochial house this evening before mass if that would suit you?"

"Thank you, Mrs McGovern, and perhaps, Paul, you will consider meeting with Josie's parents?"

"Yes, Father. I will. Thank you."

"I will show you out, Father." Mary followed him out to the cart. "I am sorry, Father. Padraig has not been himself lately."

"I understand, Mrs McGovern. But at times like these we all have to put our faith in prayer. I will expect to see you at mass and we can discuss the necessary arrangements. Good day."

Padraig was shouting loudly when she came into the kitchen again. "What the hell is goin' on with you, Paul? Ye niver iver let on ye had feelin's for Josie O'Neil and now we hear she's havin' yer wean. Yer a liar, Paul, and that wee tramp is playin' ye fer a fool."

"Don't ye dare call hur that, Da. And ye have no right ta call me a liar either. Like it or not she will be Mrs Paul McGovern and there is nuthin' ye can do about it."

"How are ye going to keep a wife and wean with only wan arm?"

Paul lunged at his father, knocking him off his feet onto the box of eggs which were wating for collection. The thin box splintered and egg yolks began to leak out onto the floor. Mary caught Paul's hand, pulling him away as Padraig struggled to get up.

"God forgive ye, Padraig, for sayin such a thing." Padraig's face was twisted in grief.

"Christ, Paul. Can ye forgive me? I niver meant to come out with such a thing."

He came and stood beside them and they embraced in silence.

Mrs O'Neil and Josie were alone in the house when Father Murphy made his promised call.

"Can I get ye a cup af tae, Father?"

"No thank you, Mrs O'Neil. Is Joseph joining us?"

"He's not back from the Fair day in Strabane Father, so I haven't had a chance to tell him." She let the lie fall, inwardly crossing herself, knowing full well Joe was in the public house. "It could be late when he's home him and the cubs are workin' for a neighbour up the valley."

"Ah, that's unfortunate. I had hoped both families could meet this evening before Mass to discuss the matter of a wedding. I have spoken to Paul and his parents and they are coming to the parochial house this evening before mass."

"Luk, Father, her Da will go mad about this." As she spoke the door opened and Joe O'Neil walked into the room, his hat sitting at an odd angle. There was a strong smell of porter.

"Father Murphy, what brings you here? Are ye checkin' up on all the sinners the day?" he laughed and pulled up a chair to the fire. "Any tae in the pot, Josie? And get the Father a cup while yer at it."

"No tea for me, Joseph. I have come to talk to you about a matter concerning your daughter."

"What about hur?" He looked at Josie and then his wife. "What's to talk about?"

"It seems Josie has gotten herself into trouble and finds herself in the family way. I have come to talk to you and Mrs O'Neil about what's to be done."

O'Neil rose from his chair letting out a roar of curses and caught Josie by the hair swinging her around slapping her hard on the side of her face. The priest and her mother pulled him away as Josie screamed in pain and blood began to flow from her nose.

"For God's sake, Joseph, stop this at once." Father Murphy was angry. "That is no way to treat the girl in her condition." This remark only fuelled O'Neil's fury and he swung his fist out again in a blind attempt at hitting Josie again. Restrained by the priest, his face purple with rage, he glared at his daughter.

"Get out, ye fuckin' whore! Get out and don't come back!"

Josie ran out of the house, her hot tears mingling with the blood pouring from her nose. She ran up the mountain road, stumbling through an open slap, her feet sucking into the wet mud and dung that lay there. She sat down on the ditch at the side of the field. The blood had stopped and dried on her face. She pulled moss off the bank and wiped herself. Then more tears came and she sobbed, her head bowed between her knees. She heard her name being called. First her Ma and then the priest, their voices echoing up the valley. She didn't answer at first but she knew she couldn't stay here and it wasn't just her. It was the wean she was carrying she needed to think about. She came down the road towards them. Her Ma wrapped her arms around her making the tears begin again.

"Don't mind yer Da, Josie. He's drunk and he'll be sorry for hittin' ye. Father Murphy wants ye to go with him to the parochial house and get cleaned up. Paul and his wans are comin' to talk about the wedding and we can't have them seein' ye lookin' like this. I have left you a dress and coat in a bag by the gate, I'll deal with yer Da."

Paul walked beside his parents up the drive to the parochial house. They had spent the last of the afternoon talking about what was to be done. Padraig was ashamed of his reaction and was now intent on making the best of what Paul wanted to do. Mary had kept her own thoughts to herself. Her nagging doubts about the truth of Paul's confession worried her. If he was lying to them, there had to be a reason. She couldn't stop herself thinking about of her conversation with Ann Johnston weeks ago that Josie was writing to William. Why would she write to William if she and Paul had been in the throws of a courtship?

Paul was shocked when he saw Josie in Father Murphy's study. The side of her face was swollen and she looked so wretched. He went to her and put his hand to her face.

"What happened to you? Who did this to you?"

"Now, Paul. Can we all sit down and see how we can make the best of this?"

"I don't need to think any more, Father. I have already asked Josie to marry me and she has agreed. What I want to know is who has done this to her?"

"Unfortunately, Josie's father was not happy with the news and got carried away, but her mother is delighted and will join us shortly to talk over the plans for a wedding."

"I'm sorry, Josie. I should have been with ye when ye told him."

"Please, Paul. I'm alright and Father Murphy has been very kind to me." She looked over to Mary and Padraig. "I'm sorry for any upset I have caused today, but Paul and I love each other and I will try to be a good wife and mother to our child."

Mary and Padraig came forward and hugged her. "You are welcome to our family, Josie, Mary and I want only what makes Paul happy."

"Thank you both."

The housekeeper knocked and Father Murphy went out, leaving them with a smile and pointing to the calendar on the wall.

"Perhaps you can talk about dates when I'm gone." Mrs O'Neil was in the hall alone.

"He wouldn't come, Father. He won't even hear hur name mentioned and the two cubs are worse. All they can talk about is not something I want to repeat, Father. They have it in for young McGovern."

"There is nothing you should hold back from me at this stage, Mrs O'Neil. Joseph and your sons will have to answer to God and the Holy Mother. I will speak to them myself. Now the McGovern family are inside and are accepting Josie into their family, which is as it should be. Are you happy to meet them now in the spirit of God's grace?"

"Yes, Father, God bless you, Father."

Christmas at Bundoran

On the 23rd of December B and C Companies
of the 9th Royal Inniskillen Fusiliers will proceed
on Christmas leave. A and D Companies will remain
behind, spending Christmas day in billets at Bundoran.
Christmas dinner with all the trimmings will
be served in the skating rink, which had been
decorated with bunting and coloured paper strings.

Tyrone Constitution, 17th December 1914

Chapter 36

William found it hard to settle in camp in the days after he had been home. Tommy and Mark were full of questions.

"Who died, Willie?" Mark had asked and he was hard pressed to be truthful with them.

"Nobody died, boys. I had a very sick friend who was at death's door. But thank God he survived.

"Was it the same wan that was goin' to join up with ye?"

"Aye. It was, Tommy."

"Why did he not join up ?"

"It's a long story, Mark, and maybe I'll tell ye one of these days." After a while they stopped asking.

He had written to Paul, but found it awkward. All the questions he had wanted to ask didn't make it unto the page and the short note he wrote hadn't deserved the stamp. Mrs McGovern had replied once on Paul's behalf but her letter was full of news about the farm and the weather, so he had no way of knowing how Paul really was.

He thought about writing to Josie, but gave up the idea. He missed her. Their time together had been what his dreams had been made of but she had turned him down. He knew that most of what she had said was true. All hell would break out in her house when they found out about the wean. But hell was a better place to be if they ever found out who the Da was.

In the camp and on the unending route marches, the Sergeant had singled him out for ridicule. Some of the men joined in, resentful because he had been given special home leave. One soldier he knew had been refused home leave to see his newborn son but admitted he wasn't married to the mother. Others tried to pick fights with him knowing he was on thin ice with the sergeant but he held his temper long enough to show them he wouldn't rise to the bait.

The bad weather was unremitting and living under canvas was a nightmare. One storm had left the Derry men in flattened tents, the officers quickly billeted to a hotel in town. Eventually, they had been moved to Bundoran's skating rink. On their first night away from the thud of the rain on canvas they slept the sleep of the dead, the only sound to be heard was their loud snores.

He had been expecting leave to go home but the sergeant took great pleasure in telling him that he would not be granted leave before the New

Year, so he resigned himself to spending his first Christmas away from home and his Ma's cooking.

The concerts were good and usually ended up in singsongs. He had never played cards before but Mark and Tommy were experts and soon he was able to play with the best of them. The girls around the town still kept their eye on them but he stayed clear of getting too close to anyone on a regular footing.

Daily route marches took them to the far reaches of the wild side of Donegal. The poverty there was a shock to many of them but the people they met were generous in their poverty and often insisted on sharing their food with them and it was hard to refuse because very few of them spoke English. William enjoyed these marches into the country away from the roar of the sea, the boggy mountains reminding him of the days spent walking in the Sperrins. A letter came for him in the mail bag in mid December. He recognised Josie's handwriting. He had not heard from her since that last day at the river and he was surprised to hear from her now.

Dear William,

I am writing this letter for Paul and for myself because we thought it best to tell you the news. Paul asked me to marry him and I said yes. We are to be married on the 19th of December and I am moving into his home place. We hope you will be happy for us and that all is well with you.

Paul and Josie

William couldn't believe what he was reading. Paul and Josie married. He stared at the page, disbelief filling him with disgust and betrayal. How could they be getting married when they meant nothing to each other? Josie never had a good word for Paul nor him for her and yet now they were getting hitched. He balled the letter up in his fist. He had not had a word from Paul until this. Then suddenly it was clear. Paul was taking on Josie and the unborn wean. He flattened out the letter and read it again. He hated himself for his bitterness. He had wronged Josie and had taken the easy option leaving her to deal with it on her own. He was jealous, he had really loved Josie, walking away from her hadn't been easy. He wanted to write back but what could he say. 'I'm happy for ye. Thanks for taking my wean.' He went to the reading rooms that night to write to his Ma. He sat for ages, staring at the blank page, then wrote:

Dear Ma,
Paul is getting married to Josie O'Neil. She is going to have my wean. I am so sorry.

He tore it up knowing that he could never say the child was his to anyone. He did not deserve it and it would hurt Paul. He ended up in the pub and for the first time in his life he got drunk.

Ann met Mary at the monthly fair day in the village. Christmas was just around the corner and the fair was busy despite the blustery weather. The stalls were full of turkeys, hanging in featherless rows their blank stares making the small children run away in fright. They stepped in under the canvas of one of the stalls to pass the time of day.

"Are you all ready for Christmas, Mary?"

"Aye. The turkey's been plucked and I'm stuffin' it tonight. Christmas is comin' early this year in our house. Ye must have heard by now, Ann."

"Aye, I heard. But stories can grow quicker than grass around here."

"Well, the truth of it is Paul is to be married to Josie O'Neil on Saturday morning. It's to be a quiet wedding and we are givin' them the wedding breakfast, well turkey and all the trimmings." She smiled through her embarrassment. "They will be living with us until they get a place of their own. She is expecting, Ann, but I would rather that wasn't spoke about just yet."

"I hope they will be happy, Mary. Can I help at all on the day? Maybe mind the house when you go to the chapel?"

"No. But thank you. It will be a short mass and Mrs O'Neil and her other daughter are the only ones comin' on Josie's side. Oul Joe is supposed to be givin' her away but that might change. The two wild brothers have taken agin' it. I feel sorry for Josie's Ma. She has had to carry it all herself."

"I will drop around a gift. Is there anything they need?"

"Not at all, ye don't need to do that, Ann. Ye have enough to be spendin' money on in these times."

"I want to, Mary, and besides, William would want to give them something. I will write to him tonight."

"Josie wrote a letter from them both to William to tell him. Has he not said?"

"No. But I'm waitin' on a letter. Sometimes when they are away on marches they stay out all night."

"I wish to God Paul was in the army with two hands and nothing to worry him. But only God knows the reason for it all. I must get on, Padraig has Oliver and no patience."

Ann watched her disappear into the crowd. She had avoided telling William the gossip about Paul and Josie mostly for her own reasons. It was better to say nothing than put fodder into the gossipmongers' hands.

William was not getting leave to come home at Christmas. It was their first without him and she was thankful he was not in France. Walter was somewhere between France and Belguim and Allison was out of her mind with worry.

Late that night, a trap came onto the street. John had gone to bed and she was reading her Bible.

She took the lamp from the table and pulled the bar on the door. Jack was climbing down from the cart. John pushed past her, pulling on his braces.

"Ye shouldn't have opened the dur till ye knew who it wus."

"It's Jack."

He came towards them into the glow of the lamp, his face etched with grief. "Can ye come over to Alison? We have...we have bad news about Walter..." He was crying silently as they led him into the kitchen,

"He was killed at Mons. That's all we know. Alison is in a bad way. I've left Aunt Tilly with her"

"When did ye hear, Walter?" John asked

"The telegram only came a while ago. I think there was five to deliver before it was our turn. The telegraph boy got lost."

Silent sobs burst out in spit and tears. She put her arms around him, her own tears falling on his hunched shoulders.

"Sit down, Jack. I'll put on the kettle." She wanted to scream. She wanted to jump on the cart and go to Donegal and bring William home. She scraped up the fire and set on the kettle.

"No time for tae, Ann. Thanks all the same. Alison is not good and I said I would be as quick as I could. Can ye come on over now, Ann?"

"Aye, Jack. I'll just get my coat. Will you see to things in the mornin' John? Bring wee John over to me if I'm not back."

"Aye, I'll be over first thing tomorrow."

"We knew this day would come, John. Ye only have to read the papers to know the slaughter that's goin' on out there. He wus only 19, only a child."

His tears came again in giant sobs. John embraced him, his eyes meeting Ann's where he saw his own fear reflected in them.

The days after, the news of Walter's death had stretched out into a long, neverending wake. There was no body, no coffin, just a piece of paper that Alison had clung to until it was a crumpled ball, wet with her tears. She had finally given it to Jack and he had placed it in the family Bible, joining the names of long dead family members.

There had been a service in the Church, one of several held in the parishes around the country. Eventually, the family cleared away the remnants of the wake house and went back to living in the midst of their loss. Allison spent long hours at her mother's grave laying flowers and sharing her sorrow with the one person she had depended on all her life. Jack was silent packing away Walter's letters, not wanting to be reminded of his son's last days and his body now laying in a muddy field in France.

The chapel was cold and empty as Paul and Oliver sat in the pew in front of their Da and Ma. Josie's Ma and younger sister sat on the other side of the aisle. Her brothers had not been invited.

The candles flickered as Father Murphy came down form the sacristy and stood beside Paul to wait for the bride.

"Good morning, Paul and Oliver. I hope the best man has the ring?" He smiled down at Oliver who blushed and and looked down at his new shoes bought specially for the occasion. Paul had insisted that Oliver was his best man although Father Murphy had expressed his disapproval that one so young could have no understanding of the duties. Oliver was delighted and bursting with pride. As well as new shoes he was wearing a new waistcoat under his coat, the ring tucked safely in the small pocket.

"Yes, Father. The ring is in safe hands and we have been practisin' and, thanks to Oliver, I am word perfect."

A cold draft from the front door made them turn to see Josie and her Da standing at the back. Father Murphy nodded and they made their way down the aisle. There was no music.

Mary gripped Padraig's arm as the mass began. Joe O'Neil's face was expressionless. He handed his daughter over to Paul, then turned, glared at the McGoverns and walked out of the chapel.

As they emerged, the early sun had disappeared and black clouds hung over the mountain. A few early massgoers stood back, their eyes downcast in silent witness of the shame the families had to endure.

Paul and Josie climbed into the waiting trap, their families following them in a cart. The wedding breakfast was being served at McGoverns. Mary had spent the days before making the preparations and now, as they all crowded into the small kitchen she began uncovering plates of fresh soda bread, boiled eggs and sliced ham and turkey. Father Murphy had arrived and, after more prayers, they all sat down to the meal. Father Murphy, along with the Bride and Groom, occupied the best seats at the top of the table, while the two younger children where squeezed onto the window sill.

Mrs O'Neil had baked a fruitcake and had brought bottles of lemonade. Padraig stood up and called for a toast to the Bride and Groom. Paul and Josie blushed. There were no speeches. Father Murphy concluded with prayers and left, taking the O'Neil family with him. Padraig saw them out and went on about the business of the farm.

Josie rose from the table to help clear the dishes, but Ann gently stopped her.

"Now, Josie, we can't have you washing dishes on your wedding day."

"I don't mind, Mrs McGovern. I want to help."

"Not today, Josie. Paul will take you down to your room so you can unpack and have a rest. It's been a busy morning."

"Thank you, Mrs McGovern, for the lovely food and all the trouble you went to."

"We want you to be happy here, Josie. To feel part of the family. I think we should begin by you calling me Mary, especially as there are two Mrs McGoverns in the house now."

They all laughed, breaking the tension that had hung around the gathering. Paul embraced his Ma.

"I'm tired too, Ma. Would it be alright if we both took a rest?" This made Mary smile and Josie blush.

"Go and do what you want, Paul this is still your home. Be happy in it."

Mary covered the food. Left the dishes in the basin, put on her shawl and went for a walk. The house was small and getting smaller.

Sports on the sand in the afternoon

With money prizes and a Christmas Concert
in the skating rink completed the Christmas
celebrations of The Royal Inniskillen Fusiliers
stationed at Finner Camp, Donegal.
A and D Companies proceeded
on leave on 28th December.

Tyrone Constitution, 1st January 1915

Chapter 37

Before going on leave, William got the letter from his Ma to tell him about Walter's death in France. He wasn't alone in getting such news. Tommy had lost an uncle and another lad had lost his brother. Morale was low and the bad weather did not help. Route marches had become a drudge, snow and hail soaking the wool of their uniforms, which never really dried out.

They had expected to move to a new camp at Randalstown in the New Year, but it was not ready for them. Then orders came to say they were being moved to Shane's Castle in Antrim. Four special trains carried them through the Ulster countryside, stopping briefly in Omagh. William had at last got his long awaited leave to go home and stood on the platform, waving goodbye to the men in his platoon.

His Da had come in Uncle Jack's trap to take him home calling at McCrea's on the way so William could pay his respects to the family over Walter's death.

Aunt Allison collapsed into uncontrollable crying when she saw William. Clinging to him and sobbing Walter's name. He was shocked at the change in her. She had shrunk to a shadow of her former self and her brown hair had turned white. He couldn't wait to leave the sadness of her distress. It was a picture that would stay with him for a long time to come.

"God Da, Alison is in a bad way."

They were in the cart making their way home.

"Aye, son. She'll niver get over it. She idolised that cub. Jack's a changed man as well. He niver was a talker but he says even less now. Mabel's man's an officer in the Belfast Brigade same as Walter's outfit. She lives in county Down. She's havin a wean soon, so they don't see much of her which is a shame. Allison could do with the company. She'll niver be the same again."

This was something that he had not thought about before. How the family would suffer if he didn't come home again. William pushed the thought to the back of his mind. It would do no good to dwell on it.

"Will I get a chance to see our Elsie when I'm home?"

"We could try. I'll ask the Provost tomorrow. Elsie is doin' two jobs these days, she's takin to learnin about nursin'. Yer Ma's not to happy about it but Elsie seems to be enjoyin' herself."

"How are you getting on there?"

"It's the best thing ever happened ta me. I help out at the mess and ferry supplies from the station. I wanted to help with shootin' practice but that's all in hand now, so I do whatever they ask."

"You still off the drink?"

"Aye, still af it and makin' yer ma a happy woman."

They pulled up onto the street and wee John flung himself at William who swept him up into the air.

"Well, will ye luck at ye? We'll have to stop callin' ye wee John. Luk at the size af ye. What have ye been feedin' him on, Ma? I could be doing with yer good cookin' in the camp." He set his brother down and embraced her.

"It's good to have you back again, son and I have a whole week to fatten you up."

He was glad to be home and able to enjoy his Ma's cooking.

After dinner, he walked down to the river. The winter gales had done their work and the Chestnut tree that had stood proud throughout his childhood had lost its grip on the land and lay crookedly across the remains of the hut. He sat down on its thick broken boughs, remembering the times him and Paul had climbed up into its thick canopy looking for the prize of the biggest and best chestnut. He missed Paul. He missed those days they had spent together in this place, days that would never return and the place that would never be the same again. He turned his back on it and went home.

"Have ye seen Paul at all, Ma?" he asked after supper that night. He had not had a letter from him since the wedding when Josie had written for them both to thank him for the wedding gift. His Ma looked up from her sewing.

"I see him and Josie on the road walking to chapel but I've not been speaking to him. Mary came over once or twice, but apart from saying Josie was well, we have not talked much. Are you going to see him?"

"I'm not sure. I don't want it to be awkward for them."

"Sure, why would it be awkward? They're married and there's a child on the way, its no secret." She looked at him puzzled.

"No reason, Ma. But sure ye know what happens when a man gets himself a wife. Things change." He laughed avoiding her obvious question. "He'll be changing nappies instead of flies soon."

"Aye, a little one will change everything. I wish them well. I have fresh trout for the tae. Your Da has taken to the fishin' since you've been gone and he's catching fish."

John came in after taking the bridle of the horse before putting it in the field for the night. Jack had told him to keep it as long as William was at home.

"I was just telling William you're a dab hand at the fishing since he left. The bailiffs have their eye on him."

"The water's a bit brown since the storm but I would like to get in a day's fishin' if we get time Da. I see the oul chestnut tree is down. We should start cutting it up for firewood."

"Time enough to cut it up til the turn af the day and the sap is down. Did ye hear David Bowman has joined the army? He was an officer training down at Baronscourt. I've met him a couple of times. He's a nice cub."

"What rank is he?"

"He was a Lieutenant, then he was promoted to Captain. He went to England. Called across to Aldershot. It's a far cry from the clergy. He was a press officer for the battalion. Our Elsie knows him." John winked: "I think he's sweet on her."

"John, stop putting ideas in William's head. Our Elsie is just friendly and wouldn't have time for such nonsense."

"Well, she could do worse, Ann."

John and William laughed. Ann bowed her head over her sewing and tried to ignore them but secretly could not deny that David Bowman's name was mentioned more than once in Elsie's letters home. In the last one, she had sounded withdrawn and Ann sensed she was keeping something back.

The following day, William decided to call up at McGovern's. He was in his civvies, not wanting to cause trouble with Paul's Da.

There was no answer to his knock. He stood for a moment listening. Then, as he began to walk away, he heard hammering coming from the barn. He stepped over towards the sound and heard Paul's voice. As he pushed the door open it squeaked and a young pup tumbled out at his feet and scampered away down the yard.

"Who the hell let the dog out? It'll be in at the hens again..." William stepped back.

Paul stopped by the open door. They stood for a second, frozen in the moment, before they were locked in an embrace, talking over each other, their greetings warm and sincere.

"Are ye on leave?"

"Aye, I'm home for a week."

"Come on in ta the house. Ma's gone into Newton but I can manage a brew."

"How are things these days?"

William felt awkward, trying to avoid mentioning or looking directly at the stump, not sure what Paul's reaction might be. "I'm sorry, I just wondered."

"Luk William, don't let it annoy ye. I'm a one-handed man now and I'm over it." He laughed and slapped William on the back. "I still can't write so don't give out about my poor letter writing. Now tell me all about the camp." They sat for over an hour, William doing most of the talking and Paul hanging on his every word. They didn't hear the latch fall until Josie was standing beside them, the pup squirming in her arms, her advanced state of pregnancy very evident.

"This boy was in with the hens again."

William stood up. She was radiant. He couldn't take his eyes of the bulge in her belly. He wanted to touch it, to touch her. He had not expected to feel this way. All he had ever wanted was her, now all he felt was a deep sadness and sense of loss. His heart was racing. She stepped past him.

"Hello, Josie. I'm sorry. It was me that let the pup out." She ignored him. "I'll be down in the bedroom when ye want me. Lock this wan in the barn." She dropped the pup in Paul's lap and left them. Paul, stood up, clutching the pup.

"I'm sorry, William. She's just surprised to find you here."

"No, it's me that's sorry. I shouldn't have come. I have no right to wander in here as if things where the same. I hope you will both be happy and all goes well." He felt sick.

Mrs McGovern was on the street when he came out of the house. "William, I didn't expect to meet you here," her smile of greeting fading as William passed her.

"Good day, Mrs McGovern. I was just leavin'. It was a mistake to come." "Wait, William." She called after him, but he had to get away.

He stopped, the bile in his throat erupting as waves of nausea erupted and he degorged his dinner onto the road. He choked, retching until his stomach had nothing more to give. He leant heavily against a tree, cleaning the spittle from his chin, on the sleeve of his coat.

He heard his name being called. He looked around and saw Paul coming towards him on a bicycle. He came to a rattled halt beside him.

"Jez, Willaim, I'm sorry. Josie doesn't mean to be crabbit. It all this wean thing. She gets moody. Come on back. Ma wants to talk ta ye."

The bile hovered at the back of his throat.He couldn't be sick again, not now. He kicked a clod of muck over to cover over the vomit. They walked on.

"Naw, Paul, it was wrong of me to come here without warnin'. You're a married man now and what's past is past."

"Can we meet down at the river so we can talk about this. I'm sorry I didn't write to you. I didn't want to say things for Josie to write down. I know the child is yours and that's alright with me. I've always loved Josie. At school I would watch her but she niver had any time for me. It was always you she wanted. She was in an awful way after you left. Her Ma found out about the child and she didn't know where to turn. It all happened so fast."

William stopped walking, and sat down on the grass verge. Paul dropped the bike and sat beside him. The back wheel of the bike slowly came to a stop. "Is that the same bike we went to Omagh on to join up?" William asked.

"Naw, sure it was a bundle of scrap to start with. It's a wonder we got there at all."

They lapsed into silence, both remembering that perfect day when they had been filled with the excitement of the adventure to come.

"Do you love her?" Paul asked, his voice barely a whisper.

"I don't love Josie. At the time I thought I did but I have no feelin' for her now. I'm glad you'll be the Da to the wean when it comes. I'll make no claim on it. I wish you both a happy future, Paul."

"Did you love her?"

"I can't answer that, Paul. I'm sorry. You're my best friend, better than I deserve. Josie an' me would niver have worked out. Our lives are too far apart. The O'Neils would have started another war if she had married me. It's better this way. I'm happy for you. I won't come again. Tell your Ma I'm sorry for runnin' off."

They rose and embraced. Then they broke apart. William walked on, crossing the ditch along the familiar fields where the river flowed gently over the broken branches of the Chestnut tree.

Epilogue

The cart bumped and swayed at every hole in the road. He shifted himself trying to get a sense of comfort. He had been travelling for three days. The pain was as bad as ever. He pulled out the bottle from his kit bag. The straw was bent and he fumbled with it pushing the top of it through the hole in the mask that covered the bottom half of his face. He sipped slowly, careful not to spill, ignoring the stinging sensation in his mouth. The heat from the liquid travelled down into his gut, warming him and in time the pain began to fade. He slept.

He woke with a jolt. Someone was calling him. He rose and looked around. He was in the wood or what used to be a wood. The trees stood stripped of their leaves, the bark black and smoking like the chimneys of a foundry he had seen in England. He heard the cry again and stumbled across the pitted ground. The smoke got thicker and he coughed, spitting blood and phlegm onto the black singed earth. He tripped and fell, landing into a hole filled with water and mud. He went under and then surfaced again. Mark's face bobbed up beside him, his eyes wide and staring, his mouth frozen in a scream. The screaming got louder. Then hands shook him and the screams came again.

"William, William wake up." He opened his eyes and stared into the face of his Uncle Jack. "You must've had a bad dream. You were screamin' and shoutin'. Are you alright? We'll stop for a while if ye like I have tae in the basket."

The cart stopped and William got down, cold sweat pouring from him. He shivered. Jack lifted the great coat and wrapped it around him.

"Sit down, cub. Here on the bank. I'll get the tae."

William sat down and bowed his head. The nightmare never left him. It was always the same, apart from the face. Sometimes it was Walter, sometimes Tommy. This time it was Mark. He shivered. They were all dead now, all except him. He had survived. But what had he survived for?

"Are ye in much pain, William?"

He raised his head, shifting the mask that covered his face. He tried to form the words with what was left of his lips but the only sound that came was a blubbering hiss. He bowed his head again and pulled the mask back over his face, the salt from his tears stinging the pockets of fresh scars.

Jack watched him as he brewed the tea.

He was a pitiful sight. He had been hit full on the face. The splinters had cut away his nose and mouth leaving a gaping raw hole.

The doctor who had discharged him in Dublin had explained to Jack that they had performed four operations on William's face and more operations would be necessary. The red and swollen areas operated on would mend and further surgery would reduce the scarring. He was to report to a new hospital over in Sidcup, England in six weeks time. Home leave was granted in order to allow him time to rest and recuperate before his next operation.

Jack thought about Walter killed in battle over a year ago. He missed him but couldn't help thinking he was better off dead than left like this. His heart went out to Ann waiting at home for her boy to come back to her. They should have warned her. But all the letter had said was:

'Your son Willam Johnston was injured in action at the front. He has been granted sick leave for the duration of six weeks.'

Pheme Glass
2017

Slang References

Reference to Irish Slang words used in the dialogue as taken from
Slanguage: A Dictionary of Irish Slang and Colloquial English in Ireland, New and Expanded Edition. By Bernard Share, published by Gill & Macmillan

Eejit – fool, idiot, simpleton (Dublin)
Hallion – clumsy boy; irresponsible person; vulgar woman (Ulster)
Wean – wee one, small one, child (Ulster)
Shugh – ditch (Ulster)
Sheebeen – unlicensed drinking place (Irish)
Cub – young boy (Ulster)
Mither – nag, scold (Ulster)
Agin – against
Yis – you (Dublin)
Wan – one (Dublin)
Naggin – small measure of whisky
Midden – dunghill, manure pit (Ulster)
Chitter – complain constantly, chatter (Ulster)
Yap – one who complains constantly (Ulster)
Proddy – Protestant
Slap – gap in the hedge (Ulster)
Pratties – potatoes (Ulster)
Cod – old fool; possibly codger
Shanagh – tell stories (Ire)
Craythur – strong drink (jocular)
RIC – Royal Irish Constabulary
UVF – Ulster Volunteer Force
IRB – Irish Republican Brotherhood

Bibliography / Reading list

Carson, *Geoffrey Lewis*

John Redmond's Last Years, *Stephen Gwynn*

John Redmond; A Biography, *Warren Bradley Wells*

The Miracle of Ireland, *expressly written by John Redmond for The War Illustrated 8th January 1916 kindly supplied by John Wyse Jackson, ZoZimus Bookshop, Gorey, Co. Wexford*

James Craig, *Patrick Buckland*

Fred Crawford – Carson's Gunrunner, *Keith Haines*

Journeying Through Irish History; Exploding Myths, *Gary McMurray*

An Olive Branch in Ireland, *William O'Brien*

The Irish Revolution 1912-23 Tyrone, *Fergal McCluskey*

The Two Irelands 1912-1939, *David Fitzpatrick*

The Irish Guards in the Great War The First Battalion, *Rudyard Kipling*

The History of Ireland in 250 Episodes, *Jonathan Bardon*

Finner Camp – A History, *Colonel Declan O'Carroll*

A Wheen of Medals, *W.J Canning*

Ballyshannon, Belcoo, Bertincourt, *W.J.Canning*

The Road to The Somme, Men of the Ulster Division tell their Story, *Philip Orr*

Friends in High Places 1912-1914, *Alan F. Parkinson*

Somme Mud, *E.P.F. Lynch*

The First World War In Omagh – A project assessing the significance and impact the Great war had in Omagh and surrounding district, *Teachers and Pupils of Drumragh Intergrated College*

Three Cheers for the Derrys!, *Gardiner S. Mitchell*

County of Tyrone 1802, A Statistical Survey, *John McEvoy*

Newtownstewart Remembered, *Billy Dunbar*

All Quiet On The Western Front, *Erich Maria Remarque*

James Craig, *Patrick Buckland*

The Blossom or the Bole